Amazon in Hiding

Amazons of Themyscira Book Three

Elizabeth Salo

Book Cover by Graphicsoul Art

First edition 2024

EBOOK ISBN: 978-1-962460-04-0

PRINT ISBN: 978-1-962460-05-7

Contents

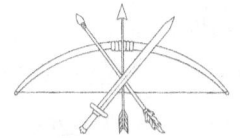

Chapter One

THE FOOTAGE WAS EVERYWHERE.

Zoe Harper sat in her office at Interpol headquarters in Lyon, France, flipping through every news outlet they had access to. She clicked the remote and watched as the large television screen across from her desk changed from one broadcast to the next, each airing the same thing.

She finally stopped flipping through channels and settled on a program called *The Truth Report*. She wasn't super familiar with the show, but when every channel was focused on the same thing, did it really matter which one she watched?

She stared at the screen and let the horror unfold again, as if she hadn't seen it dozens of times already.

Standing in the middle of the Trevi Fountain in Rome was a woman with stringy black hair and a black leather outfit best suited for a dominatrix. She was speaking to a crowd of several hundred people, all listening intently, hanging on her every word.

"People of Rome," the woman began as a hush fell over the gathering. *"My name is Nyx, and I am the rightful queen of the Amazons. That may not mean anything to you, because it has been brought to my attention that most if not all of you do not even know who the Amazons are or what our purpose is. Allow me to correct that.*

"The Amazons are fierce warriors with superior strength and power. We have existed for millennia with the sworn duty to protect others and keep them from being harmed. For centuries we fought your wars for you. We bested the toughest fighters of the era, all in the name of keeping the population safe.

"I look about me and see a population that has become soft and vulnerable." Nyx gestured to the people in the crowd, dressed in business suits, exercise clothes, and casual shorts and T-shirts. She pointed at people shoving baked goods into their mouths, causing them to slowly lower the food before dropping it entirely. *"I come before you with an offer. Clearly your current leaders are doing nothing to help protect you. Not from yourselves and not from others. I can change all of that. I can offer you something that no other ruler can. Power. The power to give up control, to allow someone else to carry your burdens and to fight your battles for you. The power to give yourself to me."*

Zoe watched the screen as another woman—one with long, curly red hair and a pissed-off expression—stepped into the fountain and stood next to Nyx. Under normal circumstances, the redhead, Selene, never would have allowed herself to be caught on camera like this. But Nyx standing in the center of Rome and exposing the Amazons' secrets to the world was far from normal.

The talking turned into yelling as the confrontation in the fountain escalated, and the women started to fight. Their movement was a blur. They jumped and dove and spun at a pace far faster than any human. Eventually Selene tackled Nyx through a window into the building next door, bringing the major action in the video to a close.

As soon as the footage stopped, a news anchor popped on screen. The man was attractive and clean-cut in a boy-next-door type of way. He had perfectly tanned Caucasian skin, light-brown hair that barely brushed his ears, and attention-grabbing blue eyes. His clean-shaven jaw was boxy, and his smile was one he clearly used to devastating effect.

"There you have it, folks, the footage that's currently breaking the internet. Many questions remain. What exactly happened in Rome? Who are these women who call themselves Amazons? For anyone listening at home, we here at *The Truth Report* took the time to do the research for you. The Amazons are a Greek myth dating back to at least two thousand BCE. According to legend, they were a race of warrior women so fierce they cut off one of their breasts to be more effective with a bow and arrow. I'm not sure how much I believe in myths"—he let out a fake-sounding laugh—"but if any woman was going to convince me she was a mythical warrior, these two would be high up on my list."

Zoe groaned as she listened to the reporter share preposterous lies to drive interest in a story she would have preferred had never been broadcast.

"Is there any legitimacy to what these women were saying, and is there any connection between their fantastical claims and the unconfirmed mysterious city that suddenly appeared out of thin air along the coast of Türkiye? I'm Jason Bloom, and you can count on us to bring you nothing but the truth."

Zoe rolled her eyes at the in-your-face tagline and hit the power button on her remote.

Well, there it was. The truth was out there for everyone to see, even if they chose not to believe it. Hopefully someone would soon present "evidence" that the whole thing was a hoax, and it would blow over. Or maybe some celebrity couple would break up in spectacular fashion and drive this from the headlines.

Not that either of those things had happened yet. It had been a week since the confrontation in Rome and the footage was still everywhere. To be fair, it had taken a few days for it to get out of the conspiracy-theorist parts of the internet and into mainstream news, but now that it had, it didn't seem like they were going to put that cat back in its bag anytime soon.

Which explained what Zoe was doing back in France, rather than in her homeland of Themyscira with the rest of the Amazons. She'd been working for Interpol for years, and her job put her in a perfect position to hide in plain sight. The Amazons needed eyes and ears on the outside, and Zoe had access the others didn't. It only made sense for her to head back to her job at Interpol, this time as an undercover double agent for her queen.

Zoe's colleague and friend Gabriel Dubois stuck his head into her office. "Harper, are you still watching that ridiculous footage that's been playing all over the place?" Gabriel asked in his thick French accent. "Bizarre, right? There's no way it's legitimate. It has to be doctored somehow."

Zoe did her best not to react and nodded at her TV. "Yeah, I just got through watching it." For the millionth time. "It does seem a bit unbelievable." Mainly unbelievable that it had been only two weeks since the magic hiding her home from the rest of the world had been removed, and yet here the Amazons were, already on the news.

Gabriel let himself into her office and plopped down into the chair across from her desk. As his butt hit the leather, his chin-length brown hair flopped in his face, and he carelessly brushed it out of his way. "How wild would it be if these warrior women actually exist-ed? I bet they would be wildcats in bed. Especially that redhead." His eyes glazed over as his mind clearly drifted to things better left outside the office walls.

"You know you're a walking HR violation, right?" Zoe said with an eye roll.

"But a charming one, oui?" Gabriel had been trying to get her to go out on a date with him for at least a year, and she'd never taken him up on his offer. It wasn't that Gabriel was unattractive. Far from it, in fact. He had warm brown eyes and just the right amount of facial scruff to give off the bad-boy vibe. Regardless of his looks, though, she wasn't personally attracted to him. Besides that, he was a work colleague, and it wasn't smart to get involved with coworkers.

"So what do you think this big meeting is all about?" Zoe asked, trying to get Gabriel to focus on work instead of her. "Do you think we're finally going to be going after the Shadow?" She named an art and antiquities thief that Interpol had been tracking for several years—someone she personally knew was out of the business, but Interpol didn't know that.

Gabriel's face lost its dreamy quality. "I doubt it. He's been a pest, for sure, but we have bigger issues going on at the moment. I bet it has to do with that place in Türkiye."

Zoe swallowed thickly. This was her opportunity. "Oh? I heard the reporter mention a mysterious new city. He seemed to think it was tied to the Amazons, but that can't be true, right? Especially not if the fight was all faked and the Amazons don't really exist. Do you think the city is real? What does Interpol know about it? I've been out in the field and haven't had a chance to dig into it yet." *Out in the field* wasn't a lie. It also didn't give away that she'd been in that very city until a few days ago.

Themyscira was her home and where she'd lived for over a thousand years. She'd been exiled—along with several of her sisters/friends—twenty-five hundred years ago, but a small band of them had recently returned to save the city and the Amazons residing there from destruction. A small paramilitary force had attacked the hidden city, and a battle had ensued. The Amazons had come through victorious, but with a price. Several of her Amazon sisters had died.

For better or worse, the battle had convinced their queen, Kalliope, to remove the protective veil that had been obscuring the city from outsiders for millennia. Which, incidentally, led directly to why Zoe was back working her job at Interpol rather than spending time with the sisters she hadn't seen in thousands of years. The fact that the veil was gone meant that anyone and everyone were now able to find the city of Themyscira, and that included world governments, military operations, and, of course, police organizations like Interpol.

"The city is real, all right, but there isn't much to go on yet," Gabriel said. "The town somehow appeared out of thin air, and no one can explain why. I mean, it's not like it's a huge place. Honestly, the photos make it look tiny and slightly backward, if you know what I mean."

Zoe bristled, even though she knew she shouldn't. Her home wasn't backward. It just hadn't been updated much since 500 BCE. The small stone buildings weren't exactly up to modern-day building codes, but they had stood the test of time. And if she wasn't mistaken, Kalli and Selene were working right this moment to bring in much-needed updates like generators and portable bathrooms.

"Photos?" she finally prompted. It wasn't a surprise that Interpol had already done or acquired reconnaissance about Themyscira. As far as she knew, they hadn't attempted to enter the city, but that couldn't be far off.

There was no way a city that appeared out of nowhere would be left to its own devices. The world powers would be coming. It was just a matter of time.

"Yeah. You haven't seen them yet?"

She shook her head. "Nope."

"Oh, well, I'm sure . . ."

Gabriel was cut off by the loud bark of their boss, Matis. "Harper, Dubois, conference room, now! You're late."

Zoe frowned at the clock on her laptop. The meeting didn't start for another five minutes, but Matis didn't like waiting. His favorite phrase was *To be early is to be on time, to be on time is to be late, and to be late is to be screwed*.

Gabriel shrugged and raised an eyebrow. As one, they both stood and left her office, joining the rest of the team in the conference room down the hall.

The conference room was mostly unremarkable, with a long wooden table surrounded by chairs, most of which were already occupied. The most exciting thing about the room was the view out the windows, which overlooked the Rhône River. Zoe and Gabriel took the last two chairs and then looked expectantly at the man pacing at the head of the table.

Matis Laurent was an older man who hadn't lost his attractiveness as he aged. His hair had long since gone gray, as had his rather large mustache and beard. He stopped pacing, then used his thumb and forefinger to trace his mustache before stroking his beard.

Zoe hid her smile. Matis had been her boss the entire time she'd been working for Interpol, and he made that gesture only when he was confused or stressed. She wondered which one it was this time.

"Okay, team. I know you've probably all heard about this city that showed up out of nowhere in Türkiye." Matis glanced at the folks gathered around the table, and everyone nodded their agreement. He pointed at the TV behind him, and a satellite photo of Themyscira appeared on the screen. "Our team has been given the mission to figure out what the situation is out there."

Relief flooded through Zoe. If their team was the one that got the assignment, she wouldn't have to work very hard to figure out what Interpol knew and feed that information back to Kalli. This was going to make her job much easier.

"As far as we can tell, none of the world powers are willing to claim this village as one of their own. Though, given the cloaking technology present, we have to assume that it's likely one of the more scientifically advanced countries. This is a level of tech we haven't witnessed before. Not sure why it broke or what exactly went wrong out there, but we are where we are. The town is now visible to everyone, and no one wants to admit what they were doing."

A woman near the front of the table raised her hand.

"Yes, Rachel?"

The woman lowered her hand. "Given where this town is located, do we believe it has anything to do with monitoring the ongoing situation in the Middle East?"

Matis nodded once. "That's an excellent theory. Honestly, we don't know enough yet to make that determination, but it very well could be."

"So what's the plan?" Gabriel asked from Zoe's right.

Matis put his fists on the table and leaned on them. "Great question. The group is going to divide up. The first team will consist of Rachel, John, and Zoe. You'll be staying here at HQ to do support work and research. The second team is everyone else: Gabriel, Anna, Olivia, and Lorenzo. You're heading to Türkiye with me to work on the ground. Wheels up in five hours, people. Let's go."

Zoe sat in stunned silence as everyone around her slowly got to their feet and headed back to their offices.

She hadn't been picked. The most important operation of her career and she wasn't on the fly-away team. This was bad. She needed to find a way to travel with the rest of the team. Back-office support wasn't going to be enough.

She bolted to her feet and dashed into the hallway. Matis had entered his office at the end of the hallway, so she chased after him, catching the door before he closed it.

"Sir, can I please speak to you?" She peeked around the door as he sat down behind his desk. With a wave, he invited her inside. She entered the room and quietly shut the door behind her.

"What is it, Harper?" He didn't sound annoyed exactly, more like resigned.

"Sir, I'd like to discuss my team assignment on this operation. I think I could be an asset on the field team. I've been to that part of the world many times and know the area well." She tried to sound convincing rather than desperate.

Her boss sighed. "I'm well aware of your field time in that area of the world. Most recently chasing after a black-market arms dealer and smuggler, if I'm not mistaken."

Zoe swallowed nervously. "Yes, sir. That's correct. Her name is Eris."

"And after all the money we threw in your direction to track her down, what do we have to show for it?"

The answer was nothing. She had nothing to show for it. Eris had been the bane of Zoe's existence for so long Zoe didn't even want to do the math. Since Eris had been a fellow Amazon, Zoe had felt like it was her responsibility to keep her in line. Or at least keep Eris's chaos from spreading too far. A thankless mission that Zoe was all too happy was no longer her concern.

However, she should have seen this coming. It wasn't exactly like she could tell her boss that Eris had died during the battle that took place in the very town to which he was now sending the team. "I am confident that Eris is no longer a threat."

Matis cocked his head to the side as his eyes narrowed on her. "Oh, you're confident, are you? That's good to know, but without any evidence one way or the other about what happened to her or where she is, that's not good enough."

He waved her off and went back to the pile of paperwork stacked on his desk.

Mild panic tried to crawl up her throat, but she forced it back down. She was good at her job. She'd done exactly what she'd said she was going to and had stopped an international threat from destroying her home. She knew she was talented, and she knew how to take care of herself.

She just needed to convince her boss.

"You're still here," Matis said after several moments of silence.

Zoe clasped her hands in front of her and squared her shoulders. "Yes, sir, I am. I'm one of the best agents on the team. I've been working for you longer than anyone else. I'm good at what I do, and I can be an asset on this vital mission. I would like to ask you to reconsider sending me with the team. I deserve this opportunity."

Matis leaned back in his chair and looked her over. "You have guts, I'll give you that. And it's not like you'll be on your own with a blank check this time." He seemed to consider his options before making up his mind. "Fine. You can go. You've got less than five hours to prepare, so get out of my office."

Zoe nodded once and fled the room before he could change his mind.

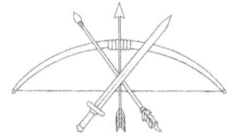

Chapter Two

D ESPITE HAVING WORKED AT Interpol for more than ten years, Zoe had never been part of an operation this large. All told, six people were traveling from France to Türkiye—the four original team members, Zoe, and Matis.

Normally they would have flown commercial airlines, but the amount of supplies they were bringing dictated that they take a charter plane instead. Zoe glanced around nervously at the sheer number of cases they were bringing. It almost looked like they were planning an invasion.

Once the gear was stored and the team was loaded, they buckled in for the several-hour flight ahead of them. As soon as they were airborne and able to move about the plane, Matis stood up and drew everyone's attention.

"Team, listen up," he started loudly, even though everyone was already watching him. "This mission isn't going to be one of those get-in-and-get-out-quick sorts of jobs. Our role is to set up a base camp outside this town and observe what's happening. Depending on what we find, we may or may not engage with whoever is living in the town, so we'll need to be prepared for that."

Matis cleared his throat and continued, "This is a fact-finding mission, people. There is no intention for this to escalate to physical violence, though obviously we do need to be ready for that if the targets initiate it. Now, do what you need to do to prepare. Once we hit the ground in Türkiye, it'll be full speed ahead." Matis sat back down.

Zoe took a deep breath and then let it out slowly. Discreetly, she pulled out the high-tech cell phone Selene had given her before Zoe had gone back to Interpol to spy on them. Selene swore that short of an electromagnetic pulse, the phone should connect.

> Zoe: *Six Interpol agents incoming, including me. Sounds like we'll be setting up a base of operations nearby to observe.*

She hit send, then sneaked the phone back into her pocket before anyone saw what she was doing.

If anyone knew she was transmitting details of an ongoing mission to outsiders, she would be locked up so fast she would barely have time to take a breath.

It wasn't like Zoe wasn't used to dangerous missions. She was an Amazon, for God's sake. This one was more complicated than usual, though. She was either going to be betraying her family or her coworkers. Neither was a great option, but she would absolutely side with her family over anyone else, hands down.

The flight passed slowly. Zoe tried to nap but was too keyed up to let herself fall asleep. She didn't dare check her phone to see if Selene had responded. Instead, she pulled out a book and tried to read it, but the words blurred on the page.

After a short eternity, the plane finally touched down in a small airport outside Samsun, Türkiye. Zoe stood and stretched her long legs, which complained after being crammed into small airplane seats for extended periods of time. Like the rest of her team, she grabbed her own bags and carried them off the plane, then helped transfer the rest of the equipment from the plane into the waiting trucks. Zoe crammed herself into one of the trucks with Matis, Gabriel, and Olivia Watson, a Brit on loan to Interpol from MI6.

The drive from Samsun to Themyscira was surprisingly short. It was a testament to the strength of the veil Hermes—the god of travel and boundaries—had placed on the town that it had remained hidden for twenty-five hundred years even though it was so close to a modern city.

The satellite photo Matis had flashed on the screen back in the conference room had shown the basic outline of the buildings and the town, but it was nothing like seeing it in person. As they came up the final rise, Zoe heard three separate gasps around her.

There it was, in all its ancient glory.

A valley spread out in front of them so suddenly that Matis slammed on the brakes and jerked the truck to a stop. In the center of the valley lay Themyscira. The town itself wasn't huge, but it wasn't tiny either. It was shaped somewhat like a cross, with the largest and most ornate building at the southern end—the farthest from the shore of the Black Sea—and the smallest buildings closest to the water. In the center, where the two arms of the cross met, Zoe could just barely see a small patch of green that made up the town square. The buildings were made of stone blocks—not a single piece of vinyl, glass, or metal on the structures anywhere.

"Blimey," Olivia finally said in her crisp British accent. "There is no way those buildings were built anytime this century, much less in the last five years."

She wasn't wrong, but Zoe wasn't about to volunteer that information. Themyscira had been standing for more than four thousand years. Buildings had been added or repaired during that time, but the layout of the city remained largely the same as it had in two thousand BCE.

"Maybe it's a decoy," Gabriel mused, but Zoe could tell even he didn't believe his own theory.

"This is close enough," Matis chimed in. "We make camp here."

The team exited the vehicle and started unloading their gear. The first things to go up would be large white tents that would not only provide them with some level of protection from the sun but also hide what they were doing from a casual observer.

Or a not-so-casual observer like the Amazons.

Setting up the command station took several hours. There was one large tent where they'd set up tables and equipment and a second smaller tent where they'd put cots and bedrolls for everyone. By the time everything was in order, it was already past dark. They set up the generators to be ready first thing in the morning, then wandered off to their cots for the evening.

Zoe fell on her bed, exhausted. Before passing out, she pulled her phone from her pocket to see if she'd gotten a response.

> Selene: *Understood. We'll be on the lookout.*

Her sisters were aware of what was going on. That was good. At least she shouldn't expect an attack from them in the middle of the night, not that she thought Kalli would authorize an attack on an unknown entity.

The next day was going to be interesting, to say the least.

>>>> <<<<

Zoe was jolted from sleep when someone smacked her feet. "Get out of bed, sleepyhead." It was Gabriel's teasing voice that accompanied the gentle whack. "Stand-up is in ten minutes. There's coffee."

Zoe's eyes popped open. "Go away, you heathen." She smiled to soften her words. "I'm awake."

She sat up, her metal-and-cloth cot creaking slightly as she did so. She stretched her arms over her head and tried to ignore Gabriel's eyes tracing her body.

"Seriously, get out of here. I'm coming." She shooed him away. Gabriel gave her one last reluctant look, then headed out to the equipment tent. Zoe quickly changed into fresh clothes, grabbed a cup of coffee, and went to meet the rest of the team.

While on a mission like this, every morning would start with a short, generally fifteen-minute meeting to go over where the operation stood and what the day's goals were. She'd been to hundreds of these meetings in her tenure as an Interpol agent, but this meeting was undoubtedly her most important to date. These meetings would set the tone of their interactions with Themyscira. Hopefully, things would remain calm and not escalate, but honestly, it could go either way.

"Listen up, people," Matis started in his slightly overdramatic fashion. "This is day one. We don't know how this is going to go, so let's take things cautiously but still work as quickly as we can. I don't need to tell you that important people are very interested in what we figure out here. It isn't an exaggeration to say that the world powers want answers, and we're the first line of defense in this information war. Let's hope it doesn't escalate beyond that."

For the first time, real fear settled in Zoe's stomach. She'd understood that they were on a fact-finding mission, and she'd mostly been okay with that. Things could always get out of hand, which she was mildly worried about, but she hadn't been afraid for her people.

Now Matis was talking about world powers and war. Yes, he'd said information war, but he also hinted that if their Interpol team didn't get the intelligence people were looking for, then it could easily escalate to military action. Military action would not end well for her people. They might be immortal mythical warriors, but they could still be killed. Old age and diseases wouldn't do it, but a bullet to the head or a tactical missile would do just fine.

"Gabriel and Olivia, you're on surveillance cameras. Figure out where to put them—discreetly, of course—and get those feeds sent back to here and HQ. Anna, you're on drone duty. Get that bird up into the air and start getting us live footage as soon as possible. Zoe and Lorenzo, you're here with me. We'll get these systems hooked up and running and make sure all these feeds are getting captured as they go live." With a loud clap from Matis, the team broke up and went to carry out their assigned tasks.

Zoe didn't know Lorenzo Gallo all that well. He was a new addition to their team, a transfer from the Polizia di Stato—the Italian State Police. His ruthless efficiency in setting up their computers and networking equipment was commendable, though. Zoe watched in mild fascination as he ran cables, hooked up their satellite modems, and took care of all their tech needs. He seemed to enjoy what he was doing, so she was more than happy to let him do his thing while she booted up her computer and logged in to their cloud-storage interface.

She monitored the system as the video feeds from the various cameras popped online one by one. The first two didn't show anything of interest, just the main street with a row of houses, but no people. When the third stream went live, Zoe jumped. A spark flew from her fingertips and landed on a nearby piece of paper.

"Shit," she said as she jumped up, dragged the paper to the ground, and stomped on it to put out the flames. She quickly glanced around, but thankfully no one was paying any attention to her. She glanced down at her hands like they'd betrayed her.

And they sort of had. It had been decades since she'd used her magic, either purposefully or accidentally. She kept it ruthlessly locked down for a reason, and it needed to stay that way. She couldn't allow anything to open that Pandora's box, especially not now with Interpol looking over her shoulder. This was not a good time to lose control.

She sat back down in the chair she'd so rapidly vacated and glanced again at the image that had made her freak out in the first place. The most recent video feed showed a clear view of the front of the Royal Hall, and standing outside the heavy wooden door were Kalli and Selene, heads bent over a piece of paper.

If she were doing her job as an Interpol agent, it would be her responsibility to report it to Matis. She had clear visual confirmation that Selene, the woman from the viral video, was in the town that had appeared out of nowhere. Clearly this was proof that the two incidents were connected.

Instead, she clicked away from the video before anyone could see what she'd seen. She wasn't going to be able to hide the truth forever, but she needed to at least buy the Amazons some time to figure out how to handle the situation.

She watched as more and more video feeds came online. The team was nothing if not thorough. They had Themyscira under a microscope, and it was only a matter of time before they saw something they shouldn't.

And speaking of the team, the heavy canvas door to their tent was pushed aside as Gabriel and Olivia entered.

"All done planting cameras?" Zoe asked, keeping her tone as neutral as possible.

"Of course, mon cher," Gabriel said as he came up beside her. He leaned down until his face was inches from hers, pretending to glance over her shoulder at the laptop screen Zoe was studiously watching. Seriously, the man was a walking sexual harassment case.

"Leave Zoe alone," Olivia said without any real heat.

Gabriel was a flirt, and everyone in the office—man or woman—knew it. He did seem to pay a bit of extra attention to Zoe, which she wouldn't mind if she wasn't trying to keep everyone from noticing what was happening in the video feeds. As casually as possible, she minimized the window on the screen she'd been looking at, then turned to face the team after Matis came up and joined the rest of them.

"Did you see anything of interest?" Matis asked, his question directed at Olivia and Gabriel.

"There were a few people walking around, but I didn't get a good look at any of them," Olivia volunteered.

"The place looks like a shithole," Gabriel offered. "It's nothing but old stone buildings. I didn't see a single modern convenience. No electricity, no vehicles, nothing. Well," he corrected himself, "I think I saw a few porta-potties."

Zoe didn't know if she should be mad that her coworker had called her home a shithole, happy that Selene's people had finally delivered the porta-potties, or relieved that Olivia hadn't been able to make out anyone's face. She settled for all three.

Matis sighed. "That's not a lot to go on, but I guess we'll have to see what happens as we monitor the feeds."

"Sir, what would you like us to do next?" Lorenzo asked.

Matis opened his mouth to respond but was interrupted when Anna Campbell burst through the tent doors. "Guys, you have to see this." Without asking for permission, she walked straight up to Zoe's computer and pulled up the same window Zoe had been looking at before, which suddenly had one new feed. The one coming from Anna's drone.

With a sinking stomach, Zoe watched as Anna clicked on the live feed coming from the drone, currently spinning in place somewhere above the town square and providing a 360 view of the entire town. The tops of every house and building, not to mention the town square and the steps of the Royal Hall, were filled with women staring at the sky as if mesmerized. And these weren't just any women, these were clearly warriors. They were clad in leather and bronze armor and holding swords, shields, and spears. Hundreds of confused and agitated faces watched the drone as it slowly circled the city.

Only two faces seemed to stick out. As the drone swooped closer to the Royal Hall, Zoe was able to make out Kalli's and Selene's faces. Unlike the rest of the population of Themyscira, they weren't surprised, but they were irritated.

Crap. She'd forgotten to warn them about the drone.

"What exactly am I looking at?" Matis asked, his voice quiet and mildly confused.

"I'm not sure, sir. But that one"—Anna tapped the screen in the vicinity of Selene's face—"appears to be the same woman from that Trevi Fountain video. If you believe what they said before they started fighting, then my best guess is that we're looking at the Amazons."

Murmurs rose from the rest of the team. They'd all seen the video, of course. But seeing it and believing it were two totally different things. "You've got to be joking," Olivia said. "That video was fake, right? Photoshop or whatever they use for video manipulation."

"I don't know. Did you see the redhead fight with the black-haired woman? No human could move that fast," Gabriel chimed in.

"Exactly," Olivia responded. "Manipulated. There's no way that was real."

"Well," Lorenzo said, "we did have that vague report from the Polizia di Stato that something happened at the fountain, but the report was light on details."

"Either way, what do we do about it?" Anna asked, looking to their boss for guidance.

Matis tried to answer, but Zoe cut him off. "I think we should try to talk to these women. You know, open up lines of communication."

Matis nodded. "Gabriel, you should go talk to them."

That was not what Zoe had in mind. "Sir, are you sure Gabriel is the correct choice?" All eyes snapped to Zoe. People didn't question Matis Laurent. It just wasn't done. Zoe cleared her throat awkwardly and kept going. "What I mean to say, sir, is look at them." She gestured to the screen, which was still full of the curious gazes of hundreds of women. "There isn't a man in sight. If you believe the legends, the Amazons are a civilization composed entirely of women. Don't you think they would feel more comfortable if a woman approached them instead of a man?"

Olivia and Anna immediately nodded in agreement with Zoe, but Matis wasn't convinced. "Perhaps, but Gabriel is our most senior officer, not including me, of course."

"I understand that, sir, and Gabriel"—Zoe nodded to each of them in turn—"but if this is Interpol's first opportunity to interact with a previously unknown race of warrior women, do we really want to wind up committing some social or political gaffe by sending the wrong person? I have nearly the same number of years of experience at Interpol as Gabriel. Send me instead, and I promise you won't regret it."

Zoe held her breath as she waited for her boss's response. It was one thing to realize that she—a person who had been alive for four thousand years—didn't need this job. It was another entirely to ensure that whatever relationship the Amazons had with the outside world, it started on the right foot. She could only hope that she'd been convincing enough.

With a put-upon sigh, Matis relented. "Fine. Harper, you're on. And don't screw this up."

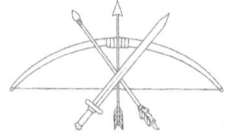

Chapter Three

J ASON BLOOM HAD BEEN all over the world—it came with the territory of being an investigative reporter—but he had never been to this part of Türkiye. He had to admit, it was quite lovely. The harsh terrain of rocks and hills was softened by the green scrubby plants and trees that seemed to grow everywhere.

The one thing that didn't fit in with the beautiful surroundings was the pair of giant white tents perched on the top of a hill overlooking the landscape below.

"I guess we found where the action is," Jason's camera operator, Noah Quinn, said as he ran his hands over his closely shorn black hair.

"Right? Are they on a fact-finding mission or are they planning an invasion?" Jason quipped back. He pulled their rental car up next to a row of trucks that presumably belonged to the owners of the tents and got out, followed by Noah.

It had been a long flight from Washington, DC, and all Jason wanted was a shower and a change of clothes. Unfortunately, that wasn't in the cards. Not if he wanted to get a jump on this unfolding story before any of the bigger news outlets showed up. This was his chance.

"This place looks really homey," Noah said sarcastically as he opened the trunk and readied his camera equipment.

"I always take you to the nicest places," Jason responded, doing his best to straighten his clothes and run his finger through his short light-brown hair in an attempt to shape it into the artfully messy look he went for when on camera.

He didn't know what to expect with this investigation, though when something was this hot off the presses, he rarely did. What he knew for sure was that a tiny town had suddenly blinked into existence on the coast of Türkiye, and Interpol was here investigating it. That was it. He had no idea who was in charge of the investigation or what they thought they were investigating.

There was no one outside the tents, and Jason wasn't about to go barging into a law enforcement structure without authorization. He would have to wait outside for someone to emerge.

"Maybe we should have called ahead to let them know we were coming?" Noah suggested, taking in the lack of people the same way Jason was.

"And give them a chance to rehearse their answers? No way," Jason replied. "We should scout the area. Let's head up that hill and figure out what the fuss is all about." He pointed toward a nearby rise after which the land seemed to drop away suddenly.

Noah grunted his agreement, hefted his camera onto his shoulder, and followed him.

The climb from where they'd parked the vehicle to the top of the ridgeline wasn't particularly long or hard to scale, but what appeared below them was nothing short of astonishing. The city laid out before them was much bigger than Jason would have assumed from the sketchy details that had trickled out so far. The north end of the town started at the Black Sea, with a small beach surrounded by craggy rocks and boulders. A dirt road led away from the beach and between rows of buildings that, if he had to guess, were most likely hundreds of tiny houses. The road continued south until it hit a large grassy area where he could see animals grazing—either sheep or goats. The square had buildings on all sides, with the southernmost building being the largest in town, which probably meant it was the most important. Behind the large building was another expansive clearing, this one containing a series of objects that looked like targets and training mannequins. On the far side of town, another line of hills turned the area into an isolated basin that could easily have been missed if you weren't careful.

Jason could feel his slackened jaw and closed his mouth. "Are you getting this?" he asked Noah, both staring down at the town in shock.

"Yep, every detail."

Noah's camera was going to get a workout with this story, that was for sure. These buildings looked like they were hundreds—if not thousands—of years old. There was absolutely no way this city had appeared overnight. "What are we even looking at?" Jason asked, not expecting an answer.

"Your guess is as good as mine," Noah said.

"Why don't you see if you can get closer and get more video. Just be careful. We have no idea who's down there. Don't get caught or kidnapped." Jason didn't need to warn his cameraman to be careful—they'd been in war zones together, after all—but that wasn't going to stop him from doing it. He had no intention of getting either of them into trouble. If he came home, so did his cameraperson. Period.

The sound of a hand smacking canvas caught his attention, and Jason turned back toward the Interpol tents. An attractive blond woman had emerged, dropping the heavy fabric door back in place behind her. She took a few steps to the side but didn't go far. Jason watched her eyes close as she took several deep breaths, a look of relief crossing her beautiful face. She pulled out her phone and typed rapidly before sliding the phone back in her pocket.

The first signs of life. Perfect.

Jason casually strolled in her direction, trying not to look too suspicious or too much like the reporter he was. Though it wasn't exactly like he had a great cover story for accidentally being in the middle of nowhere, right next to an Interpol encampment. Oh, well. He'd bluff his way through. It wouldn't be the first time.

"Hi, there. Do you think you could help me out?" he said with his best rakish grin.

The blonde shook her head slightly as if she was bringing herself back to the present. She glanced around the area, then focused on him. "Well, hey there, handsome," she said as her perfect pink lips lifted into a sexy smile. "What are you doing all the way out here?"

Jason did his best to look sheepish. "I'm lost, actually. I'm trying to find my way to Samsun, and apparently I got a bit turned around." He glanced around as if it were the first time he was seeing the tents and all the vehicles. "I have no idea what I stumbled into here, but if you could point me in the right direction, I'd be grateful."

She cocked her hip and tilted her head to the side, her eyes narrowing in on him like she was studying him for a science project. "Well, I'd tell you to jump into your car, head back to E70, and drive west, but somehow I don't think that would actually get you what you're after." She crossed her arms—which did excellent things to her breasts—and bit her lip. "So how about I say this instead? Interpol has no official comment about the situation here or what we're dealing with."

Damn. She'd clearly made him as a reporter. Maybe the situation wasn't completely hopeless yet. He dialed his charm up to eleven and ran his hand through his hair. "Sorry, you can't blame a guy for trying, right?" He sent her a teasing smile, which she didn't return. Instead, she glared at him like he was a bug on her windshield. Giving up on the charm offensive, he pulled out his phone and clicked the voice recording app. "Are you the agent in charge?" he asked, holding his phone in her direction to catch her response.

"Thankfully, no," she said before she leaned back toward the door to the canvas tent and tugged it open. "Boss, someone is here to see you."

A blustery man in his fifties, with graying hair and a rather large beard and mustache, came barreling out of the tent. "Harper, what are you still doing here? I thought I told you to—" He cut himself off as he realized a stranger was standing there.

Before Jason could offer his hand and name to the newcomer, the woman did it for him. "Matis Laurent, this is Jason Bloom. He's a reporter from America."

Jason tried to hide his shock. Not only had she figured out he was a reporter, but she recognized him. As much as Jason wanted to believe she was somehow a fan of his show, even he wasn't cocky enough to think his small-time—or was it medium-time?—news program was a must-watch for international law enforcement. Regardless, she knew who he was, but all he had was part of her name: *Harper.* Was that a first name or a last? Before he could speculate too wildly, his thoughts were cut off by a grunt from Laurent. As much as the woman fascinated him, she wasn't why Jason was there. He was there to break the story of the mysterious city. He was first on the scene, and he had to press his advantage.

"Mr. Laurent, my name is Jason Bloom, from *The Truth Report* based out of Washington, DC. If you don't mind, I'd like to ask you a few questions about what we're looking at here." He inconspicuously held his phone in the direction of the older man, trying to catch anything he might say.

Laurent sighed and said, "Reporters." He took a deep breath before putting on what Jason liked to refer to as a professional mask. A change came over people when they realized they needed to be *on*, as if they needed to don a persona to deal with the press. Whatever.

As long as Jason got the scoop he was after, it was all the same to him.

The sound of footsteps behind Jason heralded Noah's approach. A mic appeared out of nowhere, and suddenly Jason was in full beat-reporter mode, with Noah there to catch every second. "Mr. Laurent, my name is Jason Bloom," he repeated himself for the camera. "Can you give our viewers any insight into Interpol's investigation and what you think might be happening here in Türkiye? Where did this mysterious town come from, and whom do you believe to be living there?"

Out of the corner of his eye, Jason saw the blond woman slip away. Too bad. He wouldn't mind getting to know her better. However, right now he needed to focus on doing his job. He shoved her out of his mind and concentrated on what Laurent was saying.

"We don't have anything we can share at the moment. We just arrived ourselves and have not had time to make any assessments." The man turned and headed back into the tent, making sure the canvas door fully closed behind him so Jason and Noah couldn't see what they were doing inside.

Disappointing but not unexpected. If the officials weren't going to give them anything to go on, then it was going to be up to them to figure it out.

Exactly what he did best.

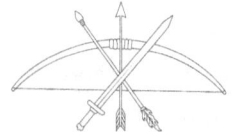

Chapter Four

REPORTERS. JUST WHAT ZOE didn't need complicating her life right now. She was already walking a fine line, trying not to let her boss and Interpol colleagues figure out she was one of the very people they were there to investigate. Now she had to worry about a nosy writer poking around for a story. Just great.

Well, there was nothing she could do about it, so it was best not to fixate on it. She shoved the far-too-attractive-for-his-own-good journalist out of her mind and focused on what she needed to accomplish.

She'd gotten Matis to agree to let her act as a liaison, which was a huge relief. Her role, at least as she saw it, was to keep both sides from killing one another. Both literally and figuratively. With any luck Kalli and Selene had been strategizing while she'd been undercover, and hopefully they had a plan.

She was about to find out.

Zoe approached Themyscira slowly. The Interpol camp was high on a rise east of town. She made her way down the hill and across the open space toward the road that led through town. She had a vague idea of where the cameras were from the brief glimpse she'd gotten watching them come online. There wasn't anything she could do about the location of the drone, however, and she was certain her coworkers would be watching her every move. It was best if she didn't appear to be overly familiar with the town and its people, even if she knew every nook and cranny and could name every inhabitant on sight.

As soon as she'd left the tent, she'd sent Selene and Kalli a text in their group chat, giving them a heads-up that she would be coming and asking them to warn the rest of the Amazons to pretend they didn't know her.

It had been only two weeks since the veil hiding the city had been removed and her sisters had been exposed to the outside world for the first time in more than twenty-five hundred years. That wasn't exactly a long time to get them caught up on everything that had changed. She was surprised no one had thrown a spear at the drone, and she wouldn't be shocked if it happened at some point.

She could only imagine what Matis would make of that.

As she made her way down the road through the center of town, people came out of their houses to watch. She was pleased that the most they did was nod in acknowledgment, though a few fell in behind her, a small crowd trailing in her wake. She approached the town square and saw that Kalli and Selene were still standing on the steps that led to the Royal Hall. Zoe walked up to them and gave a quick bow.

"My queen," Zoe said.

Kalli's eyes darted around before landing back on Zoe.

"Don't worry. They have video feeds only. No audio," Zoe reassured her.

Kalli let out a relieved breath. "Well, that's something at least. However, it's probably best not to give them much of a show." With that, she spun on her heel and went inside, beckoning Zoe to follow.

Zoe glanced around at the small gathering surrounding them before heading inside. Eventually everyone would need to be told what the plan was, but for now they would keep it among the people closest to the queen—the lieutenants Kalli trusted the most. As Zoe's eyes adjusted to the dim light, she made out not only Kalli and Selene, but also Kalli's fiancé Sam, Selene's boyfriend Colin, and four other Amazons: Melina, Frona, Psyche, and Ariadne.

"Hey, cuties, are they keeping you locked in a tower?" Zoe said as she greeted Sam and Colin with a wink.

Sam shrugged. "It seemed like the safest course of action with all the surveillance."

Sadly, he wasn't wrong. Trying to explain what a Georgetown professor and an international arts and antiquities thief were doing amid this chaos would be an added layer of hassle.

"Speaking of surveillance, what exactly are we dealing with? Apart from the drone, obviously," Selene asked as they made their way over to the long table in the middle of the room and sat down at the benches on either side. Scattered across the table were papers and maps and a laptop that looked distinctly out of place with its shiny newness.

Zoe riffled through the papers on the table until she found a map of the area. She grabbed a Sharpie and started drawing dots. "Near as I can tell, the cameras appear to be located in these positions."

Colin whistled. "Ten cameras and a drone? They're not messing around. Though there are still obvious gaps in their coverage areas if we need to exploit them." He drew his finger along several locations that would be hidden from the view of the cameras.

Sometimes it was helpful to have a thief on the team, even if the "Shadow" was on Interpol's radar. He'd given up that life to be with Selene, but his skills still came in handy.

"Let's take a step back. What exactly are we looking at here? Is this a friendly visit to introduce themselves? Or are we talking military action at some point? What do they think Themyscira is?" Kalli asked from the end of the table.

"Great questions," Zoe said. "From the brief intro we got yesterday before we packed up and shipped out, the running theory is that this is an intelligence-gathering dark site for one of the major world powers. They think there was some super-advanced cloaking device at work that failed, and now no one is willing to claim ownership of the location, especially given its proximity to the Middle East."

"Well, they aren't exactly wrong about the cloaking device, though not in the way they think," Selene said.

"Yeah, I'm not about to try to convince Interpol that the Greek gods are real. Even if they were the reason Themyscira was hidden from the rest of the world for several millennia," Zoe said.

"You said world powers," Kalli said. "As in the most powerful countries in existence right now."

"Yeah, if I had to venture a guess, something like a G7 country: Canada, France, Germany, Italy, Japan, the UK, or the US. Maybe throw Iran, China, or Russia in there for good measure," Zoe said, rattling off the countries.

"So what's going to happen when none of those places step forward and claim ownership of the town?" Kalli asked.

"What would happen if one of them *did* claim ownership?" Sam tossed out, and Kalli gave him a shocked look. Clearly that situation hadn't even occurred to her.

This whole situation was a powder keg.

"We are not prepared to fight off foreign military," Selene said.

"But we're Amazons!" Frona shouted, her fist smacking the table.

Kalli sent her a sad smile. "Yes, we are Amazons. The problem is that there are only a few hundred of us. Even with our added powers and gifts, we're no match for the thousands of soldiers they could bring, and that doesn't even include the advanced weaponry that they have access to. We may have been the most feared and most advanced fighting force of our time, but that is no longer the case."

Frona, Melina, Psyche, and Ariadne sat in stunned silence. Selene had been doing her best to educate them and the others on guns and other modern weapons, but they simply hadn't had enough time to fully grasp the world they were a part of now.

"So what do we do?" Ariadne asked quietly as she tucked her long black hair behind her pale ear. "If we can't defeat them when they come, what do we do instead?"

The defeat in Ariadne's voice broke Zoe's heart. The Amazons had always been powerful. That came with a sense of strength and worth that you could see in each of their eyes as they faced down their enemies or even just went about their days. To see that belief start to fade was distressing.

"First, we try diplomacy," Kalli responded. "I refuse to try to fight our way out of this situation when a conversation might work instead. We use Zoe as a go-between to set up a meeting between us and Interpol and then go from there."

Zoe could only hope that Kalli was right.

"One more complication," Zoe said as she pulled out her phone and opened a browser. "There's a reporter nosing around." She pulled up a picture of Jason Bloom from his network's web page. Zoe passed her phone around the table so everyone could get a good look at his face. She handed it to Frona first, who took a quick glance and then passed it along. However, unless Zoe was imagining things, Ariadne stared at his photo for a bit longer than necessary—a wistful look in her eyes—before she passed it along to Selene.

Selene reached out and grabbed the phone, letting out a long whistle. "Oooh, he looks like he'll be a fun distraction for you." She waggled her eyebrows suggestively.

Zoe rolled her eyes. "Despite what you may think, I can keep my pants on."

Colin got the phone next and glanced at the image. "Yeah, but why would you want to?" He winked and passed the phone to Kalli.

Zoe tried not to blush. She wasn't normally a blusher, but she also wasn't used to being teased by people who knew her as well as these people did. She loudly cleared her throat and said, "Anyway. Be on the lookout. He's here digging for a story, and we don't want to give him one." She accepted her phone after it finally made its way back to her.

The group spent a few hours strategizing every possible scenario they could think of and how they would approach each situation should it arise. In the end, they decided Kalli, Sam, and Selene would go to the meeting with Zoe.

Assuming Interpol was even willing to entertain the idea.

With at least a partial plan, Zoe felt a bit better about their situation. It still wasn't ideal, but there was no need for anything to escalate. Kalli was a levelheaded ruler, and she had the advantage of having lived in the modern world. It wasn't like their queen was going in with no knowledge of what she was getting into.

Zoe started her trek back through town and up the hill toward Interpol's camp just as the sun started to set over the hills surrounding the city. She hadn't even made it halfway there before Jason Bloom materialized out of the bushes in front of her. At least his cameraman was nowhere to be found.

"So, Harper, is it?" Jason asked with a smile that was far more charming than any man had a right to be.

"It's Zoe," she corrected, then mentally cursed herself for giving him anything else to work with.

He fell in step beside her as she continued trekking up the hill. "Well, Zoe Harper, you not only went into the mysterious city but came back alive."

"Never let anyone tell you that reporters aren't observant," she said lightly.

He laughed. "Touché." They walked in silence for several beats before he finally spoke again. "So how long have you worked for Interpol?"

"What makes you think I'll answer that?" she asked, turning slightly to catch his gorgeous smile in the dim light.

"Because I asked nicely?" The way he fluttered his eyelashes was so over the top she actually laughed.

"Did you ask nicely, though? I didn't hear a please." Zoe always enjoyed flirting, even if it was with someone she should be avoiding.

Jason stopped dead on the dirt road and turned to face her. He put on a puppy-dog look, staring at her with enormous blue eyes. "Pretty please with sugar on top, will you tell me how long you've worked for Interpol?"

Zoe fought back a grin. "Wow, with sugar on top even. You sure you want to waste all that sweetness on that question? What if you have a more important question later?"

He slumped dramatically, his shoulders hunching in fake defeat. "Alas, you aren't wrong. I have a list of questions as long as my arm."

Zoe bit her lower lip suggestively and traced his well-toned body with her gaze. "Why don't you try one of the other ones. Maybe you'll get lucky . . ." She watched his Adam's apple bob as he swallowed thickly.

His voice was low and raspy when he finally asked, "Can you tell me what the city is or who lives there?"

Zoe took a step closer, invading his personal space. She brought her fingers within an inch of his chest but stopped short of touching him. She leaned close to his ear and whispered, "No comment." She stepped away from him and started back up the hill.

Jason let out an undignified squawk but stayed where he was. "You're really not going to give me anything? What was the city like? How long has it been there? What are Interpol's plans?" He yelled the questions at her retreating back. Zoe smiled to herself and ignored him.

Her entire team was waiting outside the command tent when she arrived. *Oh right, cameras.* Well, hopefully they didn't watch the interaction she'd had with the delicious Mr. Bloom. If they did, oh well. Nothing she could do about it now.

"Harper, inside." Matis opened the flap to the tent and ushered her away from prying eyes and ears.

Zoe approached the makeshift conference table and sat down at one of the chairs. The rest of the team, except for Matis, settled in around her. Their boss, however, felt the need to pace around the cramped interior of the tent like a stalking lion.

"Well, come on, out with it. What happened?" Matis asked.

Zoe cleared her throat and tried not to shift uncomfortably in her seat. Gabriel sent her a wink and an encouraging nod for her to go ahead. "I spoke with their leader, well, their queen," she rapidly corrected herself. "As we predicted when we arrived and saw the primitive state of their city, this is not an installation put in place by any modern government. They aren't some sort of spy base or intelligence-collection site. In fact, I believe them when they say they are the Amazon warriors of myth and legend."

Olivia scoffed in disbelief and crossed her arms. "You've got to be kidding me. There's no way Amazons are real. It's just a story. A Greek myth like Hercules or Jason and the Argonauts. Harper, I thought you were smarter than that."

"Yeah, if these women were as strong and as powerful as they claimed to be in that video, they would have much nicer digs," Gabriel added. "No way would I settle for something like that"—he waved vaguely in the direction of Themyscira—"if I had superpowers."

Zoe tried not to get defensive or let her irritation show. She desperately wanted to defend her people and her homeland, but that wasn't her current mission. She shouldn't care what these people thought. She knew what her people were worth and what they'd struggled through over the centuries. She didn't need to prove it to others.

"I think it would be awesome if they are what they say they are," Anna said. "I'd love to meet one of them in person and pick their brain. I can't imagine what they would be like. Generation after generation of women hidden away from the world and trained in secret to be badass warriors. Maybe they'll let me join their ranks." Zoe wanted to tell her that wasn't exactly how it worked, but if Interpol didn't know about the immortality thing, she wasn't going to be the one to bring it up.

Zoe needed to get a handle on this conversation before it went too far afield. "Sir, if I may," Zoe said, cutting off Lorenzo, who looked like he was about to say something. She waited for Matis to acknowledge her before she continued. "Queen Kalliope has offered to parley with you and your team."

"Parley." Matis let out a deep scoff. "What are we, pirates?"

Zoe barely held back an eye roll. "Call it whatever you'd like. A meeting, a conclave, a summit. She would like to initiate discussions between the Amazons of Themyscira and Interpol."

That set the team buzzing again. Zoe tuned them out and focused solely on her boss. He was their leader on this operation as well as their boss, so what he said went. It didn't matter if the entire team disagreed with him or not. What Matis wanted and what he thought was the best course was what happened. Period.

After a long pause in which the excited chatter from around the table finally died down, Matis weighed in, "Set it up. We can bring them here and hopefully get more information out of them then. I'm not buying this Amazon garbage, so they better have a good story to tell me."

Zoe raised a finger to get his attention. "Sir, I think we should hear them out before rushing to judgment. They deserve at least that much."

Matis threw up his hands and stalked away. "Fine! Make it happen by tomorrow." He tossed the words over his shoulder as he strode out of the tent and into the evening air.

Ding, ding, ding. Round one was over, with no clear winners. At best, Zoe would call it a draw. Though every day that didn't wind up with a tactical nuke landing on her homeland was a win in her book.

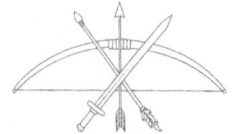

Chapter Five

NOTHING WAS GOING ACCORDING to plan.

It wasn't like Jason had expected to show up and have the authorities tell him everything he wanted to know, but the longer things went on like they were, the more likely another news agency would show up and try to scoop his story. That wasn't something Jason was willing to have happen.

Endless footage of closed white tents flapping in the wind high on a hill over the Black Sea wasn't exactly the compelling imagery he was hoping to have. Noah had sneaked down the hill again and gotten some limited footage of the town, but he hadn't wanted to get caught by the Interpol agents or the unknown inhabitants, so even that was minimal.

He'd gotten excited when he'd seen the blond woman, Zoe, come back from the city alive and unscathed. She hadn't been detained and she hadn't been injured, both of which were good things. However, it would have been much more compelling if something had happened to her while she was down there, and he'd gotten to interview her about whatever it was. Not that he was wishing her harm or anything. He just needed a juicy morsel he could dangle in front of his producers and fans to whet their appetite for more. The delicious Zoe Harper definitely qualified as a juicy morsel.

"What should we do?" Noah finally asked after several minutes staring at the closed flap of the tent.

"Make camp," Jason responded. They weren't going anywhere until he had what he was after.

Their small nylon tent wasn't nearly as nice as the huge white canvas ones next to them. The bright-orange fabric stuck out like a sore thumb among the brown rocks and green bushes, but at least it would keep them dry and out of the wind in case the weather decided to change on them. Jason pulled out their small propane camp stove and started heating some soup for dinner. Noah was sitting next to him, scrolling through the footage he'd transferred from the camera to his laptop.

When the soup was finally hot enough, Jason poured it into two bowls and tried to hand one to Noah. Except Noah wasn't paying any attention. He was squinting at his laptop screen as if it contained the secrets to the universe. "Hey, Noah. Soup's on."

Noah offered him a dazed expression. "I need you to look at this and tell me if I'm making this up." His deep-brown eyes were so focused they almost looked black, and the dark-brown skin of his forehead was wrinkled in concentration.

Intrigued, Jason set both bowls of soup on the small table next to the stove. He crossed to where Noah was sitting and peered over his shoulder at the image on the screen. It was slightly blurry and looked like it had been zoomed or enhanced in some way, but Jason could make out groups of people standing around the town square in the middle of the city. Then Noah tapped one blunt finger against the screen and pointed to two women on the steps of a large building. "Is that who I think it is?"

Even with the less-than-sharp nature of the footage, it was immediately evident to Jason who the redhead on the steps was. The shaky cell phone footage of the fight at the Trevi Fountain had been playing nonstop around the world for days. He'd talked about it on his own show more than once. And here, smack in the middle of the mystery city, was one of those impossible fighters. "Hot damn. You are not making it up. That is exactly who you think it is. This just got a whole lot more interesting," Jason said.

The wheels in his mind started spinning. The black-haired woman in the video, the one named Nyx, had clearly and articulately stated that she was the rightful queen of the Amazons and that the Amazons had existed for thousands of years.

Jason had done his research when the story at the fountain had originally broken. The Amazons were a Greek myth dating back to at least two thousand BCE. They featured in plenty of ancient stories, including those surrounding Hercules. The key word, however, was stories. The Amazons were a myth. They, like Hercules, had been fables passed down through the centuries to entertain and caution others.

Right?

There was no way an ancient civilization could have existed for more than four thousand years without anyone finding out about it. Modern technology would have made it impossible to hide. Except he'd done a search of all the aerial and satellite photography he could get his hands on, and until about two weeks ago, the area of Türkiye where he now stood had looked totally unoccupied. The city that he had seen today with his own two eyes wasn't visible on any of it.

"So which conspiracy theory are you leaning toward?" Noah asked as he finally grabbed one of the bowls of soup Jason had set down. "The one that says an ancient civilization magically appeared out of thin air? Or the one that says the Russian government has advanced enough cloaking technology that it can shield an entire city from view?"

"I'm leaning toward the one that says that it's a town built and occupied by aliens." Jason chuckled, but he honestly wasn't sure what to think. He had speculated on his show that the town might be linked to the Amazons, but he wasn't sure he'd truly believed it. The idea of a mythical race of women suddenly appearing out of nowhere seemed about as believable as the alien theory.

His gut was telling him that Zoe Harper was the key. Whoever lived in the town below—Amazons, advanced military geeks, or little green men—she had gotten in and out without being harmed. How had she done it? If it really was the Amazon civilization, and they were as dangerous as Nyx claimed they were, how had Zoe gotten in and out without coming to any harm?

All he and Noah needed to do was stick to her like glue and she would eventually lead them to something useful. He was certain of it.

⫷⫸⫷

Zoe paced nervously between the Royal Hall and the armory in one of the few camera dead zones that Colin had noted the day before. The arid ground sent puffs of dust into the air every time she stepped, but she ignored it. She'd lived in this city for long enough not to be bothered by a little dirt.

What did bother her, however, were the upcoming negotiations. She'd gone down to the city at first light after tossing and turning on her cot all night. She didn't think she'd sleep well again until these talks were over. Thankfully she'd been the first one up and about, so none of her coworkers could corner her and try to pry more information out of her about the town. Even more thankfully, except for the bright-orange lump of nylon tent, she'd also seen no indications that Jason was lurking around either.

That man made her nervous in a whole different way. The balance she was trying to strike between her chosen profession and her ancestry was already hanging by a thread. She didn't need the Fates to come along and snip that precarious string. As attractive as he was, she needed to stay as far away from him as possible. He was a reporter, and he could expose her family to the world. She couldn't allow that to happen.

Not that a romp in the hay would be unwelcome, just unwise.

She'd been pacing back and forth for at least fifteen minutes. As soon as she had arrived, she'd notified Kalli of the situation and that Interpol had agreed to meet. Since she'd barged in on Kalli and Sam still sleeping—fully clothed, thank God—it seemed wise to give them some time to wake up and get dressed.

She worked off her anxiety in the only way she knew how. Constant movement. Despite the well-worn paths already trod into the ground, Zoe was on the verge of wearing a new groove in the dry earth as she trudged back and forth.

She shook her hands by her sides, trying to loosen her tight muscles. A bright glow caught her eye, and she glanced down, horrified to see tiny sparks dripping off her hands and hitting the ground. One ember landed on a tiny, parched bush, which promptly lit up in a whoosh of flames.

Panicked, Zoe stomped on the plant, trying to crush the flames beneath the sole of her boot. Only after the fire was out did she glance around to see if anyone had noticed. Thankfully, the area appeared totally empty. No one had been around to witness her anxiety-driven meltdown.

She had no idea what was going on with her. This was the second time in as many days that her powers had gotten away from her. She'd had them locked down for decades. This was not the time for them to start going haywire. The very thought of one of her coworkers seeing flames shooting from her hands drove her anxiety off the charts.

"What on earth has gotten into you?" Kalli asked, causing Zoe to let out a slight scream and spin to face her queen.

"Um, nothing. Why do you ask?" Zoe said, desperately clutching her hands behind her back and hoping that her powers behaved themselves, at least long enough to get through the day.

Kalli gave her a pointed look but didn't push her on it.

"We're ready when you are."

It was only after Selene spoke that Zoe realized Selene and Sam were standing behind Kalli, each giving her the same speculative look that Kalli was. They were dressed casually, but Kalli and Selene each had a gun strapped to their hips.

"Right. Of course. Let's head out," Zoe responded.

Zoe and Kalli led the way out of the city. "Are you ready for this?" Zoe asked her friend.

Kalli sighed quietly before responding. "Not really, but it's the right move. I just hope that we can stave off any violence. Our people are not prepared to deal with the threat of attack from the outside. They could crush us like bugs."

Zoe made a low sound of agreement. The Amazons weren't completely helpless—they did have their preternatural abilities in addition to their strength and fighting skills—but Kalli was right to be cautious. Unless and until they could prove to the outside world that they were a force to be reckoned with, it was better to appear humble and peaceful.

As they crested the top of the hill, their small party came face-to-face with Zoe's entire Interpol team, who were waiting outside the tent. To make matters worse, the attractive-but-nosy reporter was standing off to the side with his back to them, talking into his microphone as his cameraman caught their arrival and no doubt broadcast it to the world.

Zoe slightly tilted her head in their direction, calling the others' attention to the media presence. Kalli gave a slight nod in acknowledgment.

"Let's introduce ourselves inside, shall we?" Zoe said, speaking to Matis and drawing his gaze to the camera.

He glanced at the weapons they were carrying but didn't comment. Instead, he nodded in agreement. "This way," he said before spinning around and heading into the tent, the whole team following him.

Zoe pulled back the canvas door and let Kalli, Sam, and Selene precede her into the tent. She glared in Jason's direction before dropping the flap back into place and making sure there were no gaps that a sneaky reporter could peek through. When she turned around, she was faced with a tense standoff. The whole Interpol team was on one side of the space, and the Amazons were on the other side. The plastic folding tables they were using as a conference table sat empty between them.

She cleared her throat, then said, "Matis Laurent, may I present to you Queen Kalliope of the Amazons. Queen Kalliope, this is Matis Laurent, senior agent at Interpol and the leader of this mission."

Matis and Kalli shook hands, but Zoe could tell that her boss was trying to size Kalli up and put her into a box that might make sense to him. His gaze took in her appearance, from her hiking boots to her jeans and polo shirt before landing on the silver filigree circlet containing a sapphire the size of a robin's egg, perched on top of her head. The slight widening of his eyes as he took in the massive jewel forced Zoe to quickly mask her smirk.

"It's lovely to meet you," Kalli said, smiling at the collected crowd of wary and suspicious agents. "This is my fiancé, Dr. Samuel Tread-well. He's an anthropology professor at Georgetown University." Several of the agents turned speculative glances toward Sam, but no one said anything. "And this is one of my lieutenants, Selene Blackburn."

Gabriel looked dumbstruck that Selene was there. It had to be because of the stupid video. It may have been a mistake to bring Selene, but it was too late for that. They'd brought her for a reason. She was the only other Amazon besides Kalli and Zoe who knew anything about the outside world. Plus, she owned a billion-dollar security company, so if things went sideways, Selene was a handy person to have around.

When the silence felt like it had gone on long enough, Zoe cleared her throat and nodded in Kalli's direction. Matis flinched and then said, "It's nice to meet you as well. This is my team: Gabriel, Lorenzo, Olivia, and Anna. And, of course, you have already met Zoe. Shall we sit?" Matis gestured to the folding chairs surrounding the table, and everyone took their seats.

Could this be any more awkward?

"Our team has been sent here to learn more about your town and its inhabitants. As I'm sure you're aware, two weeks ago this city didn't exist. It wasn't on any maps, it had never been seen on satellite photos, and no one had ever met one of the residents. That changed almost instantly, and now a village that looks like it has been here for thousands of years suddenly exists where one didn't exist before. Can you explain that to me, by chance?" Matis cut straight to the heart of the matter, not bothering to beat around the bush.

"I will do my best to do so, but you may find that even the truth will stretch your imagination," Kalli said, fiddling with the silver ring on her finger.

"We'll do our best to keep our minds open," Matis said, cutting off Gabriel, who was clearly on the verge of saying something else. Gabriel shut his mouth with an audible snap.

"That's all I ask." Kalli took a deep breath before she proceeded. "This town looks like it has been here for thousands of years because it has been. The city was built around four thousand BCE and has been occupied continuously since then. The Amazon race was around during ancient times, and it continues to this day."

"That's not possible. There's no evidence of that," Olivia said scathingly.

Sam shifted uncomfortably in his seat. "That's not entirely true. I've spent my entire career studying the Amazons, and I think you'll find that there's currently an exhibit at the Smithsonian National Museum of Natural History that documents all my findings that demonstrate that the Amazons really did exist."

Matis nodded at Anna, who promptly whipped out her laptop and started typing. "And how did you come to be involved in all this?" he asked Sam while Anna was working.

Sam and Kalli exchanged a quick glance, but she nodded for him to proceed. "Kalli and I met in DC, and I offered my expertise to help her with an urgent matter," Sam said, giving a watered-down version of the truth.

Matis grunted at the nonanswer, but seconds later Anna spun her screen toward Matis to show him the Smithsonian website, which had stills and teasers for Sam's exhibit. There were photos of excavated graves and ruined weaponry next to images of well-preserved clay vases, one of which depicted Kalli in full armor.

Matis took a quick look at the computer screen before waving it away like he couldn't be bothered to inspect it closely. "Even if what you're saying is true—which I doubt—that only proves that Amazons used to exist. Not that they still do."

Sam leaned back in his chair, a look of mild irritation crossing his face before it was quickly masked.

"Besides," Gabriel cut in, "none of that explains why the town suddenly appeared out of nowhere. Explain that." He leaned back and crossed his arms as if asking to be proved wrong.

Selene tried to speak, but Kalli raised her hand, and Selene backed off. "I assume you all saw the video from the Trevi Fountain. It's gone viral at this point, so it would have been hard to miss." There were nods around the table.

"What do you think that proves?" Gabriel spoke up again. "Just because she"—he gestured to Selene—"got into a public brawl doesn't prove that you are what you say you are. In fact, given her fighting style, I'd bet she had formal military training. Israeli army, perhaps? Or maybe US Special Forces?"

"A little bit from column A, some from column B," Selene said with a smirk.

Kalli sent Selene a pointed look, and she dropped the smile instantly. Now was not a good time for Selene's attitude to get them into trouble.

"I'm sorry, but Queen Kalliope, is it?" Matis asked, the sarcasm in his tone not particularly well masked. "Gabriel is correct. None of what you've told us so far explains the appearance of your town out of the blue."

Kalli's eyes narrowed as she once again toyed with her ring. Zoe knew the power that ring held. If only the Interpol agents knew it too. Maybe they would back off and be more open minded—not that Zoe had been expecting much. However modern and relaxed Kalli was, the Interpol agents were still insulting a ruling monarch, even if they didn't believe it. Hopefully Kalli's easygoing nature would prevail over any insult she might have taken from their behavior.

Zoe braced herself for whatever Kalli said next. They had debated for a long time about whether Kalli should explain what had happened with the veil. Interpol wasn't going to believe her if she tried to explain it, but they also knew it was going to be impossible to get out of the meeting without at least trying.

"You're right, it doesn't explain that," Kalli said. Zoe watched triumph spread on Gabriel's face before Kalli continued. "The town appeared out of nowhere, as you say, because until two weeks ago, the city was hidden. It was protected by a veil that cloaked its existence from anyone outside of that veil."

Matis smiled smugly. "So our speculations were right. You are hiding advanced technology in that backward town. Who gave it to you? Where are you stashing it?"

"Backward town?" Selene almost screeched, a sign of how upset she was. Selene was the first to admit to missing the modern-day comforts of living in the outside world, so to see her pissed off at someone for calling their city backward was mildly amusing.

"I'm afraid you're still wrong, Mr. Laurent. We aren't hiding advanced technology, or even modern technology. In fact, what we're hiding is exactly the opposite. It's ancient. What was cloaking our city was divine magic from the Greek gods."

Olivia let out a huge laugh as if she couldn't hold it in any longer. Matis rolled his eyes. He stood and extended his hand as if to shake. "Yes, well, thank you for your time. I'm sure you have more important matters to be getting back to, Queen Kalliope."

Matis didn't believe them. Not that Zoe had expected him to. But it did bring up the question of what came next. If Matis didn't believe what Kalli was saying to them, then Zoe had no idea what he was going to report to his superiors and what they would tell the various international law enforcement agencies and foreign governments.

Kalli slowly stood, a disappointed look on her face. Sam rose to join her.

"Oh, for fuck's sake," Selene spit out before she yanked her wicked-looking tactical knife out of her thigh holster. All six Interpol agents went for their guns, but before they could even aim them, Selene sliced her own arm from elbow to wrist.

"What the hell?" Lorenzo said, eyes wide as he watched the blood stream down Selene's arm. All eyes were on Selene as she sat in her chair and smiled smugly. Kalli merely sighed.

"Does anyone have a towel?" Kalli asked politely.

Zoe figured everyone else was too morbidly fascinated with what was going on and went to fetch one herself. She handed the piece of terry cloth to Selene, who inspected her arm briefly before wiping off the blood.

The cut was gone.

Matis sucked in a surprised breath, and Olivia muttered "There's no way" under her breath.

Zoe was pretty certain she'd heard Anna gasp in delight.

"Anyone care to discuss the possibility of magic now?" Selene asked in a falsely sweet tone.

"Selene, that was unnecessary," Kalli said. She turned to address the confused agents. "I apologize for my lieutenant. She gets a bit carried away at times."

Selene coughed out the words "Worth it." Zoe glared at her.

"Now, I realize that this might be a bit of a shock to everyone," Zoe said, "but perhaps we can take our seats again and continue to talk this through." She gestured to the folding chairs that everyone but Selene had vacated.

Anna and Lorenzo happily plopped back down, but the rest were far more reluctant. Just as Matis was starting to lower himself into his chair, half the cell phones in the room dinged simultaneously. All the Interpol agents, including Zoe, pulled out their devices to see what it was.

It was a news alert. Specifically one from Jason's program, *The Truth Report*. Someone obviously clicked the notification, because Jason's smooth voice filled the tent. Zoe clicked the link herself so she could see the video, but she muted the audio.

"Welcome back, viewers. If you're just joining us, I'm Jason Bloom, and what you see behind me is a camp set up by Interpol. If you've been watching our show for the last day or so, you know that we're in Türkiye, tracking the story of the mysterious village that seemingly appeared out of nowhere. Interpol has been on-site for two days so far, and we've learned that they appear to be having a meeting with the local town leadership." The video stream cut to a clip of Zoe, Kalli, Sam, and Selene walking up the hill to the tents before flashing back to their intrepid reporter. "You may recognize one of the women in that party as the same woman who was involved in the fight in the Trevi Fountain just over a week ago. While the woman named Nyx claimed to be part of an ancient civilization known as the Amazons, most experts believe the Amazons never existed and that the story was completely faked for as-yet-unknown reasons.

"However, we here at *The Truth Report* are relentless in bringing you nothing but the truth. That is why today I'm excited to show you actual evidence that not only are the mythical Amazons real but hiding among us in plain sight."

Zoe's stomach dropped. What on earth was Jason talking about? There were no Amazons hiding in plain sight. The only people that fit that description were in this very room.

Oh no . . .

The stream cut to a series of clips of her face. There was one of her talking to Matis, another where she was walking up the hill from town, another of her talking to Kalli and Selene. But the most damning shot of them all was a clip of her pacing wildly next to the Royal Hall that morning. The on-screen version of her shook her hands, sending flames scattering on the ground and catching the bush on fire. Zoe watched herself panic and stomp out the small blaze, then look around frantically before the video cut out.

"There you have it folks, definitive proof that these so-called Amazon warriors not only exist but might have more than meets the eye in the way of special abilities." The video feed cut from Jason's face and went back to someone in their home studio.

Every gaze in the room zeroed in on Zoe.

"Harper, you're one of them?" Matis asked. For the second time in five minutes, five Interpol agents went for their guns, but this time they were aimed at her.

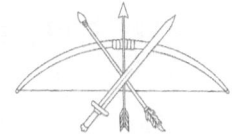

Chapter Six

As soon as Jason got the all clear that they were no longer broadcasting, he let out a loud whoop. He felt like he was flying. He wanted to throw his microphone in the air in celebration but decided against it at the last minute. No need to damage expensive equipment.

"Now that's what I'm talking about!" Jason crowed as he reached out and high-fived Noah. "That is the type of story we always need to be reporting." He grabbed Noah in a bro hug, careful not to damage his camera equipment.

"Hell yes. I can't believe we managed to break that story. EBC and TNN aren't even here yet. This is totally getting us raises," Noah said, his deep voice rising with excitement. He did a little dance and twirled in place, making Jason laugh.

The English Broadcasting Corporation and Top News Network almost always scooped them. It was a huge rush to turn the tables on the other stations. "EBC and TNN can eat their hearts out. This is our story." The adrenaline was still pounding through him. "I can't believe you captured whatever was happening with Zoe Harper and the fire. Freaky, right?"

Noah nodded. "For sure. I have no idea what was going on, but whatever it was, it wasn't normal. There was no lighter or matches in sight. Those flames were just flying off her hand."

The pair moved away from the Interpol tent and toward their own gear. Whatever talks were going on inside were most likely going to take a while. They probably had some downtime before they needed to be ready to go again.

"Matis, please be reasonable." The voice came from the tent door.

Maybe they didn't have as much time as Jason thought. With a quick hand movement Jason gestured for Noah to start filming again. Noah was way ahead of him.

Jason stood, microphone at the ready, as he watched Zoe and the small party from the village back out of the tent with their hands raised above their shoulders. Zoe looked desperate, the fiery redhead—Selene, according to the Trevi Fountain footage—looked pissed, the brunette wearing the tiara looked resigned, and the only man among them looked freaked out.

And he had reason to.

The tent flap was pushed wider as five armed Interpol agents emerged, Matis Laurent at the front of the group. Every agent had guns pointed at not only the visitors but Zoe too. Which didn't make any sense. Zoe was a member of Laurent's team. Why would they threaten her?

"Matis, I can explain," Zoe tried again.

"Oh really? I'd love to hear this explanation." He flexed his jaw, making his beard and mustache twitch. "Tell me how I have some sort of Amazon freak working on my team, standing beside us day after day, hiding right under my nose. Someone who knew exactly what was going on here—and in Rome—yet didn't see fit to tell me."

At the word *freak* Zoe's expression went from desperate to blank. It was as if all emotion washed off her face and a stone statue stood in her place. "Would you have believed me if I tried?" she asked quietly.

"Hell no," an attractive man with brown floppy hair said.

"Stay out of this, Gabriel," Matis snapped.

"So I guess this means our peaceful discussion is over?" Selene sneered, and the brunette shushed her. "What? You know I'm right, Kalliope. My queen." The redhead made a quick bow.

Kalliope took a deep breath, then slowly lowered her hands to her sides. The man standing next to her made a sound of distress, but she shook her head. "Don't worry, Sam. These people aren't going to do anything to us."

"How do you figure that?" Gabriel asked.

"Them, for one," Kalliope said, gesturing in the direction of Jason and Noah. Matis looked frustrated, as if he had forgotten about the media presence and was annoyed to be reminded. "But there's another reason. Mr. Laurent here knows that doing anything to us would be a calculated risk. He's seen what Selene is capable of. Thanks to our friends with the cameras, he's seen what Zoe is capable of. Unfortunately for him, he has no idea what I'm capable of. So there's a decision to be made. Can he and his team of agents take us out or capture us before we can retaliate? And even if he was that bold, is he willing for it to be broadcast on prime-time news? If you think the last video went viral, what do you think would happen to this one?"

Damn. Their queen was not only smart but tricky. He had to give her props for that. She'd trapped Interpol in a tight little box. If they did anything other than back off, they were either publicly ruined or dead.

Well played.

Jason watched an array of emotions cross the senior agent's face before he lowered his gun and tucked it into his hip holster. The rest of the agents followed suit.

The queen smiled. "There now, isn't that easier all around?" Zoe, Selene, and Sam slowly lowered their hands and looked around warily. "You may not have believed me when I told you where the veil cloaking the city of Themyscira came from, but I would ask you to truly give it some thought. The Amazons would like to have peaceful relationships with the outside world. In fact, it's my utmost goal to get to a place where we can work together and not be at odds. However, Interpol—in fact, the entire modern world—is dealing with something they have no knowledge about. I urge you to do your research, but keep in mind, the written histories do not contain all there is to know about my people. Now, if you'll excuse us, we'll be going." She lifted her hand aloft, and the ring on her finger started to glow. A blue light spread from the small band and surrounded her group like some sort of energy barrier, standing between them and the murderous-looking agents.

Kalliope and her people turned and headed back toward town, leaving the agents—not to mention Noah and himself—with gaping mouths.

"Harper, you're fired!" Matis screamed at their retreating backs. He spun on his heel, sent a scathing look in Jason's direction, then stormed back into the tent, his team following somewhat more slowly.

In the ringing silence, Jason turned to Noah with a huge grin. "Is it Christmas?"

"Christmas in the spring? I'll take it." Noah's matching smile lit up the morning. "We should probably shoot a quick outro clip of you talking, and then we need to get this footage to the producers ASAP. I'm sure they're going to want to run it as soon as they can."

Jason agreed and put on his serious, camera-ready expression. Noah pointed at him, and he dove right in. "Folks, what you just saw was a confrontation between the Interpol team on-site here in Türkiye and the delegation from the village we have just learned is named Themyscira. We recently showed you footage of one woman who appeared to be able to create fire from her bare hands. Now we have evidence that the Amazon queen also appears to have some sort of magical gifts. We're not sure what that blue glow was or what it was capable of, but it appeared to be emanating from a piece of jewelry the queen had on her finger.

"It seems that the peaceful talks initiated less than an hour ago have already broken down. The delegation from Themyscira has departed and not on good terms. We'll keep you posted as more developments arise."

"And we're clear," Noah said as he turned off the camera and lowered it to his side. "I'll work on getting this sent off to headquarters."

Jason nodded. "You do that. I'm going to try to track down Zoe and see if I can get her to tell me anything else."

Noah's eyes narrowed. "You really think that's such a good idea?"

"What do you mean?" Jason asked.

Noah set his camera down on its case and crossed his arms, tilting his head to stare at Jason slightly sideways. "Dude. You got her fired. You also outed her as an Amazon to the entire planet."

Jason's stomach sank. Oh yeah, he had done that, hadn't he? It was probably fine, though, because how mad could she be? She was an Amazon, so what was the point of hiding it? And if she was an Amazon, did she really need to work for Interpol?

Okay, so maybe he was oversimplifying it. Either way he now wanted to talk to her more than ever. He needed to explain why he'd done what he'd done. Surely she'd be okay with it once he gave her his reasons.

Though come to think of it, what reasons could he possibly give her for his actions? He was a reporter and truly believed that people deserved to know the truth about what was going on in the world. If there was a race of superpowerful warrior women out there, people had the right to know.

But if he was being honest with himself, was that really the only reason he'd done it? Deep down, he knew he had ulterior motives in addition to his passion for bringing the facts to the general population. He was happy with what he was doing, but in the grand scheme of the news world, he was small potatoes. *The Truth Re-*

port was a reputable program on a network with a relatively middle-of-the-road political stance. It wasn't, however, nearly as well known as EBC or TNN. Jason wanted to be a household name, someone the average person would associate with hard-hitting stories and excellent reporting. The only way to get there was to continue to push boundaries—to be the first to report.

It was ruthless, but it was how the game was played. There was no place for second-guessing himself or regretting what he'd done.

Even if he truly was sorry that his actions had hurt Zoe. He didn't like stepping on people to get what he wanted. "Yeah, I should try to apologize." With a sigh Jason ran his hands through his already windblown hair.

Noah just shrugged. "Your funeral, man." He turned away and grabbed his camera before walking to the folding table they were using as a makeshift work desk.

Jason tried to think of the best way to approach Zoe, especially now that she'd retreated with the others back to town. If only he'd followed them when they'd left. Perhaps she would have been willing to talk to him, or maybe she would have set fire to his head—you know, either way. He wanted to reach out to her, though, if only to clear his own conscience. Even if she didn't accept his apology, at least he would know he'd tried.

There was no time like the present. Jason headed down the hill toward town, apprehension weighing in his gut. He was walking into an unknown situation with armed and possibly hostile citizens. If he'd been thinking at all, he would have grabbed his Kevlar vest from his bags before starting down this path, but he didn't particularly want to turn back now. Hopefully the Amazons were reasonable people. Queen Kalliope had brought up wanting to have a peaceful relationship with the outside world. With any luck that meant not killing reporters.

The closer he got to the town, the more fascinated he became. The buildings were clearly ancient, the stone and mortar structures not particularly advanced or modern in their design or construction. He made it to the first set of small dwellings and started down the road through the center of town. There had to be enough small houses for hundreds of people.

Out of nowhere he was surrounded. Women wearing a strange blend of leather and bronze armor with modern tactical gear and Kevlar were everywhere he looked. They were on top of buildings, blocking his path down the road, and coming up behind him. Stranger still were their weapons. Not one of them held a gun. They had glinting swords, long wooden spears, and delicate—but likely still deadly—bows and arrows.

Guess I should have gone back for that bulletproof vest after all. He slowly raised his arms. "I'm here to speak to Zoe," he said, mildly proud that his voice didn't waver. Having never been on the pointy end of a blade before, he hadn't realized how terrifying it would be to suddenly have dozens of them pointed in his direction.

The Amazon in front, with dark skin and long braids coiled on top of her head, stepped forward. "We know who you are, Jason Bloom," she said as she lowered her sword. "You will come with us. Ariadne, Psyche, with me."

"Yes, Frona," two of the Amazons wearing modern clothing chorused. Sadly, these two didn't lower their weapons.

He'd never had an armed escort to speak to someone before. He could check that one off his never-want-to-do-that-again list.

Jason fell in step with the Amazons, who led him through the center of town, across the central square, and up the steps to the large building where they'd first seen Queen Kalliope and Selene. He guessed it was probably some sort of government building. It looked like he was about to find out.

He stepped inside the stone structure and blinked at the dim lighting, hoping his eyes would rapidly adjust. It was a large room with a long wooden table taking pride of place in the center and flanked by simple benches on either side. At the far end of the room was a carved wooden chair that sat on a small, elevated platform. In that chair—surrounded by a bickering crowd of people—sat Queen Kalliope.

All eyes turned toward him and his escorts as they entered the room.

"You!" Zoe yelled as she pivoted toward him. "This is your fault." Her hands bunched into fists, and she attempted to lunge at him but was restrained by Selene and a lean man with brown hair and hazel eyes.

"Zoe, no. You don't want to do that," the man said calmly.

Zoe pinned her captor with a scathing look. "Are you sure about that, Colin? What would you do in this scenario? What if he'd outed your big secret on prime-time news?" Zoe continued to struggle, but between Selene and Colin they seemed to have her immobilized.

It was probably a good thing for his safety that they had her pinned. He had a feeling she was going to be upset, but her reaction was fairly extreme. He put his hands up slightly, palms out. "Zoe, just give me a moment."

"Why should I?" She lashed out at him. "You have no idea the extent of what you've done!" Color rose in her cheeks as her eyes pinned him in place like a bug on a corkboard.

Jason glanced at the queen, who appeared grim, then to Sam, who stood next to her, looking concerned. Selene looked almost as angry as Zoe, despite the fact that she was holding Zoe back from attacking him. Only the newcomer, Colin, had any sort of sympathy and understanding on his face.

Jason was definitely missing something. But when in doubt, fall back on professionalism. He turned to where the queen sat on her throne and gave her a bow. "Queen Kalliope, forgive my intrusion. I came to apologize to Zoe."

Kalliope raised one eyebrow, then gestured with one arm for him to proceed.

With a quick nod of thanks to the queen, Jason turned to fully face the gorgeous and ferociously pissed-off blond woman in the middle of the room. "Zoe, I would like to formally apologize for my actions. It was unprofessional of me to share your secret on the news without getting your permission first. I had no idea that my story would come at the cost of your job." He bowed his head to her as well, then waited.

Zoe stopped struggling against the people restraining her and stared at him slack-jawed. "My job? That's what you think this is about?" Venom practically dripped from her words.

Jason froze in place, suddenly uncertain. "Isn't it?"

Zoe finally broke free of her captors and slowly paced toward him. "I'm over four thousand years old. Do you think I give a rat's ass about a job I've had for ten years? This has nothing to do with getting me fired."

Shock ricocheted through Jason. "Four thousand years old . . ." He tried to interrupt her to ask about that important fact, but she barreled on.

"Our city has been invisible to the outside world for thousands of years. None of those powerful countries that exist outside of these borders were even aware of our existence, which is exactly how we wanted it. Kalli hid our city on purpose all those years ago for this exact reason. We were too big of a target. Other countries and their rulers figured out who we were and what we were capable of, and they came for us. In droves. Our people started to die out. We had no choice but to lock ourselves away out of a sense of self-preservation." She finally came to a stop in front of him and jabbed her index finger into his chest hard enough to leave a bruise.

"Now here we are. We were hoping that we could reintroduce the Amazons to the modern world in a way that was slow and controlled. And most importantly"—she gave him a pointed stare—"informed by outside intelligence about what those outsiders were thinking and planning. Intelligence I could have provided through my position at Interpol."

He was starting to understand the ramifications of what he'd done, but as soon as he opened his mouth, she cut him off again.

"The last thing we wanted was to paint a giant bull's-eye on Themyscira and the people living here. And with one fell swoop, *you* undid all our careful planning. You destroyed the only access we had to what those foreign governments might be planning. We're flying blind in a world that might want to kill us, and it's entirely *your fault*." She punctuated her point with another sharp jab to his chest.

Zoe was inches from his face, but he refused to back down.

She was right, though. He hadn't seen the long game. He'd seen the secret society of mythological warriors and thought just far enough along the path to believe that the population should be aware of them and the potential threat they posed. He hadn't given a single thought to what the Amazons were risking in the interaction.

His shoulders slumped, and his gaze dropped to somewhere around her navel. He felt about two inches tall. He deserved everything she was throwing at him and more. "You're right," he said quietly. He felt awful about the role he'd played in this situation, even if he was just doing his job. "There aren't enough words in the English language to express my remorse for the consequences of my actions. If there is anything I can possibly do to make this up to you, please let me know." Jason didn't bother looking at Zoe. His eyes went straight to the queen. "Queen Kalliope, if there is anything I can do to make this situation better, either as an individual or as a reporter with access to the world's media, please don't hesitate to reach out." He pulled a business card out of his pocket and slid it onto the table.

The queen stood from her throne with a sad smile. "Thank you for your offer, Mr. Bloom, but I think you've done quite enough for one day." She gestured to his guards, who hadn't ventured more than two feet away from him during the entire confrontation with Zoe. "Psyche, please escort Mr. Bloom out of the city."

"We're not tossing him in jail?" Selene asked.

Colin chuckled. "Not everyone deserves to be thrown in jail, love."

"Especially not with Interpol and the international media watching," Sam said.

Jason cast one last look over the gathered group, but his eyes came to rest on Zoe. "I am sorry. Maybe someday you'll find it in your heart to forgive me." With one last nod, he left.

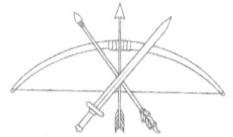

Chapter Seven

ZOE COULDN'T BELIEVE THE nerve of Jason. Showing up unwelcome and uninvited. "How dare he come into Themyscira less than an hour after he potentially signed its death warrant?" Zoe felt overheated, and flames raced under her skin. She glanced down and realized that her powers were once again rearing their ugly head. Only this time there were no tiny embers that she could quickly douse. This time her hands were fully engulfed in flames.

"Has that been happening a lot lately?" Colin asked casually as he stared in fascination. "I can't say I've ever seen someone spontaneously combust before."

"It's not the usual way I like to send men up in flames," Zoe said sweetly, making Colin smirk.

Kalli crossed the room until she was standing next to Zoe. "All jokes aside, has this been happening frequently?" Kalli nodded at Zoe's flaming hands, which she still hadn't managed to extinguish.

"Other than the incident that was caught on camera this morning, I mean."

Zoe pinched her lips. Like she needed to be reminded that her powers had been caught on camera. "Only one other time. While we were setting up camp yesterday." She took a deep breath and closed her eyes, willing the flames to retreat.

Finally she felt the heat leave her hands. When she opened her eyes again, the fire was gone, but her queen's concerned gaze wasn't. "And before yesterday?"

Zoe's stomach twisted in discomfort. She felt like a bug under a magnifying glass. "It's been a very long time," she said quietly. Now was not the time to get into why she'd stopped using her powers. They had bigger issues at stake. "So what do we do now?" Zoe asked, trying to change the subject.

"That's an excellent question, considering option A blew up in our faces. Literally." Selene gave Zoe a sideways glance. "What's option B?"

Everyone fell silent as they tried to come up with an answer. They had placed all their hopes on being able to talk some sense into Interpol and ensure they had the time they needed to convince the world they weren't a threat. Now that that option was gone, they needed a backup plan, and they needed it now.

"Can we do a show of force? Make them realize that it would be a mistake to try to invade Themyscira?" Frona asked.

Kalli was already shaking her head. "Sadly, no. They have access to weapons unlike what you've ever seen or even imagined. Our entire town would be dust within seconds."

"If we can't go on the offensive, then we need a stronger defense," Sam said. "You all have gifts. Could any of them be used to defend the city in case the worst happens?"

All the Amazons looked at Zoe, but she shook her head. "Not an option." Sam and Colin didn't know the full extent of her abilities, but Kalli, Selene, Frona, and Ariadne did. While some of her abilities could potentially do what Sam was proposing, there was no way she was willing to open herself up like that again. Not happening.

"What about the fleece?" Ariadne asked quietly. She bit her lower lip and lowered her eyes as if she was expecting to get pounced on for asking.

"The fleece?" Sam asked skeptically. "You mean the golden fleece?"

Ariadne glanced around the gathered crowd of people, and when no one cut her off, she continued talking. "Yes, the golden fleece. The one stolen by Jason and the Argonauts. It was rumored to have protection spells imbued into it. If we brought it back to Themyscira, maybe it could help protect our borders?"

Silence rang in the air for several moments before a bunch of people started talking at once.

"There's no way it's still around," Selene argued.

"Really? You're going with that argument while wearing that?" Colin asked in amusement as he pointed at the leather-and-bronze belt wrapped tightly around Selene's waist. The belt that Selene and Colin had tracked down after it had been missing for more than three thousand years.

Selene's eyes narrowed. "That's different, though. The belt was trapped in a magically protected vault. There's no way sheepskin from 1300 BCE is still around in this day and age."

Colin cracked up laughing, earning him a glare from Selene.

Zoe didn't know what to think. She wasn't as dubious about the fleece's existence as Selene appeared to be, but it seemed like a long shot. Not to mention, the stories about the fleece's powers were just that, stories. There was no guarantee that it could do what it was purported to do.

Oh, but if it could . . .

Zoe imagined the relief of knowing that the borders of her homeland were safe. Safe from a threat she'd accidentally brought to their shores. She'd heard the stories of the fleece just like anyone else who had been alive at the time, not to mention the thousands of scholars who had studied its existence since then. If there was even a chance that it was still around, she had to try. It was the answer to all their prayers.

"I'll go," Zoe volunteered, interrupting the argument that she'd conveniently tuned out. Everyone in the room stopped talking and stared at her, but Zoe pressed on. "It's my fault that we're in this mess. It's my responsibility to fix it," she continued.

"Zoe, you can't take responsibility for this situation. It isn't your fault. If the fault lies with anyone, it's with me. I'm the one who chose to remove the veil that had hidden our city for millennia. I'm the reason the outside world is suddenly aware of our existence," Kalli said, a deep vee forming between her brows.

"It was the right thing to do," Selene argued. "Our people had a right to know about the modern world."

"I can't say I disagree. I never would have met this one had you not done it," Colin said, then winked at Selene. She sent him a cheeky grin back.

"Be that as it may," Zoe said, interrupting Kalli before she could start speaking again. "What's done is done. The barrier is down, the outside world knows of our existence, and I just pissed off one of the most powerful law enforcement agencies on the planet by lying to them. You can stay here and brainstorm a plan C in case I fail, but I'm going to go see if I can find a shiny piece of wool and leather that might save our asses."

Zoe's righteous anger carried her out into the baking afternoon sun. She got as far as the middle of the town square before she stopped dead. She had no idea what she was doing. If she'd been thinking more clearly, she would have asked either Sam or Colin to come with her on this wild-goose chase. Sam was an anthropology professor with a specialty in Amazon history and Greek myth. Colin had been his PhD student. Both knew way more about ancient history than she did, despite her having lived through it. They lived and breathed history. She'd merely survived it.

It wasn't too late to turn around. The Royal Hall was only a few dozen feet away. She could head back inside and either give up the foolish quest or ask for assistance. Both options seemed smarter than blundering off on her own. But that would mean admitting she was in over her head and that she was unwilling or unable to get herself and her family out of a mess of her own creation. Because no matter what Kalli wanted her to believe, at least part of this was Zoe's fault. Perhaps there had been another way to approach this situation that hadn't involved her lying to her coworkers. Or maybe she could have found a way to explain the situation and herself so that they wouldn't have been so angry.

That felt like a good place to start. She could go back to the Interpol base camp by herself—no other Amazons in tow—and see if they would hear her out. If they would, perhaps she could still salvage this situation and she wouldn't have to go off chasing shadows.

With a new plan, Zoe made the journey back through town and up the hill to where she could see the white canvas tents flapping in the wind. For the second day in a row, she climbed the steep incline as the sun was setting behind her, turning the sky blushing shades of orange, pink, and blue. The peace of the scene was almost enough to make her think everything was going to be fine.

Until she saw her suitcase, neatly packed, sitting in the middle of the clearing fifteen feet away from the tent, as if waiting for her to claim it. Or maybe hoping someone would steal it.

She sighed and glanced at the door of the tent. Maybe there was still a chance. She'd known Matis a long time. If she could just talk to him now that he'd had some time to cool down, she might stand a chance.

"I wouldn't go in there if I were you," a purring voice said from behind her.

Zoe spun around in surprise, her hands coming up to defend herself, if necessary.

Gabriel straightened from where he'd been leaning against a tree, his hands in front of him in a calming gesture. "It is fine, ma chérie. I'm not here to attack you. I probably couldn't best you if I tried." He raised one eyebrow in question, as if waiting for her to confirm that she could kick his ass.

Zoe's heart rate slowed as she watched her friend and former colleague approach slowly. "How bad is it?" she asked, nodding toward the tent as if there were any mistaking what she was asking about.

Gabriel's attractive mouth pinched into a grimace. "Laurent has been on the phone for an hour. No one knows who he's talking to, but based on the small snippets of conversation we have overheard, it's probably someone pretty high up at work. Your name has come up a few times." Gabriel winced as he said it.

Zoe crossed her arms and sighed. "Well, there goes any hope I had of trying to resolve this situation quickly."

Silence stretched between them. As Zoe was prepared to leave, Gabriel finally blurted out, "Is it true? Are you really an Amazon?"

Zoe couldn't tell if he wanted the answer to be yes or no. Earlier he'd been unimpressed and somewhat derogatory about her people. She wasn't sure whether confirming she was one of them would improve his opinions of the Amazons or lower his opinion of her. Either way, it didn't matter in the end. "Yes, I really am." There was no sense in hiding it. Everything had been caught live on camera by Jason and his trusty sidekick.

Gabriel nodded as if he'd expected her answer. "There was always something different about you. I never could figure out what it was."

He shrugged. "I'll do my best with Laurent and the others. I can't promise you anything, though."

It was far more than she'd been expecting, so she'd take it with gratitude. "Thank you, Gabriel. You're a good friend."

He smiled sadly. "Even if that's all I'll ever be." With that, he sent her a quick wave, then headed back inside the tent.

Zoe grabbed her suitcase and was about to return to Themyscira when yet another voice made her jump. "Please tell me you never slept with that guy." Jason emerged from the direction of the orange tent that Zoe assumed he and his cameraman were sharing.

"What's it to you if I did?" she asked. She had no idea where the totally inappropriate question was coming from.

Jason shrugged as he stopped just out of her reach. "He seems like a tool. Someone like you could do much better than him."

If she hadn't been pissed before, she was now. "Someone like me?" She tossed his words back at him. The last thing she needed right then was someone making snide comments about her and her people. "You mean an Amazon?"

Jason flinched. "What? No. I meant someone as attractive and self-confident as you are. On a scale of one to ten, you're a fifteen. That dude is no higher than a seven on a good day."

Zoe wasn't sure if it was better or worse being judged by her looks instead of her heritage. "Well, as flattering as that may be," she said sarcastically, "I need to be going now." She spun on her heels and headed back toward town.

"Wait, where are you going?"

"To locate something that might help me fix this mess," Zoe tossed over her shoulder as she walked away.

Much to her annoyance, Jason jogged up behind her and matched her pace. "What can I do to help?"

She sent him a sideways look. "I think you've helped quite enough, thank you."

His face fell. "Okay, I deserved that one. But seriously, I want to help fix things. I didn't have any idea that my story was going to blow up the peace talks so spectacularly. I would never have wished for that to happen. I'm willing and eager to help in any way I can."

Zoe paused halfway down the hill to face Jason more fully. His blue eyes sparkled with honesty, and his far-too-attractive face displayed a tentative smile. She could almost feel the regret pouring off him. She was happy that he'd finally realized the extent to which his intervention had screwed them over, but she had no use for a nosy reporter following her around, especially while she was chasing after something as important as the golden fleece. She also had a hard time believing that his motives were as pure as he made them out to be.

"Let me get this straight. You have exclusive access to the one of the biggest breaking news stories on the planet, and you're willing to give that up to help me run an errand?" It was an oversimplification of her actual mission, of course, but it made her point.

Jason was already nodding. "By this time tomorrow—if not earlier—this place is going to be crawling with other news stations. In fact, I'm surprised they're not here already. Whatever exclusive access you think I have is going to go up in a puff of smoke. My network can send someone else to take this story. I'm more interested in the up close and personal. Who are the Amazons? What do they want? What are they capable of?" His eyes went dreamy for a second before his gaze snapped back to hers. "That's why I want to follow you. Well, that and to help fix the situation I unintentionally threw a grenade into."

And there it was. He wanted to do a story on her. She couldn't even muster one iota of surprise that he had ulterior motives for wanting to help. "I think you've put me in the spotlight quite enough already. No thanks." She resumed her trek down the hill. This time he didn't follow her.

"Don't you want to tell your side of the story?" he asked quietly.

She froze in her tracks a second time. She glanced back at him and saw his earnest expression, his eyes almost pleading with her. "What do you mean? And speak clearly, since I'm already annoyed with this conversation."

Jason nodded and approached her slowly, hands out in front of him as if he were approaching a wild animal. "What if I promised to help you get your message out into the world? Think about it. Wouldn't it be better if you could tell your side of the story and not be forced to rely on whatever skewed view will be coming from the other side? If you trust me, I can help you with this. Think of it like an image campaign. One the Amazons desperately need."

"No thanks to you," Zoe muttered sarcastically.

She contemplated what he was offering. She'd had passing interactions with the media over the years while she worked with Interpol, and most of them were out for their own stories and to make a name for themselves. It seemed like too far of a stretch that she'd found the one reporter in the whole world who wasn't hoping that his next story would be his next big break.

As if sensing that her resolve was weakening, Jason's voice dropped and turned silky and impossible to resist. "You could even look at this as a way to get back at me for exposing your secret to the world. Besides, don't you want a chance to win the world over to your cause? The more supporters you have, the worse it would look for some overly ambitious world power if they decided to take things to the extreme, you know what I mean?"

She knew exactly what he meant. If there was any chance that having this reporter with golden retriever energy tag along with her would help stop the US or any other country from blowing up her homeland, she had to at least consider it. She held up one finger to Jason and pulled out her phone. She called Kalli and quickly filled her in on Jason's idea. Unsurprisingly, Kalli was supportive and wanted her to play nice with the reporter. Apparently she now had a shadow.

"Fine. Let's go."

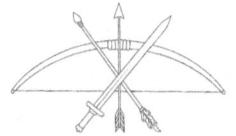

Chapter Eight

H AD JASON REALLY HEARD what he thought he'd heard? He'd been hoping to convince her to let him tag along on whatever mission she was leaving for, but he'd never expected her to agree. Not one to look a gift horse in the mouth, he simply said, "Give me five minutes to grab my stuff."

She rolled her gorgeous blue eyes and flipped her long blond hair over her shoulder as if it was in her way. "Fine. Meet me there." She pointed to a spot near town where he could barely make out a few large SUVs hiding behind a building. "If you're not there in six minutes, I'm leaving without you." With that, she flounced off.

Jason raced back up the hill to the tent he was sharing with Noah. The other man looked startled at Jason's sudden appearance, but he had no time to explain. Jason started frantically shoving clothing into his bag. Some of it might not even have been his. Whatever. "Sorry, Noah. I'm going to have to ditch you here. Don't worry, I'll call and warn the station that they need to get someone else out here

ASAP. I have a lead I can't pass up. I have no idea when I'll be back." He grabbed his laptop, his phone, and his chargers, and was hoping that wherever Zoe was heading, it had access to fast Wi-Fi.

"What on earth are you talking about?" Noah asked, his eyebrows somewhere near his hairline.

Jason took one last look around their meager campsite and then sent his cameraman and friend a jaunty salute. "Sorry, my man. Duty calls." He left Noah spluttering behind him and raced down the hill, his bags smacking him on the ass. No way was he missing the chance to follow the lovely Zoe around because he couldn't run fast enough.

With fifteen seconds to spare he finally skidded to a stop next to the hulking black vehicle. He wanted nothing more than to heave in giant breaths—he longed for oxygen—but Zoe's unimpressed stare had him doing whatever he could to downplay how out of shape he was. "Ready," he gasped out. He was fairly positive he'd blown whatever semblance of cool he might have possessed, but oh well. Breathing was sort of necessary for life.

"Fine. Get in," Zoe said as she climbed behind the wheel without looking at him.

Jason tossed his bags into the back seat and then climbed in next to her. "So," he tried once his breathing had started to slow back to a normal level. "Where are we headed?"

"Greece."

Huh. He wasn't sure what he was expecting, but Greece seemed like a random place to be traveling during what was likely to turn into a very tense standoff. "Do you mind if I ask why we're heading to Greece?" Jason asked, glancing at his traveling companion out of the corner of his eye.

"Maybe I want a quick getaway with a sexy American," she said with a wink.

Jason chuckled. "Not that I'm not flattered, but since you had this little jaunt planned before I invited myself along, I tend not to believe you. You do realize that if I'm going to be doing a story on you and the Amazons, it's only going to work if you and I actually talk, right?"

"Believe it or not, I do realize that," she said before falling silent.

"Okay, then." He let her have the silence. She was clearly uncomfortable talking to him. He needed to find a way to ease her into it. Maybe he could come up with questions that didn't feel like an invasion of her privacy. He was a skilled reporter. He should be much better at this, but something about her was throwing him for a loop. It had nothing to do with her earlier truth bomb about being four thousand years old—though they would absolutely be coming back to that at some point—or even about her being an Amazon—someone who could somehow conjure fire from nothing. No, this had a far simpler explanation.

She was fucking hot.

Jason had never had trouble getting women. He was confident enough to admit that he was no slouch in the looks department. It was almost a job requirement for being on camera for a living. But the woman seated next to him was intimidating on a whole new level. It was a level he was going to have to get used to, though, since they were traveling together for however long it took them to chase down whatever she was after.

"Cats or dogs?" Jason asked as Zoe pulled onto the highway.

"Huh?" she asked, glancing at him quickly before looking back at the road.

He shifted around in the passenger's seat until he was looking at her head-on. "I figure if we're going to be spending some time together, we should probably get to know one another. So which do you prefer, cats or dogs?"

She chewed on her lower lip like she had to think about it. "Cats, I guess."

"Figures. The strong, independent woman likes the animal that can't be bossed around. Me, I'm a fan of dogs. They're trainable, so they listen to what you say, but they're also the sweetest companion you'll ever have. Nothing shows affection quite like a good dog," he said. "Snowy mountains or sunny beaches?"

She expertly maneuvered the car through the light traffic as they headed toward the nearby city of Samsun. "Beaches, duh. You've seen my hometown."

Zoe's icy demeanor was starting to thaw, and Jason was here for it. He smiled. "Of course, how could I have picked such a silly question. Let me see . . . London or Paris?"

"Paris," she answered instantly. "The Louvre, the Eiffel Tower, the Arc de Triomphe. Even if they are tourist destinations, you can't beat them."

Jason made a sound like a loud buzzer going off. "Incorrect answer. London is clearly superior. Buckingham Palace, Tower Bridge, and of course the London Eye." He listed a few sites off the top of his head, though he didn't really have a preference between the cities. Both Paris and London were equally magical. Mostly he wanted to pick the opposite of what she did to needle her.

"Favorite myth or legend," Zoe prompted.

"The Amazons, obviously." Jason winked at her, pleased that she was playing along.

"I guess I walked right into that one."

He could have pressed her for more information with the opening she'd given him, but he didn't. She was starting to let her guard down, and he needed to earn her trust. Even more than that, he wanted her to like him. He didn't want to examine his reason for that very carefully, though. "Queen Bey or Tay Tay?"

This time she laughed out loud. "Going for the pop culture reference, I see. Should I feel stereotyped?"

Jason gasped and put his hand up to his heart like he was offended. "I'll have you know that both Beyoncé and Taylor Swift are near and dear to my heart, thank you very much."

Zoe rolled her eyes at him. "And it has absolutely nothing to do with them being supremely attractive women."

"Of course not. They're both extremely talented musicians."

"On that we can agree," Zoe responded. She took the exit to the airport, then pulled into a parking lot and cut the engine. "Last stop." She hopped out of the vehicle and grabbed her luggage. Jason did the same. Instead of going to any sort of ticket counter or passing through a terminal, Zoe walked up to a security checkpoint at an outside gate and flashed her ID. Once they were through, she led him to a small private jet.

"Is this yours?" he asked, his voice rising in surprise.

Zoe scoffed. "Nope. You can thank Selene for this. I don't know where or how she gets most of what she acquires, and I probably don't want to know. Though now that I think of it, if I no longer work for Interpol, I guess it doesn't matter if I know what illegal stuff she and Colin get up to." She tipped her head to the side as if she was considering. Eventually she shrugged and climbed the steps to the small plane.

Jason had only ever flown commercial. To say this was a step up was an understatement. There were a few comfortable-looking leather seats, a small kitchenette, and what appeared to be a bedroom at the rear of the plane. He guessed the rich really were different. Zoe plopped herself into one of the seats as a hulking man in all-black clothing came out of nowhere and stowed their luggage for them. Jason chose a seat across the aisle from Zoe.

"Thank you, Marcus," Zoe said.

The man nodded and offered them each a beverage and then gracefully departed into the cockpit. They were airborne minutes later.

After the pilot came over the speakers and did his spiel, Jason took advantage of the fact that he had Zoe trapped and unable to escape him. He studied her exquisite profile while she studiously ignored him. She had a narrow patrician face that might have been described as dainty if it were on another woman. She, however, was at least as tall as he—making her at least five ten. She had long blond hair that she'd twisted into a braid that fell to the middle of her back.

After several minutes, she finally turned toward him and asked, "What?" Exasperation was evident in her voice.

Jason shrugged. "Nothing in particular. I'm just trying to figure you out. You're an Amazon, a former Interpol agent—sorry, again—and you can conjure fire. Oh, and don't think I forgot about that four-thousand-year-old comment either."

She blushed. "Yeah, I shouldn't have tossed that out there. Sorry about that." God she looked adorable. He probably shouldn't mention that, though.

He noted that she hadn't denied her age. He cocked his head and squinted as if he could see into her thoughts. "Is it true?" he asked casually, as if it were a normal, everyday occurrence to ask someone whether they were thousands of years old.

Zoe's gaze darted around the plane like she was expecting someone to jump out and yell *boo*. Unsurprisingly, no one appeared out of thin air. The only other people on the plane were locked behind the cockpit doors. Finally she sighed and slumped lower in her chair. "Yes. We're all that old."

"All the Amazons," he clarified, though he really didn't need to. There was no one else in this scenario who could possibly be that old. Not that it made sense for anyone to be that old. *How was it even possible?*

She nodded. "Yes. We're actually immortal."

There was no way. She had to be yanking his chain or something. "Immortal. So you can never die?" He could hear the skepticism in his own voice, so it made total sense when she narrowed her eyes at him.

"Did I say invulnerable? No. We can die. We just won't ever die of natural causes. A bullet to the heart or a missile launched by some trigger-happy first-world nation would take care of us real quick." She crossed her arms and huffed.

Jason put his hands up, palms out. "Sorry, I didn't intend to offend. I'm just trying to figure out the new rules here. Most of us alive today can only hope for eighty years or so, if we're lucky. Four thousand feels a bit like an eternity from where I'm sitting." Did he really believe that she was as old as she said she was? What benefit would there be in her lying at this point? This situation could easily escalate to one where her small hometown of a few hundred preternatural soldiers faced off against the rest of humanity. He supposed anything she could say to make her own people look more fearsome would only be a check in the plus column for them.

"So what's with the fire thing?" he asked when she didn't say anything else. He gestured to her hands like she didn't know what he was asking about. *He was an idiot.*

Her eyebrows winged up. "What about the fire thing?" She didn't move, her hands remaining tucked under her armpits like she might never remove them.

"Can you really conjure fire? Can all Amazons make fire? Can you show me?" He leaned closer to her, even as he mentally cursed himself for sounding like an eager nine-year-old.

She gave him a stare that made it obvious exactly how much of a fool she thought he was. "Are you seriously asking if I'll summon flames from my hands? On a plane filled with fuel? While we're thousands of feet in the air?"

Right. Explosions were bad. He knew that, but excitement coursed through his body at the idea that magic really did exist in the world. The fact that he was in the presence of someone who could wield it was astonishing. He wanted to know everything he could possibly know.

"No, obviously that would be a bad idea. But, you know, maybe later?" He grinned like a kid in a candy store. She rolled her eyes at him but didn't say no, which he decided was a maybe. Her phone dinged, which surprised him given that they were airborne. *Did private jets have Wi-Fi?*

Whatever the message said, she clearly wasn't particularly pleased with the contents, if her scowl was anything to go by.

"To answer your question, no. Not all Amazons can conjure fire. That's sort of a me thing."

He could tell she was reluctant to talk about it, but he was pleased that she was anyway. "To what do I owe the honor of your sudden willingness to answer my questions?" he teased, hoping to get a smile out of her. Instead, she waggled her phone in his direction.

"Direct orders. Kalli thinks that talking to you and having you tell our side of the story is a brilliant idea. So here we are. I'm supposed to be honest with you." Zoe practically grimaced.

It was obvious to Jason that Zoe wasn't super comfortable talking about her personal history. Too bad. As far as he could tell—and from the short time he'd known her—she was born for the spotlight. "I promise to make the process as painless as possible."

She looked at him slyly. "You promise? It's my first time, after all," she practically purred.

It finally occurred to him exactly what he'd said and how it had sounded. He felt heat rising in his cheeks but did his best to ignore it. He cleared his throat awkwardly. "So where are we headed?"

The sultry smile slid from her mouth, leaving only a serious, get-down-to-business expression. "Volos, Greece."

Well, that was both specific and delightfully vague. "Any particular reason we're going to Volos, Greece?" He had no idea what he'd gotten himself into, but at least he had an intriguing companion along for the ride.

She smiled again. "Yep. I'm looking for a sheep."

What. The. Hell?

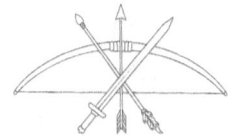

Chapter Nine

S TILL ANNOYED THAT KALLI had wanted her to play nice with the slimy reporter—who wasn't all that slimy once you got to know him—Zoe took her time and drew it out just to torture him. She had to have her fun where she could get it, after all.

"Exactly how well do you know Greek mythology?" she asked.

He shrugged his muscular shoulders and cocked his head. "A little, I guess. I mean, I watched the Disney version of *Hercules*, does that count?"

She rolled her eyes at him. Something she seemed to be doing a lot of. "You get like five percent credit for that. Do you happen to know the story of Jason and the Argonauts?"

Jason shook his head. "Nope, but I gotta say, whoever named him had great taste."

Zoe wanted to roll her eyes again, but she felt a small smile cross her lips instead. He could be quite charming when he wanted to be. "Well, consider this your crash course in your namesake. Once upon a time, a young boy and his sister were on the verge of being sacrificed in a ritual to the gods. At the last moment, a winged golden ram swooped out of the sky and carried them away. The ram carried the boy to the land of Colchis, though his sister tragically died on the journey. The boy eventually grew up, married, and sacrificed the ram in gratitude for the hospitality shown to him by the king of Colchis, preserving the ram's golden fleece in the process. The king, however, eventually grew paranoid that the young man would betray him. The king preemptively killed the man and nailed the fleece to a tree. He then placed two fire-breathing oxen and a dragon near the tree to protect the magic fleece from anyone who might steal it and the fertility and protection it provided to the king's lands.

"Years later, in a distant land, a man named Jason sought to reclaim the throne that was stolen from him by his uncle Pelias when Jason was a baby. When adult Jason confronted his uncle, Pelias told him that he would willingly give up the throne, but only if Jason first acquired the golden fleece from the king of Colchis. Jason gathered a band of warriors—including your pal Hercules—and set out on a quest aboard the mighty ship *Argos*, making the name for themselves of Jason and the Argonauts. The warriors faced many trials along their path but did eventually acquire the golden fleece and returned home."

Jason listened in rapt attention. When she got to the end of her story, though, he sent her a confused look. "That's a lovely tale—well, sort of, with all the death and all—but what does that have to do with you, me, and Volos, Greece?"

"We're looking for the golden fleece," Zoe said as she watched Jason's mouth drop open in shock.

He shook his head like he was trying to clear it. "I'm sorry, did you say that we were searching for a fictional sheepskin from a myth that's thousands of years old?"

Zoe just blinked. "Who said the fleece was fictional?" She paused, amusement draining from her. As much as she enjoyed tormenting the newbie, this was serious. "The biggest problem isn't that the fleece didn't exist in the first place. The problem is that no one knows what happened to the fleece after Jason returned and presented it to Pelias. Jason and his wife—a sorceress named Medea, who also happened to be the daughter of the king of Colchis—didn't live happy lives after they returned to Jason's home."

She could practically see the wheels turning behind Jason's eyes. He was struggling to believe what she was saying. She didn't blame him. If she hadn't been steeped in this history and lore for thousands of years, she probably wouldn't believe it either. Unfortunately, she needed him to get on board sooner rather than later. It wouldn't help the public image of the Amazons if the person charged with broadcasting their message didn't believe a word they were saying.

"Right, so . . ." Jason trailed off.

She filled in the blanks for him. "Pelias was the king of Iolcus in the region known as Thessaly—known in modern times as Thessalia. Iolcus doesn't exist anymore, at least not under that name. It's now known as Volos. It seemed like it made sense to start there." Zoe didn't bother to bring up the fact that Sam and Colin had been texting her helpful hints that pointed her in this direction. What Jason didn't know wouldn't hurt him.

"I'm following your logic on the location. It makes as much sense as any of this does. But what about the fleece? Even if it had existed back in the day, what's to say that it's still around today?" Skepticism laced his words.

Zoe shrugged. "Because if it doesn't, Themyscira is screwed." Ever since they had left her hometown on this—admittedly reckless—journey, Zoe had been racking her brain for an alternative. Anything that would help her hometown and her people protect and defend themselves against the unknown threats the modern world presented. Nothing came to mind, which was aggravating. Zoe had lived in the outside world longer than she'd had the opportunity to live in her home. It frustrated her beyond belief that she couldn't come up with an alternative plan that had a higher probability of success than the Hail Mary she was currently chasing.

Jason fell silent, and she took the opportunity to grab a few minutes of shut-eye. Once they landed in Greece, there was no telling what they would find or how soon they would be able to return home.

What felt like no more than minutes later—but logically could have been a couple of hours—the pilot's voice came over the speakers to tell them that they were descending into Greece. Zoe rubbed the exhaustion out of her eyes. It was the middle of the night. Both she and Jason would need more sleep. Tomorrow was soon enough to tackle whatever lay ahead of them.

They landed at a small airport about half an hour from Volos. Thankfully Selene's team had already made them hotel reservations. They checked in, the clerk handing them each a room key, and Zoe turned to Jason. "I guess I'll see you in the morning?" It was a statement, yet somehow came out more like a question.

He nodded at her. "Looking forward to it." He said as they went their separate ways.

Zoe opened her hotel room door, dropped her luggage on the carpet, and face-planted into the soft bedding. If today hadn't been the longest day she'd ever lived, then she would eat her suitcase. She passed out before she'd even bothered to change into pajamas.

A bright beam of sunlight shining through the curtains she'd failed to close woke Zoe. She glanced at the clock and realized she'd slept almost ten hours. Perhaps having your whole life turned upside down and rearranged without your permission could really take it out of a person.

Zoe was tempted to stay in bed—metaphorically burying her head in the sand—but someone pounded on her hotel room door, startling her. "Up and at 'em, Zoe. There are people to save and sheep to herd."

Zoe pressed her smile into the smooth sheets of the pillow she was clutching. Jason obviously still had no idea what they were up against—neither did she, to be honest—but he was more than willing to run heedlessly into danger. She had to admire him for it. "What if I left my sheep-mucking boots at home?" she called out, her stomach swooping as she waited for his response.

"I've heard there are a number of wonderful shops here in Greece that sell such items. If we get a move on, we may even get there before everyone else snatches them up."

Jason's wry humor warmed something inside her. With a smile he wouldn't be able to see, she dragged herself out of bed. "With an offer like that, how can I possibly refuse? Give me a few minutes and I'll meet you outside." She heard the soft sound of footsteps on carpet as Jason retreated. Zoe took a quick shower and then changed into fresh clothes.

Jason was casually leaning against the hallway wall when Zoe emerged from her room. It wasn't remotely fair that he looked fresh and rested, not to mention extremely attractive, while she still felt slightly flattened and exhausted. Well, it wasn't exactly like his people were the ones on the brink of extinction, right?

He pushed off the wall when he saw her emerge from her room. "It's a bit late for breakfast, but I figure we can maybe grab an early lunch and then head out. Where exactly are we going first?" He fell in step next to her, his bag casually draped over his shoulder.

Zoe wasn't even sure what their next step was. "Good question." She fished her phone out of her pocket and found it flooded with text messages. If she had to guess, Colin and Sam were having some sort of unofficial competition or one-upmanship, trying to see who could help her out the most. Or, more likely, Sam was trying to be helpful, and Colin was still trying to prove he was better than Sam. Oh well, that wasn't Zoe's problem to deal with. As long as they sent her stuff she could use, she didn't care what dick-measuring contests they engaged in.

Scrolling through the pages of text, it appeared both had suggested going to the Archaeological Museum of Volos. It was as good a place to start as any. "My sources say there's a museum in Volos that has artifacts that date back to the time of the Argonauts—some even date before that. We should start there."

"Your sources?" His voice rose in skepticism.

"Fine. Sam and Colin both think we should start there." They reached the hotel parking lot and located the black rental sedan that Selene had arranged for them—sometimes it paid to know someone with Selene's connections.

"What's their story? Obviously they're Kalli and Selene's partners, but what do they know that you don't? Didn't you live through history?"

Zoe stowed her suitcase and slid behind the wheel. Jason climbed into the other side of the vehicle. "I did indeed. But Sam and Colin both concentrated on this era of history for their PhDs. Sam's a professor at Georgetown." It probably wasn't a good idea to let on that Colin had taken his studies in a different direction and was an internationally known arts and antiquities thief. At this point, she'd take whatever either of them could give her in the way of tips, tricks, and ideas for where to start looking for the fleece.

They ran through a drive-through before starting the thirty-minute drive to Volos. When they arrived, Zoe managed to squeeze the car into a curbside spot right next to the museum. The building wasn't huge, but its yellow paint was cheerful and offset nicely with a red entryway and a blue door. The museum was only open for a few more hours, but given the small size of the place, that would be plenty of time to check it out.

They climbed the white steps and entered the dimly lit but well-kept interior. The beige walls set off the neatly displayed exhibits inside. The artifacts on display spanned civilizations that lasted more than a thousand years, from ancient pottery and tools to dioramas of what buildings would have looked like at their peak. There was an extremely large map painted on one wall, highlighting the locations where each of the artifacts had been discovered.

They came around the last corner and Jason stopped dead. Zoe had to quickly pivot so she didn't run into his back. "What are you doing?"

"Am I seeing what I think I'm seeing?" Jason asked, pointing at a large glass case in the center of the room.

A case that held a giant golden sheepskin.

"Honestly, I have no idea. It can't be this easy, can it?" She stared up at the animal skin in front of her. Never in a million lifetimes would she have expected to find the fleece at the first place she happened to stop. Her luck was never that good.

"You call that easy?" Jason asked, gesturing to the reinforced case that surrounded the fleece. "I don't know about you, but I don't know anyone who has the skills to break that out of there. And I sort of doubt the museum is just going to give it to you if you ask nicely."

Maybe they'd have to bring in Colin after all.

They approached the display cautiously, as if someone was going to jump out and yell "Just kidding!" at the top of their lungs. However, the closer they got to the half-inch-thick glass that surrounded the object, the more certain she was that something was wrong.

All magic was a form of energy. It took energy to cast magic, and it released energy when spells were used. The golden fleece—the real golden fleece—was imbued with multiple layers of magic. Not only the magic of the golden flying ram it came from, but from the added layers that Medea—Jason's wife and a powerful sorceress—had added to it to strengthen it.

The object in front of her had no magical energy whatsoever. Even through the glass case she should have been able to feel something, especially from an object as strong as the fleece. Instead, she felt nothing.

"I wish this sign was in English. Sadly, I don't know Greek," Jason said, pointing to the placard that described the exhibit.

"Luckily for you, I do." Zoe skimmed the card and then sighed. "It's a replica. Valuable in its own right, apparently, but not the real fleece."

"The real fleece?" a quiet voice asked. Zoe turned to find a slim, black-haired woman who looked to be in her mid-forties. She was wearing a navy suit and had a name tag that said Maria. She obviously worked for the museum. "My dear, the myth of the golden fleece is just that. It's a wonderful tale—we have multiple different versions of the story in the museum gift shop if you're interested—but the fleece itself never existed. A flying sheep, can you imagine?" Maria smiled to herself as if she was imagining that very thing and it tickled her pink.

Jason's eyebrows rose, but he didn't say anything. He gestured for Zoe to take the lead. "Right, of course. How silly of me. Do you know the myth well?" Zoe asked.

The docent clasped her hands in front of her and smiled widely as if Zoe couldn't have asked a better question. "Of course! I studied it carefully in school. It's one of the reasons I chose to work at this museum in particular."

Perfect. Sam and Colin were great, and obviously knew how to do their research, but maybe this woman knew something they didn't. Maybe she could fill in the blanks of what Zoe already knew. "According to the legend," Zoe started, "Jason and his band of warriors acquired the fleece—with Medea's help, of course—and then set sail for home. When they arrived—"

"Don't forget the various trials they faced on the way back," Maria interjected, counting each on her fingers. "There were the sirens, who lured men to their deaths with their beautiful singing voices; Scylla, the six-headed monster; and Scylla's counterpart Charybdis, a deadly whirlpool—and don't forget the bronze giant Talos."

"Right, how could I forget Talos?" Zoe asked tongue in cheek. She was fairly certain Maria didn't realize Zoe was being sarcastic, because the woman only nodded enthusiastically. "So after they got past all those trials, they arrived back in Iolcus and presented the fleece to Pelias. What happened after that?"

"Oh, it was tragic, really. Pelias killed Jason's father. In revenge, Medea used her sorcery to trick Pelias's daughters into killing him. With Pelias out of the way, Jason was finally able to take the throne. Of course it didn't last long. The people of Iolcus were afraid of

Medea's powers and didn't want her as their queen. Jason was forced to abdicate the throne to his cousin. Jason and Medea eventually fled."

Finally. Now they were getting somewhere.

"Where did they flee to?" Jason asked.

"Corinth," Maria supplied. She pointed at the large map on the wall behind her. Corinth was halfway across the country.

"And, in your expert opinion, would they have taken the fleece with them when they left?" Zoe asked, pouring on an extra-thick layer of flattery.

Maria spread her hands in front of her, palms up, and shrugged. "There's nothing about that in the lore, but if you'd spent all that time and faced all those dangers acquiring something that valuable, wouldn't you take it with you?" She said then walked away to greet other museum visitors.

"I guess we're going to Corinth?" Jason asked.

"I guess we are," Zoe responded. They made a quick stop in the museum to buy one copy of every version of the Jason and the Argonauts story the museum sold. Who knew? Maybe one of them would come in handy.

Zoe took a quick moment to text an update to the group chat she had going with Kalli, Selene, Sam, and Colin. She had every confidence that by the time they arrived back at the airfield, the jet would be gassed up and ready to go.

Most of the ride to the airport was spent in silence, Zoe and Jason each lost in their own thoughts. As they pulled through the gates, Jason finally spoke. "So I've been thinking. If we're going to keep going on this clearly epic quest to find the fleece, we may need to upgrade our ride."

Zoe cocked her head sideways, glancing between Jason and the private jet they'd pulled up to. "The fancy plane isn't enough?"

He smiled. "Oh, it's fantastic, but maybe it needs a new name." He pointed at the back of the plane, where the tail number was painted. "Instead of G5J28K, what do you think of calling it the *Argos*?"

Zoe laughed. "I'll ask Selene to change it the next time I see her. Let's just hope we have better luck than the original Argonauts did on their journey."

"Hot chicks with excellent singing voices? Where do I sign up?" Jason chuckled.

"With any luck, nowhere. Now let's get a move on. The sooner we find the fleece and return home, the better."

Chapter Ten

THE SECOND RIDE IN the private jet was as exciting as the first, though this one lasted less than an hour. Must be nice to have enough money at your disposal that you didn't have to drive the four hours and instead could take a quick jaunt in your plane. Jason planned to enjoy it as much as he could, since once he was back on the Jason Bloom budget—rather than whatever Selene had going for her—there was no way he was ever riding in something this nice again. They touched down on the small airfield, and once more a car was waiting for them. Without a second thought, Zoe slid behind the wheel, and they were off.

"Where to this time?" Jason asked.

"Sam and Colin did some digging while we were in the air. They think they have a general location for where Jason and Medea might have lived." They bypassed the modern city of Corinth, and even the ancient Roman city of the same name. Slightly farther along was a large flat-topped mountain. Just barely visible, several hundred feet in the air, were the ruins of an ancient structure.

When they approached the site, Jason's mouth dropped open. "This is where they lived? It's huge!" Zoe parked the car, and they got out, looking around with interest. Crumbling stone walls spiderwebbed off in every direction. The path to the top was steep and made of cobbled stone, but the views of the surrounding cities and the Gulf of Corinth were breathtaking.

"Not exactly. This is the Acrocorinth. It's a fortified structure that's been built, torn down, rebuilt, added on to, etcetera, for thousands of years. Most of what you're looking at was built after Jason and Medea lived in the area, but perhaps there's still something that might point us in the right direction."

"Good thing I have decent walking shoes," Jason muttered as they began the trek up the mountain.

According to the signs around the site, one of the primary structures of the Acrocorinth had once been a temple to Aphrodite. In later centuries an Orthodox church was built on the site, as well as a mosque. Jason could feel the generations of ancient history seeping into his bones as they explored the site, all the while keeping an eye open for anything that might give them a clue as to where Jason and Medea might have lived.

"Stop." Zoe's voice was jarring after spending the last few hours in near silence as they conserved their energy for climbing around the rocks and ruins.

Jason stopped walking and turned back to face her, grateful for the break. "Did you see something?"

She shook her head. "Not see, exactly." She backed up a few steps in the direction they'd come from and started waving her hands like she was feeling for something right in front of her but just out of reach.

"Um, Zoe?" he asked tentatively. He wasn't sure what to make of her bizarre movements. She looked like a mime trapped in a box.

"Right here," she said and took a step into nothingness.

Jason watched, mouth agape, as Zoe vanished into thin air. He spun in place, frantically looking around, but Zoe was gone.

Just as he was starting to panic, Zoe's arm appeared out of the void, grabbed his, and yanked him after her. With an uncomfortable buzzing sensation, Jason stepped through what he could only call an energy barrier of some kind, one that separated the very real ruins on one side from a lush, forested glade on the other side. He turned to look behind him, but the mountain had disappeared.

"Did we bend the space-time continuum? Did Scotty beam us up? Or maybe we traveled the rainbow bridge to Asgard. If you folks know how to teleport, you should share with the rest of the class." He glanced around at the vibrant green trees lining a path that led to an enormous circular clearing. The expanse in front of them was bright green with grass that would have looked out of place in the dusty fortress ruins they'd left behind.

"No. Of course not. We're still standing on top of the same mountain we were standing on before. We didn't travel anywhere," Zoe explained calmly.

"If we didn't go anywhere, then I'm going to need another explanation. No way does this place look anything like the ruins of a temple to Aphrodite." He gestured to the lush vegetation surrounding them.

"It's an illusion. A trick for your eyes and mind. Medea was a powerful sorceress. She must have hidden this place away from prying eyes. Yet here it remains three thousand years later." Zoe started to wander around, her wide eyes and her gaze swiveling quickly to take it all in.

"You've mentioned the whole Medea-is-a-sorceress thing a few times, so I'm tracking that—at least as much as any person with no experience with any of this can be. The part where I'm getting lost, though, is how you were able to find this place. If a superpowerful sorceress hid it back in the day, how would anyone be able to find it here and now? Unless that person were also a powerful sorceress." He chuckled, but Zoe didn't join him. Jason stopped dead in his tracks, but Zoe kept walking. It was obvious she was avoiding him. "Zoe," he called after her.

She finally stopped and her shoulders slumped. She looked so defeated. He almost wanted to give her a hug, but he needed answers more than he needed to comfort her. She didn't turn around, but he heard a quiet "Yes."

"Bzzzt," he responded with an angry buzzer sound. "I'm sorry, that's not good enough. Try again. Yes what?" He crossed his arms and waited.

After what felt like an eternity of silence, Zoe spun around, her arms flailing as she gestured to everything around them. "Yes, I'm a sorceress. Yes, I can do magic, though no, I can't cast illusions like this one. I can, in fact, conjure fire from my hands." Her arms stopped moving as flames burst from her hands before she yanked the fire back inside her. "No, I can't teleport, though yes, I do have some level of telekinesis." She gestured with her hand, and a small branch lifted off the ground nearby before she flung it away.

He watched her pace back and forth, not interrupting what was clearly a full head of steam that she needed to vent.

"Yes, there's more to what I can do, and no, I won't tell you what it is. I don't usually use my powers, and there's a reason for that. Your camera guy caught me at a stressful moment, when I wasn't fully in control, and now everyone is going to be terrified of the woman who can shoot fireballs." She glanced down at her hands like they had betrayed her. Her eyes started leaking tears, and she brushed them away with agitated swipes.

When it seemed like she was finally done with her tantrum, Jason slowly approached her, expecting her to bolt at any second. "I'm not afraid of you." He probably should have been, but for some reason he wasn't. He had no idea the extent of what she could do, but even the little she'd shared with him would have been enough to scare a normal person. Apparently he wasn't normal. He looked at her and didn't see a powerful sorceress. He saw Zoe. The flirty oddball who cared more about her people than Jason did about anything in the world. Not even his job or his parents—whom he admittedly hadn't seen in years—could compare to how she cared for her sisters. He finally got close enough to reach out and nudge her chin up with his finger, forcing her to look at him. "Hey. Did you hear me? I'm not afraid of you."

"Maybe you should be," she whispered.

"Zoe." She looked so heartbroken he did the only thing he could think of to distract her. His lips found hers, softly at first, asking for permission to kiss her. She didn't move for a few seconds, and Jason panicked that he'd misread the interest he thought he'd seen in her eyes. As he was about to pull back, her hands landed on either side of his neck, and her fingers dove into his hair. She kept their mouths fused together, tasting and sampling. A tiny moan came out of her, and Jason wanted to cheer.

Even though he felt like he could kiss her for hours, he slowly eased back, the kisses getting lighter until he finally pulled away.

"Why did you stop?" She sounded confused, and her pupils were blown wide with desire.

He rested his forehead against hers, breathing in her scent—strawberries and something uniquely Zoe. "As much as I'd love to keep kissing you for the next week or so, we're on a bit of a time crunch. Lucky for us, however, I think I know something that might help."

"Oh?" Zoe asked.

With a slight nod, Jason drew her attention to the center of the clearing. Standing tall and proud was a tree that had to be at least ten feet in diameter, and hanging from that tree was a golden ram's skin. Flanking the tree on either side were large stone sculptures of bulls, and between them—blocking the path to the fleece—was a statue of a dragon.

Something was tingling in the back of Jason's mind. "Something about this setup is familiar . . ." Jason tried to figure out what he was missing. "Do you have one of those books we bought at the museum handy?" he asked.

Zoe reached into her backpack and retrieved one, then handed it to him. Jason flipped the pages open and located the portion of the story he'd been trying to remember. "It says here that when Jason arrived in Colchis and asked the king for the fleece, the king knew he couldn't outright refuse. Instead, he agreed to let Jason have the fleece, but only if he completed a trial first. The king gave Jason a set of dragon's teeth and then told him that he needed to harness two bronze fire-breathing bulls and use them to plow a field and plant the teeth." He paused and looked at the tree and the statues. "Do you think the statues are there to commemorate Jason's retrieval of the fleece?" he asked hopefully.

"With a sorceress as powerful as Medea? I doubt anything we see is decorative," Zoe responded.

"Right," Jason said. "Duh."

Zoe studied the glade. "Well, there's no field in the vicinity, nor is there a plow. Plus, these statues are stone and not bronze. Maybe we need to somehow retrieve the teeth from the dragon statue, and then . . ." Zoe was clearly at a loss for what they were supposed to do with the teeth once they had them.

Nothing around them even hinted at what they were supposed to be doing. Surely Medea had planned it that way. She would have wanted to ensure that even if someone managed to see through her illusion the way Zoe had, they still wouldn't be able to just walk up and retrieve the fleece.

They didn't know what to do, and standing around wasting time wasn't going to help them. "What the hell," Jason said as he handed the book back to Zoe. He marched into the clearing, eyes on a swivel, looking for any signs of danger, but nothing flew at him or jumped up in front of him. As he approached the dragon, he noticed something odd.

It didn't have any teeth. In fact, it had holes in the dragon's jaw where its teeth should have been, almost like they had already been removed.

Out of the corner of his eye he noticed a slight movement. Glancing at the bull on his left, he realized that the statue was transforming. Starting near the tail of the creature and slowly moving toward its head, the bull was morphing from cold gray stone into shiny bronze.

Jason froze, watching the change happen. He'd seen Zoe do magic before, but it was still new to him. Nothing about the situation he found himself in was normal. What did it mean that the statue was mutating? Was this another one of Medea's spells? He wanted to touch the statue and see if he could sense the magic flowing through it.

He had reached his hand out—hoping to run a finger down the bull's nose—when Zoe's voice penetrated the stupor he'd fallen into.

"Jason, get down!" He sensed motion coming at him quickly, and then with a thud he was flat on the ground, Zoe pinning him in place.

"What the crap?" he asked, rubbing his shoulder where he'd landed.

"We have to go!" Zoe was already on the move. Her hand wrapped around his wrist, and she yanked him forcibly to his feet.

Jason followed her as she tore around the clearing back toward the gap where they'd first entered the glade. He felt heat on his back and glanced over his shoulder as he ran.

The two stationary stone bull statues were now completely bronze. But more than that, they were pawing the ground angrily and shooting fire in Jason and Zoe's direction.

"I don't think they're following us." He panted as they reached the spot where they'd kissed.

Zoe stopped running, allowing Jason to keel over, hands on his knees as he dragged in deep breaths and tried to lower his heart rate.

"That didn't go as planned," he finally managed.

"You think? What was going through your head that you thought it was a good idea to walk up to a magical artifact while in a hidden grove that's protected by a sorceress's magic?" Zoe took a deep breath, then gestured to the angry bulls behind them and continued, "Medea must have had the ability to animate inanimate objects."

"When you put it that way, it wasn't that great of an idea. But at least we know more than we did before." He finally stood tall, once again looking at the bulls and the dragon.

"Other than the fact that the bulls are going to try to kill us?" Zoe asked sarcastically.

Jason nodded. "Yep. Apart from that. The dragon statue doesn't have teeth to steal. But it does have spots for teeth to be placed. So maybe the trick is that we need to find the teeth and put them back in the dragon's mouth."

Zoe's eyes zoomed to the dragon, as if she could see its mouth clearly from a hundred yards away. "Hmm," she said, tapping her finger against her lips.

"Come on, we can work this out," Jason said. He rubbed his hands together and started pacing. "The bulls must be there for a reason, right? They're not coming after us, so they're not there to chase people away. What purpose do they serve?"

"You mean apart from breathing fire on anyone that approaches?"

Jason nodded. "Exactly."

"Another question: If we're supposed to be putting the dragon's teeth back in its mouth, then where are the teeth?" Zoe asked.

As one, Zoe and Jason turned to face the pissed-off cows. Directly between the front feet of each of the bulls, almost unnoticeable from this distance, were small boxes. "Bingo," Zoe said, giving Jason a wink that did funny things to his stomach.

Now was not the time for that. He could sort out his magnetic draw to Zoe when they weren't facing down fire-breathing cattle.

So now they knew—or at least suspected—where the dragon teeth were, and they knew what they were supposed to do with them once they'd retrieved them. The problem was how they could manage either of those things without getting roasted by the bulls.

"Tell me more about your own fire magic," Jason said. "If you can create fire, does that mean you're fireproof? Can you walk through the flames, grab the teeth, and put them in the dragon's mouth?" What were the odds that he was with someone that had literal fire power? This was going to be a piece of cake.

Zoe was already shaking her head. "I'm not fireproof. Fire resistant is probably closer to accurate. Too long in contact with the inferno those two are putting out could cause some real damage. Plus, given the magical nature of everything in this illusion, who knows what effect those magical flames would have on me."

His stomach sank. He'd been counting on her fire magic to help them out of this. "What do you suggest?"

Zoe continued to pace, but he just watched as she covered the same six feet over and over. He could practically see the gears turning in her head. After several seconds—which felt like minutes—she finally spoke. "I might be able to redirect the fire so that it won't hit me."

Hope surged in Jason's stomach. Maybe they could solve this puzzle after all. "Awesome. So once you've redirected it, you can grab the teeth, right?"

Her grimace said he hadn't fully understood what she was saying. "Um, no. It's going to take all my energy and power to redirect the flames so they don't hit us."

Us. There it was, the word he had been dreading. He was going to have to go back in there. He glanced at the bulls, who were glaring at them aggressively, smoke bellowing from their noses. While it had been stupid of him to blunder in there the first time, he'd done it anyway because he hadn't realized what he was up against. Now he knew. Five thousand pounds of angry animated bronze cows with deadly horns and the ability to scorch the unwary.

In for a penny, in for a pound.

"Let's do this." He was glad his voice didn't waver. Terror was trying to claw its way up his throat, but he swallowed it down. Zoe was a sorceress. Surely she could keep them both safe—right?

Zoe glanced at him one more time, as if to confirm he wasn't going to back down. He nodded once, firmly. Her eyebrows rose, but she didn't comment. Instead, she turned around and eyed the challenge in front of them. "I'll go first. Once I successfully redirect the blast, you do what you need to do. And try to hurry," she said.

Jason watched as Zoe slowly approached the bull statues. He stayed at least ten feet behind her at all times since he couldn't put "fire resistant" on his LinkedIn profile the way Zoe could. The bulls got more and more irritated as they approached. They began pawing at the ground, tearing up large chunks of grass and dirt and sending them flying with their dinner-plate-size hooves. Jason barely held in a shudder. It probably wasn't great to show weakness in front of something that could easily smash him to bits, right?

With an unexpected battle cry, Zoe charged between the bulls, one hand pointed at each of their mouths. As expected, the bulls immediately ignited, shooting flames straight for her.

Jason held his breath, ready to dive out of the way if those deadly infernos suddenly shot in his direction. To his utter astonishment, the flames hit Zoe's palms and then ricocheted away from her, aiming for the sky.

"Now!" she yelled.

Jason dove into action. He ducked under her arm and grabbed the box from in front of the first bull. The creature eyed him as if debating whether it should attack him rather than Zoe, but before it could make up its mind, Jason had already ducked under the second bull and retrieved that box as well.

He cast one last look at Zoe—who was sweating and almost collapsing under the pressure of holding off the magic of both statues—and then set to his own task. Flipping open the boxes, he discovered that they did indeed contain teeth.

He dashed over to the dragon statue and froze in place. There were dozens of holes of different sizes. He glanced down at the teeth in the boxes and realized that some were larger—more like fangs—and some were smaller. Of course, none of them were labeled. Not having a clue what order the teeth were supposed to go in, Jason took his best guess, frantically putting them into the holes in the dragon statue's mouth.

Zoe groaned in pain. "Anytime now."

Risking another glance, he saw that she was almost on her knees from the weight of the magic pressing in on her. Jason swore under his breath and picked up the pace. Finally only one tooth remained. He slotted it into the last remaining spot.

Nothing happened.

Jason stared in frozen shock at the dragon's mouth—now grinning at him cruelly—not sure what to do. This was supposed to work.

"Jason!" Zoe's scream startled him.

She was on the ground completely surrounded by fire. There was no way she could survive that much heat and intensity. "Zoe, hang on!" He frantically shifted the teeth around in the dragon's gaping maw. He said a quick prayer and placed the last one in its slot.

The sudden silence was deafening. He'd had no idea how loud the roaring flames had been until they vanished.

Jason spun around, frantically hoping Zoe was still alive. She was resting on the ground—smoke slowly dissipating from around her—but she blinked at him with a tiny nod. They'd made it through. With a huge grin, Jason crossed to the giant tree and grabbed the surprisingly heavy fleece off the peg it was hanging from.

He ran his hands over the golden wool reverently. He wasn't sure what he'd been expecting, but it was both softer and firmer than he'd thought it would be. Not quite as fluffy as actual wool, but not as hard as true gold. The shimmer that reflected the sunlight above was mesmerizing.

They had done it.

"You have to check this out," he exclaimed as he spun back around and came face-to-face with a living, breathing dragon.

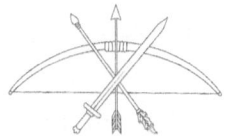

Chapter Eleven

Z OE WAS GLAD SHE was already kneeling on the ground, because there was no way she would have remained standing when confronted by an enormous black dragon.

The creature was the size of a semitruck and had black scales that glowed with internal fire. It had a handful of spikes on either side of its face, each the length of her hand, and two horns at the back of its head that were longer than her arm. Bony plates that looked like lethal versions of shark fins formed a ridge down the dragon's spine, from its neck to the tip of its tail. The dragon's feet were easily bigger than she was, and its talons looked razor sharp.

Jason's shout of excitement drew the dragon's attention. Smoke started pouring out of its nose and mouth as it turned to face him.

Great. Not this again.

She'd used up most of her magic stores holding off the bulls. She wasn't sure how much she had left in her if the dragon decided to start shooting flames everywhere. It was much bigger than the bulls and would do much more damage.

Before she had time to figure out how to stop the dragon from attacking Jason, the ground started shaking violently. Deep rumbles came from beneath her, as if the very mountain was angry and expressing its displeasure. The good news was that the intense trembling momentarily distracted the dragon as it tried to figure out what was happening.

The bad news was that the illusion that Medea had woven began failing. The bright-blue sky seemed to dissolve and reveal the overcast skies they had left behind on the Acrocorinth. The trees started to sway and topple, the wood cracking and creaking as they fell. The ground beneath her split open, creating fissures large enough to swallow her whole.

Zoe launched to her feet and raced across the ground, jumping over the ruptures as they formed. The dragon stood between her and Jason—not to mention the fleece—so Zoe headed straight for the giant lizard, despite the risk. There was no way she was leaving Jason behind. Following her had gotten him into this mess—even if he had invited himself along for the ride. She was going to do everything she could to get them both out of this alive.

Jason stood frozen in shock at the base of the giant tree in the middle of the clearing. His head swiveled as he glanced from the dragon to the illusion crumbling around them to Zoe and back again. Unfortunately he wasn't paying attention to the giant tree ready to collapse on top of him. She threw her hand out and tried to use her telekinesis to push the tree away, but nothing happened.

Telekinesis wasn't her strongest ability on a good day, and after draining her magic wells using her fire gift, today was not a good day.

"Jason, move!" Zoe yelled and gestured for him to get out of the way of the falling tree.

He did an almost comic double take at the tree behind him, then darted in her direction. Zoe latched on to his hand in a death grip. Whatever happened, she didn't want them separated.

"What now?" Jason yelled over the creaking and groaning of the trees as they dodged the collapsing ground beneath them and headed back in the direction of the tear in the illusion.

"We just need to—" Zoe was cut off abruptly as something wrapped around her torso and wrenched her upward.

"What the hell!" Jason screamed as he was scooped up by the dragon's other foot, the fleece crushed in his tight fists.

The dragon's hide was remarkably smooth and almost silky, but its talons were deadly, sharp, and in the general vicinity of Zoe's vital organs. As much as she would have loved to have time on any other—preferably very calm—day to inspect a dragon up close, today was not that day.

With an earsplitting roar, the dragon crouched and used its powerful hind legs to launch itself into the sky, tearing through the failing illusion like it was tissue paper. The dragon circled the top of the mountain and the ruins, the heavy flap of its wings a beating heart promising only destruction. The dragon was flying low enough that Zoe could make out the terrified faces of tourists as they screamed and scrambled out of their cars. The movement below seemed to startle the dragon, who sucked in a lengthy breath and then spat a plume of fire in the direction of the parked cars. The people below panicked and dove to the side, but the dragon's aim was true. The flames hit several of the vehicles and a series of explosions rocked the side of the mountain. Dust and rock flew into the air as the rental car Selene had arranged for them was propelled into the air before it flipped and landed several feet away.

Zoe didn't know how to process what was happening. Not only was she clutched in the claws of a real-life dragon, but that same dragon was raining fire down on innocent people. Innocent people who all had smartphones, and several of whom appeared to be recording the action.

The midnight-black beast suddenly pivoted sideways. Instead of circling the mountain, it headed east over the Greek countryside. With a nausea-inducing lurch, the dragon dove, barely skimming the tops of the trees that led down the mountainside.

Zoe heard Jason's shriek and wanted to do the same, but she forced herself to focus. She and Jason were being held captive by an enormous flying reptile. They had no way to know where it was going or when it would land. Unless Jason was a really good actor, he wasn't hiding any special gifts that might help them, which meant that it was up to her to get them out of this situation.

The wind pelting her face made it almost impossible to keep her eyes open and figure out where they were going. The dragon appeared to be heading for one of the nearby bodies of water. If she had to guess, it was one of the many gulfs that would eventually empty into the Aegean Sea.

Even if she could figure out how to get the dragon to drop them, falling hundreds of feet over land was a death sentence. Falling over water wasn't much better, but maybe if she could somehow get the dragon to drop lower, the fall wouldn't kill them.

The problem was that the only option she had for making the dragon do anything was something she'd sworn she would never do again. Her fire magic wouldn't have any effect against a dragon that could spew flames right back at her. Her mild telekinesis wasn't going to do anything either, even if there was anything within her radius that she could manipulate. That left one choice. The one power she had refused to show Jason in the grove.

She could bend other people and animals to her will.

Small animals like birds and mice weren't that complicated. More intelligent animals like dolphins and humans were another thing entirely. It was one thing to direct an animal that didn't have a lot of sentience of its own to do something it wasn't already planning to do. Something as smart as a dragon or—heaven forbid—a person was a totally different situation.

A situation Zoe had personal experience with and had hoped never to repeat again. But what other options did she have?

A pair of warm brown eyes swam in front of her vision. She could practically hear Max's soft laugh. But she could also never forget the sound of his scream and the hail of gunfire that accompanied it.

She shook her head and brought herself back to reality. The dragon wasn't Max and would never be. The dragon wasn't even human. And while the dragon wasn't exactly her enemy, it wasn't totally innocent either. The beast was carrying them off to who-knew-where, and it was her job to do everything she could to prevent that. There was nothing to worry about, right?

A sudden jolt from a buffet of wind and a yelp from her left brought Zoe back to the present. Jason was flailing as he tried to grasp on to the smooth scales of the dragon's fingers, but he was sliding through the lizard's grasp. Unfortunately, in his desperation to not fall, he also let go of the fleece. Zoe watched in growing horror as the fleece plummeted toward the earth, thankfully landing on a boat rather than in the water.

They still weren't low enough. If the dragon let Jason fall, it would be lights out. There was no coming back from that.

Zoe had to take action—now.

She closed her eyes and tried to tune out everything around her. No razor-sharp claw was digging into her torso. The wind wasn't rocking her back and forth every time it changed direction. Jason wasn't about to fall to his death. Her mind was a blank screen.

Her powers would have come to her much more easily if she'd been using them rather than ignoring them for the last fifty years. Too late to change that decision now.

Once her mind was calm, she reached out with her senses. Her thoughts brushed Jason's panicked mind and immediately let go. She couldn't let his fear and desperation affect what she was trying to do. Pushing slightly further, she encountered a strange consciousness that felt so foreign she knew instantly that it had to be the dragon's.

Subtly—so as not to spook the creature—Zoe slipped into the dragon's mind. The thought patterns were different enough from a human's that she had trouble following what it wanted and what it was thinking about. Eventually she was able to make out basic concepts like food, shelter, and mate. She could work with that. Zoe started pushing visions of fish into the dragon's mind: large fish, small fish, jumping fish, tightly packed schools of fish.

Zoe's stomach told her they were dropping altitude. She opened her eyes long enough to determine that they were close enough to the water that she and Jason would probably survive the fall, and then pushed one last forceful thought into the dragon's consciousness.

"You can swim, right?" she shouted.

"What?" Jason's response was confused and slightly panicked.

"Deep breath!" she yelled as the dragon loosened its grip and let them go.

The deep plunge into the sea sent Zoe's stomach somewhere in the vicinity of her throat. She tried not to flail when she hit the water so she wouldn't get disoriented and forget which way was up. She kicked her way to the surface and dragged in a huge breath, refilling her lungs with desperately needed oxygen. The chill of the water immediately seeped into her bones.

Glancing around, she realized that Jason hadn't resurfaced. She spun in frantic circles, looking for him. Just as she was about to start to panic in earnest, a head of brown hair surfaced no more than five feet from her. With a relieved breath, she swam the few feet to him.

"Holy crap. Let's never do that again," Jason said, focusing on something off in the distance.

Zoe followed his gaze and realized the dragon was taking her suggestion and scooping large quantities of silvery fish into its mouth. At least she hadn't screwed that one up. But now they had a new problem. They were floating in the middle of the water, and it wasn't exactly the Caribbean. They needed to get to shore or a boat before they tired out or the chill of the water affected them too much.

Thankfully they weren't far from a marina, where boats were tied in an anchorage off the coast of a small island. "That way." Zoe nodded toward a small yacht, on which she could barely make out a golden glint.

Several hard minutes of swimming later, they finally reached the stern of the boat. Zoe pulled down the ladder and ushered Jason in front of her. Once he was on the swim platform, she followed and collapsed in a heap. Without thinking, she snuggled up next to him. They were just sharing body heat, she assured herself.

After several long moments of nothing but the sounds of deep breaths and their own heartbeats, Jason said, "So today I learned dragons are real."

Zoe busted out laughing and Jason joined her. After everything that had happened in the last several hours, the relief of finally being somewhere relatively safe, where nothing was trying to kill them, was unbelievable. "Me too," Zoe responded when she was finally able to stop giggling. "Trust me, massive flying lizards were not a normal part of my youth either."

He rolled his head so he could look her in the eyes. "Oh no? I figured that was par for the course for someone like you." His teasing smile made it obvious he was joking.

She answered him anyway. "Nope. Though now I guess we're going to have to figure out how to deal with one, since we released a dragon on the unsuspecting world."

"Oh, right," Jason said. He sat up, forcing Zoe to move from where she'd been cuddled up next to him. He turned to face her, but his shoulders were hunched, and he was staring at the yacht's deck. "And then there's the part where I dropped the fleece over the sea. I'm sure it's on its way to meet Poseidon by now. I'm so sorry, Zoe. I know that you were counting on that fleece to save Themyscira. If there's anything I can do to make it up to you, just name it."

She reached out and squeezed his hand. "There is one thing I can think of. Come with me." She stood, ignoring the disgustingly wet jeans and shirt plastered to her body. She climbed the metal ladder that led from the narrow swim platform at the back of the boat onto the main deck. She kept going until she led Jason to the bow of the boat where, as she had hoped, there was a sparkle of tantalizing gold. "Recognize anything?"

Jason pushed past her in the incredibly skinny walkway and darted to where the fleece was splayed out on the front deck of the yacht. He tugged it into his arms and revealed the—thankfully intact—deck beneath it. If the fleece had been any heavier, it could have done some serious damage.

He turned to face her, practically hugging the weighty fleece to his chest. "We were ridiculously lucky that the fleece didn't land in the water."

Zoe wondered whether it was more than that. "Maybe. Or perhaps there was a tiny bit of divine intervention." She winked at him as his jaw dropped open. "Come on, we have to get moving. We need to get that shiny bit of wool back to Themyscira."

Jason followed her inside the main cabin of the surprisingly roomy yacht. "Are we going to try to catch a flight back to Türkiye?"

Zoe entered the lower helm and after a quick search realized that it was her lucky day, because the keys were already in the ignition. She turned them as she passed by, then nimbly scampered up the ladder to the flybridge. She waited until he'd followed her up before speaking. "Nope. If you haven't noticed, we're not exactly at a marina. In order to get to land"—she pointed at the distant shore—"we'd have to either take a dinghy or swim. Unfortunately, the dinghy for this boat is missing. It's likely already at shore where the owners left it. And since I don't fancy taking another swim in the sea right now…" She sat down behind the wheel, hunted for a moment, then pressed the button to fire up the engines. Once she knew they were both on, she hit the button to start raising the anchor. "Can you do me a favor and head back down to the front of the boat and let me know if the anchor gets stuck on anything or brings anything up with it?"

Jason stared at her dubiously. "Are we stealing this boat?"

"Do you have a better idea?"

He gave a resigned shrug before he went to play lookout.

They couldn't travel by boat for long—it wasn't an efficient or speedy mode of transportation—but they could cross the gulf and get close to Athens, then hop a plane from there. In the meantime, she needed to touch base with Kalli and Selene. Zoe wanted to know what was going on back at home, and they needed to know that she'd found the fleece. Oh yeah, and that they'd released a dragon. *You know, the small stuff.*

While she waited for the all clear from Jason, she tugged her very waterlogged cell phone out of the pocket of her wet jeans. Her phone was still functioning thanks to Selene's endless supply of new age technology, but sadly Zoe didn't have a signal this far away from the mainland. She set her phone down and rummaged around through the helm's compartments, hoping to find something useful. She was not disappointed—and only mildly surprised—when her search turned up a satellite phone. She sent a quick prayer of thanks to Hermes—the messenger of the gods and the god of travel, among other things—and typed in Selene's phone number, then waited for it to connect.

Jason arrived back at her side as Selene answered the call, so Zoe put it on speaker.

"Hey, it's Zoe."

"According to the news," Selene drawled, "there's some sort of strange bird or wacky cloud formation around Corinth, Greece, that happens to look exactly like a dragon. But that couldn't be true, because dragons don't exist. Right?"

Jason blanched, but Zoe plowed on. "Yeah, about that, um . . ."

Selene started cackling like she thought the situation was hilarious, and Zoe could just barely hear Colin's voice in the background, asking if he could come to Greece to see the dragon.

Zoe rolled her eyes, even though it would do absolutely nothing via phone call. "It's not a puppy, for crying out loud."

"Zoe, report." Kalli's crisp voice came through loud and clear and made Zoe want to snap to attention, which wasn't a great idea, considering she was currently piloting a boat.

"My queen," Zoe said, "we went to the Acrocorinth as Colin and Sam suggested." She recounted the situation with the illusion, the fire-breathing bulls, and finally the dragon.

"A dragon? What a nightmare," Kalli said. "What about the fleece?"

Zoe grinned at Jason. "On that, my queen, we did not disappoint."

"You found it?" Sudden excitement laced Kalli's voice.

"We sure did." Zoe glanced down at her navigation screen and turned the boat in the direction of Athens.

"That's amazing. How soon can you be back here?" Kalli asked.

Selene interrupted. "I can have the plane ready at the airport in twenty minutes."

"It's going to be a bit longer than that, I'm afraid." Zoe was suddenly regretting her choice of transportation—which was going to top out at around 10 knots or twelve miles per hour—though maybe not enough to want to potentially encounter a dragon while inside a small metal tube in midair.

"Where, exactly, are you?" Kalli asked carefully.

Zoe rattled off their latitude and longitude and winced while waiting for their reactions.

"That's in the middle of the sea," Selene said. "What are you doing there?"

Zoe nibbled on her lip. "Borrowing a boat?" The silence on the other end of the line went on for far longer than she would have liked.

"You mean like Colin borrowed his boat?" Selene asked.

"I told you I intended to give it back," Colin said exasperatedly.

"But you didn't," Selene said sweetly.

"Focus, people," Kalli said, interrupting their good-natured bickering. "So what's your plan, then?"

Zoe appreciated that Kalli didn't question her. Instead, she trusted that Zoe had a plan that would get them out of their current mess and back on track. "We're currently on a course for Athens. That's only an hour or so away, so if everything goes smoothly, we'll only be a little delayed."

"Why on earth would you say that? You've tempted the Fates, and now things are bound to go sideways," Selene chimed in.

Zoe shook her head for Jason's benefit. "Overdramatic much? We'll be fine. How's the situation there?" Zoe changed the topic before Selene could respond.

"Not great," Kalli said. "We have more unwanted visitors. Tents are popping up like little mushrooms."

"More reporters?" Jason asked, chiming in for the first time.

"Not exactly. More like foreign government organizations. Not entirely certain which country they're from, though. We haven't tried to talk to them yet." Kalli was clearly trying hard to keep her tone neutral and calm, but tension radiated through the airwaves anyway.

"How many?" Zoe asked with a pained expression. She suddenly regretted her decision to be the one to go on this absurd mission to get the fleece. Of all of them, Zoe was the one with the most experience dealing with law enforcement, military, and government officials. Maybe she should have stayed behind after all. She and Jason had retrieved the fleece, but at what cost? What might happen to her people if she wasn't there to help smooth the path?

"Two so far." This time it was Sam chiming in. "Depending on how many more decide to show up, we could have our own United Nations meetup right here in Themyscira."

Zoe chewed on her bottom lip. "Have they shown any signs of aggression or tried to make contact with you?"

"Not yet. But the clock is ticking. We'll try to hold them off with diplomacy, but you need to get back here ASAP. On the chance that diplomacy fails, we need to have a plan B," Kalli said. "Be safe, Zoe. And come back alive."

The phrase that they had said to each other thousands of times resonated through Zoe, giving her strength. "I always do, my queen."

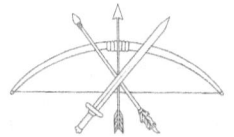

Chapter Twelve

J ASON WAS DESPERATELY CURIOUS about the slight sadness he'd seen on Zoe's face when she ended the call, but then again, they'd had what any normal person might refer to as an extremely bizarre day.

It was ridiculous to think that only that morning they'd been casually walking around a museum in northern Greece. Since then, they'd flown across the country, walked into an illusion, fought fire-breathing bulls, gotten kidnapped by a dragon, and stolen a yacht. If he wasn't so exhausted, he would assume he was asleep and that this was all some sort of wacky dream. In what reality did dragons, illusions, and golden fleeces exist?

His, apparently.

He was desperate for a nap. "How long did you say we had before we arrived?" he asked Zoe.

"At least an hour. Why don't you head down to the galley and see if the owners left any nonperishable food."

As soon as she mentioned food, his stomach rumbled. They hadn't eaten since breakfast, and it was now almost sunset. Dinner sounded better than a nap. "Where's the galley?"

"This boat isn't that big. I'm sure you can find it," she said.

Right, of course. He'd never been on a yacht before, but it wasn't like it was an enormous cruise ship or anything. He snagged the sat phone and headed down the metal ladder to the main cabin. From there he descended another short flight of steps, and lo and behold, there was a small sitting area, a table with chairs, and a kitchen. The fridge was empty, which made sense, but he lucked out in the pantry. He found an unopened—and barely expired—bag of tortilla chips, a can of refried beans, and a jar of salsa. Minimalist nachos it was.

As he waited for the beans to heat up in the microwave, Jason took the opportunity to call Noah. He felt bad that he'd left him without any real explanation. Plus, maybe Noah would be able to give him the inside scoop on the new arrivals Kalli had mentioned.

"This is Noah Quinn," Noah answered brusquely, his deep voice resonating through the phone.

"Noah, it's Jason." The timer went off on the microwave, and he pulled the beans out, then went on a quest for a plate and a spoon.

"Jason, man. Where the hell did you disappear to? The studio sent Trent out to cover the beat after you took off, but they didn't tell me where you went."

On the other end of the line, the chatter of loud voices started to fade as Jason assumed Noah walked away from whoever had been talking. "I'm doing a one-on-one interview with Zoe Harper. She's allowing me to tag along on a small retrieval job she's doing." Well, that was one way to describe it.

"Exclusive up-close access to the Amazons. Nice score, dude. No other news station has that. This is your ticket." Noah knew all about Jason's ladder-climbing ambitions, and he was hoping to come along for the ride.

Jason set about layering chips, beans, and salsa on a plate, then brought it to the small couch he'd passed on the way down. "Yeah, maybe. I've got a few notes I can type up and send when I get a chance. I'd love to send through some video as well, but it may not come through. I'm borrowing a satellite phone since we're on a boat in the middle of the sea at the moment."

"What are you doing on a boat?" Noah's curiosity was definitely piqued.

Jason crunched down a few chips while he stalled for time. "I'd rather not say yet, but trust me, it's big. Like mind-bendingly big." The world needed to know about the things he was experiencing. There was a dragon flying around Greece, for crying out loud. People needed to be able to keep themselves safe.

On the other hand, he knew exactly how fantastical everything was going to feel to the average person. Seeing two super-strong and incredibly fast women fighting in a fountain was one thing. The human mind could brush it off and assume they were both really into CrossFit or something. But a giant flying, fire-breathing dragon was something that wasn't as easy to explain away. People weren't going to want to believe it, so when Jason broke that story, he needed to do it in a way that was as unassailable as possible. He wanted to be a top-notch reporter, not a laughingstock.

"Fill me in on what's going on there. I've heard that you had some new arrivals?" Jason changed the topic.

"Yeah, the Turkish government sent some folks to stare over Interpol's shoulders. So did the US. I wouldn't be surprised if the Brits and the Germans aren't far behind. Everyone wants to know what's going on and who these Amazons are. That is, if they even believe the Amazons are who they say they are. Home base is saying that they're getting a lot of blowback, saying that our footage of that Zoe woman starting a fire was doctored. We're being accused of shoddy journalism. A few other news teams have shown up, too, and they're all prowling around, hoping to catch a glimpse of something fantastical. It's probably a good thing your girl got herself out of here. This situation is getting really heated. Like one little spark and BOOM."

Damn it. It was worse than he feared. He'd expected people to doubt the clip of Zoe lighting the bushes on fire, but he was hoping to have something else from his time with Zoe that he could broadcast to back it up. Something that would humanize the Amazons and make the world realize that whoever or whatever they were, they were still just people.

"Hey, thanks for the update, man. I'll try to send you some stuff soon. Gotta keep the big bosses happy." He hung up with Noah and tried to fiddle around with his personal phone and the satellite phone to see if there was a way he could transmit any of the photos he'd taken, but he couldn't seem to make it work. Oh well, it would have to wait until they were back on dry land.

By his best estimate, they still had at least forty-five minutes before they were going to arrive in Athens. He should probably bring Zoe some food, since she hadn't eaten since breakfast, either, but now that he'd gotten some food in his stomach, exhaustion was setting in. It wouldn't hurt for him to rest for a few moments, especially since the couch was surprisingly comfortable.

When he came to, the room was pitch black. He rubbed his eyes, but nothing changed. Jason couldn't see much of anything. There was a pale-silver glow from the moon outside the cabin windows, but other than that, it was relentlessly black.

Something was definitely not right. Zoe had said that it would take them only an hour or so to get to Athens. They should have been there long before the sun fully set. Slightly panicked, Jason fumbled around until he found a lamp and switched it on. He darted back to the ladder and scrambled up.

As soon as his head was outside, he heard it. The ethereal melody was unlike anything Jason had ever experienced. He couldn't tell if it was just a haunting tune or if there were words and he couldn't understand them. His steps slowed as he finished his ascent. The music wove through him, luring him with its beauty and serenity.

He glanced around and saw Zoe exactly where he'd left her, sitting behind the wheel of the ship. She was seemingly steering the boat as if by muscle memory, but something was very off. Zoe's face had gone slack, her eyes wide and dreamy. Jason took the two steps needed to get to her side and shook her, but she didn't respond. "Zoe!" Jason yelled, but she didn't even look in his direction.

Frantically trying to ignore the distracting song that was burrowing itself into his brain, he glanced at the yacht's controls, but he'd never driven a boat in his life. He had no idea what he was looking at or what to do.

He felt a tiny niggle in the back of his mind. Something about this seemed familiar, but he couldn't figure out why. He could guarantee he'd never been in this situation before.

"Zoe, seriously. Wake the hell up!" Jason tried again but still didn't get a reaction. She clearly wasn't asleep. Her eyes were wide open and staring off into the distance. In the dark it was impossible for him to see what she was looking at—or if she was looking at anything at all instead of just staring off into the distance—but he had to try. Her eyes didn't seem to be focused on anything on the boat, but rather something in the distance.

He noticed a switch on the control panel, helpfully labeled spotlight. He flipped the toggle, and a beam of light shot out from the front of the boat.

Jason was expecting to see nothing but open water, since they were nowhere near the port of Athens. Unfortunately, the beam illuminated something much worse. Rocks. Big, sharp boulders that stuck out of the water and were directly in their path. Worse than that, those rocky outcroppings were attached to an island. If Jason couldn't wake Zoe or figure out how to steer the boat, they were going to crash.

The otherworldly music washed over him again, dragging his mind along with it. The song was practically serenading him. It cut through his frenzy like a sharp knife. It was soothing and made him want to sit down on one of the deck loungers and take it all in. Surely nothing bad could happen while such an amazing melody was playing.

Just as Jason was about to give in to the temptation to lie back and relax, the spotlight caught on something shiny, almost metallic. He strained his eyes to catch another glimpse, and sure enough, there was movement. Almost like a fish flapping its fins or tail. But this was large. Much larger than any fish he'd seen before.

The object shifted, and Jason caught a glimpse of a woman who practically radiated ethereal beauty. It didn't make sense that there would be a woman swimming at night around all these razor-sharp rocks, but it was unmistakable. She had incredibly pale skin and long black hair that was barely covering her naked torso. Her hair was so long that it reached her waist where, if he wasn't mistaken, she had the tail of a fish instead of legs.

Before Jason's brain could process the idea of a singing mermaid on a rock, more heads popped out of the water. They each climbed to the top of a boulder and continued to sing their dreamlike chant.

He had to go to them. They were astonishing. He needed to meet them, maybe even join them on their island. Surely that was where paradise was.

The boat shuddered as a particularly big wave hit its side, knocking Jason a few steps sideways and breaking his trance. Memories of the books he'd crammed on the plane that morning came flooding back to him, and he suddenly knew exactly what they were dealing with. These were no mere mermaids.

They were sirens. Beautiful mythical creatures that lured unwary sailors to their deaths by using their voices and melodies to cause the sailors to crash their ships into the sirens' island.

In the tale of Jason and the Argonauts, the crew survived because one of the men happened to be a musician. He played his lyre so loudly that it drowned out the sound of the sirens' voices, allowing the crew to escape their pull. Unfortunately Jason wasn't a musician, and even if he were, the yacht didn't exactly have a stash of electric guitars lying around.

What it did have was a speaker system. The boat was several decades old, but the owners had made some modern upgrades. Jason grabbed his cell phone, turned on Bluetooth, and powered on the boat's sound system. He cranked the volume as high as it would go and hit play on a random playlist he had downloaded. "Highway to Hell" came blaring out of the hidden speakers and completely drowned out the sirens' song.

Jason turned back to Zoe and lightly smacked her cheeks. "Zoe, come back to me. I don't know how to drive this thing!" He grabbed the wheel and tried to at least steer it clear of the closest visible rocks, but he was worried about the ones he couldn't see. The last thing he needed was to tear a hole in the ship's hull and strand them on an island with potentially murderous sea creatures.

"What's happening?" Zoe's groggy question was sweeter music than the sirens' song could ever be.

"Talk later. Drive the boat now," Jason said as he gestured wildly to the rapidly approaching island.

"Holy shit!" She immediately flew into action. She cut the throttles to stop their forward momentum and then threw it into reverse. She looked at a screen that showed the sea depth and the location of underwater hazards before carefully turning the wheel to slowly back them away from the island.

Once they were in deep enough water to not have to worry about grounding the yacht, she cut the engines, letting them float for a moment. She reached for the volume knob, but Jason reached out and stopped her.

"Not that I don't love AC/DC, but can you tell me why we have to listen to them at eardrum-splitting levels?" she shouted over the music.

"It's drowning out the sirens," Jason yelled back.

Zoe looked baffled. "What sirens? The yacht doesn't have any alarms going off, and there aren't any other boats around."

Jason was already shaking his head. "Not that kind of siren. The kind that lives in the water and lures unwary travelers to their deaths." And that was a sentence he never would have thought he'd ever utter, especially not at the top of his lungs. "They had you in some sort of trance. I couldn't wake you up, and we were about to crash. We need to get as far away from here as possible."

"Where are we?" Zoe asked.

He shrugged. "You tell me. We're obviously not in Athens."

Zoe pulled up an app with location tracking, and they both stared at it in shock. Not only were they nowhere near Athens, but they were already in the Aegean Sea, at least ninety nautical miles past where they were supposed to be. It would take them hours to get back to Athens if they turned the boat around. "At this point we might as well continue on to Türkiye. We're halfway there already."

"Works for me. Hey, does this thing have autopilot?"

Zoe hunted around on the console in front of her and pointed to a switch. "Yeah, why?"

"Because you haven't eaten in hours, and you've spent the last God knows how long under the spell of creepy mermaids. You need rest, and since I don't know how to pilot a boat, it's probably better to leave it in the hands of the machines."

With a small shrug, Zoe plotted a course for İzmir, Türkiye, turned the engines back on, and took her hands off the wheel. The boat started cruising along without her guidance.

As soon as she stood from the captain's chair, Jason yanked her to his chest, wrapping her in his arms, and buried his face in her hair. He shook slightly as the adrenaline left his body. Now that they were no longer at risk of crashing or being lured to their deaths, it suddenly hit him how close they had come to danger. Again.

"Hey, we're okay," Zoe murmured into his ear. "You saved us both. I honestly don't know what would have happened if you hadn't been here."

"Thankfully I was. We make a good team." He pulled away and smiled at her. "You do the driving, and I'll pick out the tunes."

She chuckled. "Let's go, DJ Bloom. I'm famished." She shoved him in the direction of the hatch back to the main level, and he went willingly.

They left the music blaring loudly. Better safe than sorry.

Chapter Thirteen

Z OE WAS FAMISHED ALL right, but not for food. She was craving Jason's touch and wasn't about to jump his bones on the uncomfortable lounge chairs on the flybridge when there was a perfectly comfortable bed belowdecks.

Plus, even though she had lived through history, she wasn't used to dealing with dragons and sirens. Her brain couldn't quite comprehend that they were real. Believing in Heracles—or as Jason knew him, Hercules—and Jason and the Argonauts was one thing. They were living people that Zoe knew had truly existed. In fact, the Amazons had faced down Heracles and his men in battle and come out the worse for it. And while in theory she knew that there were other mythical creatures that had existed in the past—Heracles was well known for killing lots of them—it wasn't something she'd had to think about in a long time.

She needed a break, something to shut her mind off completely. Knocking boots with the luscious reporter sounded like the exact medicine the doctor ordered.

"Hey, I thought you were hungry," Jason said as they reached the galley, and she walked right past it.

She turned around and gave him a sultry smile. "I am. But not for anything you can find in a kitchen." His eyes went wide as she beckoned him with one finger. "I think we could both use a little release, don't you?"

He swallowed thickly. "Are you sure about this? This wasn't what I had in mind when we came down here."

She grabbed his shirt and pulled his body flush with hers. "Maybe not, but it was on mine." She captured his mouth with hers, and he leaned into her body, giving as good as he got. His hands cupped the back of her head to keep their lips pressed together.

Slow, drugging kisses kept them pinned in place for a short eternity. Zoe's hands flattened on his chest, rubbing the soft cotton of his T-shirt as she traced the muscles beneath. One of his hands slid down her spine to her butt and tugged her toward him until not even a piece of paper would fit between them.

She made an impatient noise and tore her mouth from his. "Bed. Now." She spun on her heel and led the way down to the aft cabin nestled in the lowest part of the boat. It was decorated with a nautical theme, with a blue-and-white-striped comforter and a throw pillow sporting an anchor and the phrase *Home is where the boat is parked*. Cute but in the way. With a swipe of her hand, she flung the pillow onto the floor on the far side of the queen bed.

"In a hurry?" he asked with a soft chuckle.

"Aren't you?" she asked coyly as she slowly lifted her shirt over her head. She heard his sharply indrawn breath and had to swallow down a laugh.

"I am now."

Jason whipped his shirt over his head in the way that horny men all over the world seem to have perfected. As she enjoyed the show, Zoe teased her fingers around the waistband of her jeans and slowly—very slowly—popped open the button and tugged down her zipper. His eyes were riveted to her movements, his hands frozen over his own fly. She stepped out of her pants and kicked them sideways, leaving her in nothing but a pale-blue lace bra and panties.

"You joining me?" she teased. She gestured to his pants.

Without hesitation, he stripped off his jeans and boxers in one motion, leaving him bare to her hungry gaze. Not to mention hard as a rock and standing at attention.

She stepped closer to him, her hand encircling his stiff cock. She gave an experimental pump that had him groaning, then pressed a quick kiss to his lips. "How do you want me?"

His eyebrows winged up. "You're letting me pick?"

"Why wouldn't I?" Zoe knew she came across as a bit controlling and maybe even demanding, but here, in these circumstances, she was up for whatever he was in the mood for. She took her hands off him and stepped back. "What will it be?"

Jason took the time to study her from the top of her hair to where her toes curled into the carpet. His gaze was a scorching heat that she could practically feel on her skin. He stepped closer to her and traced his finger over the lace that barely contained her breasts. "Not that I don't love this, but why don't you take it off, then lie down and close your eyes?"

Zoe did as he asked, removing her bra and panties before sweeping the blankets back and crawling onto the mattress to put herself on display for him. Jason didn't immediately follow her. Instead, he stood at the foot of the bed and stared at her as if he were content to do no more than stand around and enjoy the view. The anticipation was killing her.

Jason finally climbed onto the bed, slowly crawling up her body until they were face-to-face. He lowered himself onto her until their bodies were flush with each other's. His mouth swooped down and captured hers, ravishing her lips.

Zoe kissed him back fiercely. Her arms snaked around his neck, and her fingers dove into his hair. Jason was an amazing kisser, using just the right pressure and tongue to tease and tempt. He broke the kiss, and she let out a whimper, but he didn't go far. He tipped her head sideways and kissed his way down her neck to her shoulders, his tongue laving her collarbone.

She started to squirm underneath him, but he had barely begun. He planted kisses across her chest until he finally captured one of her nipples in his mouth, licking and flicking it with his tongue. He caressed her other breast with his hand, squeezing her nipple into a tight peak before swapping to ensure each breast got equal treatment.

With one last squeeze he continued his journey, pressing feather-light kisses to her stomach and tonguing her belly button. He kept going, and just as she expected him to land exactly where she wanted him, he jumped to her thighs, beginning a torturous journey of nuzzles and pecks down one leg and back up the other. When he once again skipped over her clit, she let out an audible growl.

Jason chuckled. "Do you want something, Zoe?"

She wiggled, trying to shift so that he was stroking her where she desperately craved his touch. "You know what I want," she said through panted breaths.

He moved back up her body so they were once again face-to-face. "Yes, but I'd like to hear you say it."

She groaned. "Touch me, Jason. Damn it, just touch me."

His hand immediately went between her legs, putting her out of her misery but starting a whole new ache that only he could satisfy. He twisted and flicked and rubbed in a way that had her dying for more.

She was done being passive. Jason's slow and steady pace was like exquisite torture, and while there was a time and place for that, she needed more, and she needed it now. She reached between them and grabbed his dick, stroking it tightly until she'd pulled a moan out of him. He choked out a groan as she twisted her hand over his sensitive tip.

"Turnabout is fair play, lover," she whispered in his ear before removing her hand and trailing it lightly over his hip rather than where he was hard for her.

He tipped his head until their foreheads met. "I yield. Please touch me."

"I have a better idea," she said as she opened her legs wider so that his knees hit the mattress and he was perfectly positioned at the apex of her thighs. She grabbed his cock and tried to guide it to her entrance, but he froze and pulled back.

"What about condoms?" he whispered.

She smiled and planted a quick kiss on his lips. "Unnecessary. Amazons can't bear kids, and we're immune to human diseases."

He returned her smile. "Handy." He plunged inside her with no further waiting.

The invasion was sudden but so welcome. Zoe groaned her pleasure as Jason set a relentless pace. It seemed the teasing was over. She wrapped her legs around him, digging her heels into his lower back, keeping him from fully withdrawing. Not that he was going anywhere.

His lips met hers, his tongue plunging inside her mouth as thoroughly as his cock was doing below. She felt herself climbing higher and higher, the pleasure dancing and swooping inside her. He slipped his hand between them and reached for her bud, rubbing it in circles.

Zoe shattered, her orgasm washing through her. Jason gave a few more thrusts, then moaned as he followed her over the edge. He collapsed on the bed next to her.

"Holy crap," Jason panted out.

Zoe felt as wrecked as he sounded. "No kidding."

"Is it always like that?" Jason rolled over so his head was on one of the pillows.

"Is what always like that? Sex? Or sex with an Amazon?" she asked, only somewhat teasing.

His eyes narrowed, and he propped himself up on his side, his chin resting on the palm of his bent arm. He met her eyes. "Sex with you."

That mollified her somewhat. "Well, I can't say I've ever had sex with myself, so I'm not exactly the best judge of that."

"You should try it. Ten out of ten, would recommend." He flopped back down on his pillow.

Zoe laughed, which was a novel feeling. She'd had plenty of sex in her life and enjoyed it immensely. She couldn't remember ever laughing quite like this, though. The tension she'd been holding in her shoulders slowly let go, allowing her to drift into a dragonless doze.

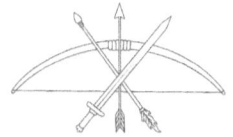

Chapter Fourteen

THE SUDDEN BLARING OF a siren—the boat kind this time—jolted them out of their haze and sent Zoe flying out of bed. She tugged her panties on and grabbed her shirt, throwing it on as she went running above deck, leaving the rest of her clothes in a heap on the floor.

Jason had no clue what was going on, but if Zoe was running, he probably should be too. He pulled on his boxers, grabbed his T-shirt, and then bolted after her. She raced to the top deck again, and he panted as he sprinted behind her. "What is it?" he asked loudly after they emerged on the top level of the yacht.

"It's the AIS alarm," she yelled as she smashed the power button to turn off the music that was still blaring. "It's a warning signal that goes off to prevent collisions when other boats are in the area."

The sun was starting to peek over the horizon, but as far as Jason could tell, there were no boats anywhere around them. There was an island coming up—in front of them and slightly off the right side.

It appeared to be uninhabited, at least the part they could see, and there were no docks or marinas where a boat would be parked. They both scanned the water as far as they could see in every direction, but there was nothing.

The yacht felt like it was starting to pick up speed, but neither of them had touched the controls. "You feel that?" he asked Zoe warily.

She nodded. "Yeah, I do. It shouldn't be doing that." She sounded worried. She crossed the floor to the control panel and started going over the instruments and settings. "Nothing's changed. I have no idea what's going on." She mashed a few buttons, but nothing happened. "And I can't clear the AIS alarm either. It's convinced there's another boat out here."

Jason didn't know anything about boats, but it seemed strange that the collision alarm would randomly start misfiring in the middle of a voyage. Given their luck, there was nothing random about this. Something was setting the alarm off; they just couldn't see what it was. He had opened his mouth to ask a stupid question about the likelihood that a boat could turn invisible when Zoe lifted her hand in a silent gesture to stop.

"Do you hear that?" she asked, her eyes narrowing. She left the control panel and walked to the railing to once again search the water.

He could just barely hear a rushing noise over the beeping alarm. It sounded vaguely familiar, but he couldn't place it. "What is it?"

She chewed on her lower lip but didn't respond.

Suddenly something appeared in the distance slightly off to their left side. It was far enough away that he couldn't quite make out what it was. It looked like a tower of some kind, except the object wasn't standing straight up but was listing to one side. It also looked like it was moving.

"Is that some sort of offshore wind farm?" Jason took a stab in the dark. He was pretty sure he was wrong, since there was only one object instead of several, and giant fans didn't usually tilt sideways. "Or maybe an oil-and-gas platform?" That wasn't likely, either, since it looked like a single post. He couldn't make out what it was connected to.

"At a guess, neither. But whatever it is, that's exactly what the AIS system has been warning us about." She tapped on the screen. "It seems to think it's a sailboat, but I don't see any sort of hull."

Their boat continued to gain momentum the closer they got to the object. Zoe disengaged the autopilot and tried to steer them to the left of whatever it was so they didn't hit it.

The boat didn't respond. No matter how hard Zoe cranked the wheel, the boat didn't turn. She tried slowing their speed, going so far as to cut the throttle entirely and then throw the ship in reverse.

No response. The boat kept cruising toward the object in the water.

"Um, Zoe?" Panic rose in his throat as he watched her hands fly over the controls to try to get the boat to respond. "Are we dead in the water?"

She was already shaking her head, but her voice was strained. "No, not exactly. The boat is fine, but whatever current we're stuck in is drawing us in. The engines can't seem to overpower it."

The boat picked that exact moment to shudder under the rush of the water hitting the hull, making Jason stumble. He braced himself against the railing. "So we're going to crash into whatever that thing is?"

Zoe spun the wheel in the other direction, aiming for the island rather than the object in the water. It wasn't a great solution—it wasn't like they wanted to crash into the rocky cliffs that ringed the spit of land—but at least the boat responded. It seemed like the current would let them steer in one direction, but not the other. It didn't make any sense.

The faster the current pulled at the yacht, the louder the rushing sound became. The sun was finally high enough to illuminate the object in the water. It was a ship's mast. The AIS system had been right. Unfortunately, it didn't tell the whole story.

"Holy Mother of God," Jason said, his jaw dropping open.

A large sailboat was trapped in a gigantic whirlpool that was sucking it closer and closer to the middle. As Jason watched in horror, a piece of debris hit the center of the angrily swirling vortex and was crushed under the pressure of the churning waves before being sucked underwater. The sailboat was pulled in next, shattering into kindling under the unrelenting force of the water. The AIS alarm shut off abruptly.

"Holy shit! Abort, abort! Whatever it is that boat people say. Get us the hell out of here!" Jason yelled. He could feel the panic clawing its way up his throat. He had no desire to drown somewhere in the Aegean Sea—or anywhere, for that matter—so getting away from the sucking void of the depths was the only option. Even if they did have to skirt the rocky island to get around it. Possible hull damage was still a safer bet than certain death by whirlpool.

"What do you think I'm trying to do?" Zoe screamed back. She was cranking the steering wheel as hard as she could, her muscles straining as she fought the relentless pull of the water. Every time it seemed like they were making progress, the boat would get sucked back into the current. They crested a particularly steep wave and came crashing back down. Finally, though, they were gaining ground. If they could get closer to the island, they might survive.

A loud crash behind him had Jason spinning around in place. He got a brief glimpse of dark scales and rows and rows of pointy teeth before the creature's head vanished into the low-hanging cloud above them. "What the fuck was that? Did the dragon find us?"

Thwack. Another noise reverberated from the front of the yacht. He caught a glimpse of a giant reptile head before it retreated.

"That's not a dragon," Zoe panted out. "It's Scylla. We're so screwed. She has—" Zoe was cut off as a mossy green head that resembled a dragon dropped right in front of them, mouth open to reveal three rows of razor-sharp teeth waiting to tear into them.

Another head appeared to their left, a third one on their right. A fourth one appeared behind the first, and by the sound of it, more had appeared behind them, though Jason wasn't about to turn around and look. Each head was attached to a long, sinuous neck that snaked back into the fog above them.

"Six heads!" Zoe choked out the rest of her thought.

Jason groaned out loud. "Are you kidding me?" He wanted to scream, though his question was moot. His mind flashed back to the books from the museum. Zoe's memory was spot-on. Jason and the Argonauts had been forced to sail between Charybdis—the giant whirlpool-creating monster—and Scylla—a dragon-headed snake-like creature of doom that came at them from above. As far as Jason could tell, it was basically a choose-your-mode-of-death type of situation.

The six heads roared, bringing Jason slamming back into their current situation. Saliva dripped between Scylla's teeth and ran off her open jaws to pool on the deck. Several of the heads started chomping their teeth, the others moving closer as if trying to smell them. Jason had no idea why Scylla's many heads hadn't attacked yet, but that luck probably wouldn't last much longer.

"We need to get out of here and get down the ladder as quickly as we can. I'm going to cut the engines and transfer control below. Then I'm going to jump down that hatch. You better follow right on my ass, you copy?" Zoe's barked orders were oddly comforting, even among the chaos of the thundering water and the howling monster. At least he could be confident that one of them had a plan.

"Copy," he yelled back.

She gave him a sharp nod, then threw the boat engines in neutral. The yacht immediately got sucked back into the swirling whirlpool behind them, losing some of the ground they had managed to gain. Zoe slapped her hand on a button and then did exactly as promised. She launched herself into the hatch, sliding down the ladder like it was a firefighter's pole.

Scylla didn't take too kindly to Zoe's escape. Before Jason could move an inch, one of her many heads swung in his direction, using its neck to knock him off his feet. He had several steps to go before he could reach the hatch, and the creature's ugly maw now blocked his path. He reached behind himself and felt some sort of pole. It was going to have to be good enough. He gripped it with all his strength and lashed out. With more luck than skill, he managed to get the hooked tip straight into the creature's eye, causing it to rear back with a roar of pain.

Jason didn't hesitate. He dove for the opening and followed Zoe's lead by not bothering to use the steps. Sliding was much faster. He wasn't nearly as graceful as she was, but down was down. He sprawled on the floor of the lower helm and watched through the still-open hatch as Scylla's many heads tried to figure out where they'd gone. With one last burst of bravery, Jason climbed just high enough to grab the hatch door and slam it closed.

The creature growled, and it was clear it was coming from more than one of the heads simultaneously. The boat shuddered as Scylla slammed her many snakelike necks and dragon-like heads into the top deck. There was definitely going to be damage.

Out of the corner of his eye, Jason saw Zoe slam the throttle forward, revving the engines and once again aiming for the island. "What are you doing? We need to get away from this Medusa-headed beast," Jason said as he picked himself up off the floor and sat next to Zoe on the bench behind the console.

"We can't go back. We'd get sucked into Charybdis's whirlpool and be crushed. Our only option is forward." Zoe's jaw clenched, and her eyes narrowed. "The only way out is through."

As much as he didn't want to admit it, she was right. Through the front windscreen, he watched Scylla's many heads slam down on the bow of the boat, making the entire fiberglass frame shudder and quake. The deck surface, which had withstood the force of the fifty-pound fleece slamming into it from hundreds of feet in the air, suddenly cracked and creaked under the impact from the monster's reptilian heads. One of the heads swung around and smashed into the glass windscreen they were staring through, thankfully not destroying it but leaving a spiderweb of cracks that made it difficult to see.

"This bitch needs to chill the fuck out," Zoe said through clenched teeth.

Jason could see Zoe's strained muscles as she gripped the steering wheel and guided them away from the deadly whirlpool, yet far enough away from the island that they didn't crash into the rocks.

The bangs and shudders from above continued but became less frequent. After one final smash to the rear of the yacht, they were far enough away from Scylla that she could no longer reach them. A sudden burst of speed made it obvious that the current had subsided, and they were no longer being pulled toward the certain death of the swirling vortex.

Jason let out a long breath, lowering his shoulders from where they'd been tensed up somewhere near his ears. The silence stretched between them as they both caught their breath. The suddenly smooth sailing was almost anticlimactic after their most recent fight-or-flight situation.

"Well, that was . . ." Jason was not even certain how to describe it. Exhaustion swamped him, and he slumped in his seat.

"Scylla and Charybdis," Zoe said, finishing his thought.

"I was going to say 'terrifying,' but sure. Let's go with that." Now that his brain wasn't in survival mode, he could think more clearly about the situation. He recalled the story of Jason and his crew facing the pair of sea monsters. In fact, if his memory served, they faced them after they had successfully evaded the lure of the sirens.

"Zoe, do you think it's a coincidence that—" Zoe didn't let him complete the full thought. She left one hand on the steering wheel and threw her other arm around his neck and pulled him down into a drugging kiss. He almost forgot his question, so distracted by how right it felt to be kissing Zoe and how relieved he was that they had come through unharmed.

His hands settled on her waist and tugged her as close to him as he could get while she still had one occupied hand. He was alive. She was alive. They had both survived their most recent—and hopefully last—brush with death. They deserved to relax for a moment. It had been a tense few hours.

Unfortunately, they both knew what had happened the last time they'd let their guards down. They probably couldn't afford to do that again. At least not while they were still vulnerable to attack. Maybe once they got back to Themyscira things would be different. Slowly, gently, he lightened their kisses until he was able to give her a small peck on the corner of her lips and pull back.

Her eyes were dazed, pupils blown wide with desire. "As much as I would love to follow up on the promise your eyes are making right now, perhaps we should focus on the fact that we survived another attack?"

Zoe shook her head, the fog clearing from her eyes. Unfortunately, she also pulled away from him, turning on the bench seat to face forward once more. "Of course. My mistake."

She thought he wasn't interested. He couldn't have that. "Zoe, let me be clear." She glanced at him out of the corner of her eye but didn't turn to face him. "If we were somewhere safe and not, say, floating through a sea of monsters, I would happily drag you back down to the bed and have my way with you once more. But maybe, just maybe, we should get off this damn yacht first?" he asked hopefully.

She visibly relaxed and sent him a half grin. "Rain check."

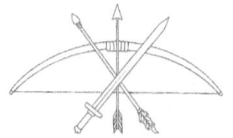

Chapter Fifteen

T HE YACHT WAS PRETTY much drifting on fumes by the time they reached the marina in İzmir, Türkiye. Zoe gently guided the boat to the dock and explained to Jason what he needed to do to run the lines. As soon as the boat was tied off and secure, Zoe took the deepest breath she'd allowed herself in days.

She walked around the yacht, taking stock. It was definitely the worse for wear. All the top surfaces—including the flybridge and the bow of the ship—looked like someone had taken a sledgehammer to them. Which something basically had. Zoe felt bad that the yacht wasn't in as good shape as when she'd liberated it, but since she'd piloted it to a foreign country and had every plan on abandoning it there, she doubted the original owners would ever get it back anyway. Maybe she should have Selene buy them a new one.

She was utterly exhausted. If you didn't count whatever trance the sirens had put her under—and since she had technically been awake, it really shouldn't be included—Zoe had been awake for over a day, closer to a day and a half. She needed food and she needed sleep. Possibly not in that order.

İzmir was the third-largest city in Türkiye, so there would be plenty of hotels and restaurants. One short car ride and she could finally relax. They could regroup, recover, and find a way to charge their now-dead cell phones so she could check in with Kalli and Selene.

The only thing that belonged to either her or Jason on the entire boat was what they'd been carrying when the dragon kidnapped them, two small backpacks and the golden fleece. Since they couldn't exactly go wandering through a city of several million people with a shiny sheepskin on display, they rolled it up—shiny side in, of course—and Jason carried the tube propped on his shoulder as they disembarked from the yacht. As they casually strolled through the marina, Zoe spotted an oversize trash bag. She snagged it before anyone saw what she was doing and helped Jason feed the fleece inside and tie it off.

They hailed a cab and headed to find a hotel near the Kemeralti Bazaar. Zoe hadn't been there in decades, but the colorful marketplace—which had been growing and expanding since the sixteen hundreds—would be as good a place as any to find food, a hotel, and a bit of entertainment should time allow for it.

Zoe approached a woman with dark hair and a neatly trimmed uniform behind the hotel's front desk, leaving Jason a few steps behind her in the lobby. "Excuse me, do you have any rooms available?"

The woman glanced from her to Jason and back. "Will you be needing one room or two?" The clerk's fingernails tapped away at her keyboard.

Zoe glanced over her shoulder and caught Jason's smirk. "One is fine." Seconds later she was armed with a hotel key, and they were riding the elevator up to their floor. She opened the door to their room and immediately took inventory of everything in the space. One bed, a small desk and chair, a stand with a TV, and a bathroom. Pretty basic stuff. She spotted a bag of complimentary snacks and fell on it like a starving woman.

She finished her pretzels and barely stifled a yawn as she tossed the wrapper in the trash bin. As much as she wanted to take Jason up on the sneaky grin he'd given her in the hotel lobby, the fluffy pillows were calling her name. "I know I said rain check, but it's probably going to have to wait a bit longer. I need to get some sleep before my body makes that decision for me."

Jason crossed the short distance between them and planted a light kiss on her lips. "There's no rush. It's been a hell of a day and night. We both need to crash."

Without further discussion, they both stripped down to their underwear and crawled under the sheets. Zoe fell asleep instantly.

It had been early evening when they'd fallen asleep, but they'd needed the rest, because when Zoe came to, she realized they'd slept for over twelve hours. She grabbed her phone off the charger she'd gotten from the front desk the night before and turned it on. It lit up like a Christmas tree as dozens of notifications flashed on her screen. Most of them were ever-increasingly-panicked messages from Kalli and Selene, wondering why Zoe and Jason hadn't shown up to meet the plane in Athens.

As she was about to hit call on Kalli's number, news alerts started pinging her phone. She glanced at one and was surprised to see her face staring back at her. With dread filling her stomach, she clicked on the link to take her to the article.

Amazon on the Warpath

by Jason Bloom

To an outside observer, Zoe Harper may seem like a bundle of contradictions. She's a—now former—Interpol agent, an intelligent and savvy negotiator, and an Amazon warrior who can conjure fire from her hands. Yet if you talk to her neighbors, she's also a sweet and loving person who is just as likely to help an old woman pick up groceries from the store or cat-sit for a friend. She enjoys long days on the beach and loves visiting Paris. In short, she's just like the rest of us, at least in many ways.

But what about the things that set her apart? A self-proclaimed sorceress, Harper has several different otherworldly abilities that can only be described as magic. According to her, however, she is the only one of her Amazon sisters with these abilities, though that information is still being verified.

What this reporter can say with certainty is that ever since he met Harper, she has been nothing but a consummate professional with the solitary goal of protecting her home, Themyscira, and bringing the situation brewing there to a peaceful and beneficial solution to all involved parties.

Follow along with us as we spend time with one of the most interesting people in the world today. This is the first of a multipart series providing a close-up look into the Amazons. Are they a dangerous threat or a group of women trying to defend their homeland? You decide.

Zoe seethed. *Who was he calling a "dangerous threat"?* She slammed her phone down on the bed.

"What's going on?"

A groggy voice pulled Zoe's head out of the article. Jason was awake. Perfect. Just the man she needed to talk to. "What is this?" she asked, grabbing her phone and shoving it in front of his bleary eyes.

He blinked several times and squinted to read the tiny screen. "Oh, my article?" He sat up in bed, scrubbing his face with his hands. He leaned against the headboard and looked at her in confusion. "What about it? You knew I was writing a story. You even said that Kalli had forced you to go along with it."

The thing was, he wasn't wrong. She'd known what she was signing up for by bringing him along, so she couldn't figure out why she felt so wrong-footed when he followed through and did exactly what he'd said he was going to do. She fell back on the one thing she couldn't quite figure out. "When did you even have time to write this and get it published?"

He shrugged, and the sheet that had been tucked around him slowly slid down his chest to his lap. "I started it that first day on the plane. Added to it here and there along the way. Whenever we had downtime. I tried to send it to Noah when we first got on the yacht, but the signal wasn't working. Not sure when he finally got it."

She crossed her arms and looked at him, not sure what to say. She didn't have any right to be upset. If anything, she was the one in the wrong for getting on his case for just doing his job.

"Wait." He paused and stared at her. "Are you upset about this? I thought we were on the same page."

They were, at least in theory. Whatever was going on, it was all in her own head, and she had to be the one to deal with it. "No, I'm not upset. Well, I am, but I understand that I don't have the right to be. I'll get over it, I promise. I'm not used to having my life all out there in the public eye. I've been hiding in plain sight for thousands of years. Deliberately putting myself out there for the world to see and pick at isn't my forte."

"And that is where we differ. All I've ever wanted was to be in front of the camera. I briefly thought about going into acting but decided I cared about the news and reporting the truth far more than making people believe the clever lie that goes along with telling fictional stories for movies and TV." Jason leaned in and planted a soft kiss on her lips, not bothering to push for more. "Don't worry, I'll help you through it."

She felt herself softening. "You promise to be gentle?" She teased.

His face split into a wide grin. "Only if you ask nicely." With that parting quip he pushed out of bed and made his way to the bathroom.

Zoe tried—and failed—to hold back a grin. Before she could get distracted again, she tapped Kalli's contact info on her phone and put it on speaker while it was ringing.

"Zoe, where are you?" Kalli's concerned question preempted even saying hello.

"We're in İzmir. Both Jason and I are safe and sound." She watched as Jason left the bathroom—his magnificent chest on full display as he crossed the room in his boxers—trying not to get distracted from her purpose.

"Why are you in İzmir?" Selene asked. Kalli must have had her phone on speaker too. "You were supposed to be heading to Athens. That's where I sent the plane."

"Yeah, about that. We went a bit off course," Zoe said.

"İzmir and Athens aren't even in the same country! That's more than a little off course," Selene said.

"What caused you to go off course?" Kalli—the more levelheaded of the two—asked.

"Sirens," Jason spoke for the first time.

The silence on the other end of the line stretched for longer than normal. "You mean like the kind that sing and lure sailors to their death?" This time the question came from Sam.

"Those very ones," Jason said. He recounted how he'd fallen asleep, then woken to find Zoe in a trance and the yacht about to crash. He regaled them with the tale of how he'd blasted the radio to get them out of there. "Now if only we could send those sirens on a highway to hell."

"That's a great story and all," Colin added, "but last time I checked, there weren't any reports about sailors going missing and crashing their ships somewhere in the Aegean. I'm pretty sure that would have made the news."

"True story," Jason said with a cheeky grin.

"Which means that the sirens probably haven't been there long," Selene mused. "But why would they be there now? They've been gone for thousands of years. Why resurface now?"

Zoe grimaced even though she knew that only Jason would be able to see it. "There's more." She recounted their encounter with Scylla and Charybdis.

"I would have loved to see that," Sam said in the awestruck way he always seemed to get whenever they discussed the topic of myths coming to life.

"Would you really?" Selene asked sarcastically. "Almost getting sucked into a whirlpool or being eaten by a multiheaded snake monster? Are those high up on your bucket list?"

"Oh, right. Sorry. I'm sure it was terrifying." Sam cleared his throat, but Colin laughed at him.

"The real question," Kalli interrupted them to ask, "is where are all these creatures coming from? The beasts we're discussing—dragons, sirens, Scylla, and Charybdis—they're monsters straight out of myth. While they may have existed thousands of years ago, they don't anymore. Well, at least they didn't. So what changed?"

"That's obvious," Jason said, drawing Zoe's gaze to where he was sitting next to her, looking rumpled and adorable. "Us. Specifically, Zoe and me."

"What do you mean?" Zoe asked, squinting in his direction.

"Think about it, Zoe. We were walking around on the top of a mountain that millions of people have visited over the last several thousand years. While I'm sure they all enjoyed their time there, I'll bet my future Pulitzer Prize that none of them located the illusion you found. And that illusion led us to—"

Zoe cut him off as she picked up his train of thought. "The fire-breathing bulls, the dragon, and the fleece."

"Take us through it again," Selene demanded. "From when you entered the illusion until right this moment."

So they did. They went over every aspect of their last two days with a fine-tooth comb.

"It had to be when the illusion shattered," Zoe said, still formulating her idea even while she was trying to explain it. "Medea was powerful. From what I can tell, she was far more powerful than I am. It was her magic that animated the bulls and brought the statue of the dragon to life. Breaking her illusion must have sent some sort of shock wave through the world. Her magic either conjured creatures long since lost or somehow unwove an illusion that had been hiding them."

Silence spread, only their harsh breaths breaking the stillness.

"That means there could be more," Kalli said.

"Damn it," Selene said. "I can mobilize my special operations team. We can be on the lookout for anything out of the ordinary and can be on-site anywhere in the world in a matter of hours."

"I'm not sure that's going to be enough," Kalli said quietly. "If Zoe—a powerful sorceress and Amazon—could barely escape these creatures, what hope do your men have?"

"To step in on behalf of the entire human race for a moment, it wasn't the all-powerful Amazon that got us away from the sirens. That was little old me, the human," Jason piped up.

He wasn't wrong. Zoe had been helpless against the sirens. If Jason hadn't been there, she would have crashed into the rocks and sunk. He'd saved them both.

"And how would you have fared without Zoe against the dragon?" Selene's saccharin tone made Jason wince.

"The truth of the matter is that we all have different strengths. Humans can't fight these creatures without the Amazons and quite possibly vice versa." Kalli took command of the conversation. "Zoe and Jason, hang tight. Selene will send the plane to you, and then you get back here with that fleece as soon as possible. Your first story didn't exactly have a calming effect on our government babysitters. We may need to defend ourselves sooner than we'd anticipated, so we could really use that fleece."

"Uh, guys?" Selene said. "All that may have to wait. Turn on the news."

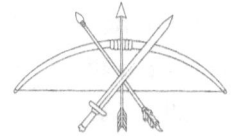

Chapter Sixteen

Jason grabbed the TV remote and flipped to the first English-speaking news network he could find. *Giant Bronze Robot Terrorizes City*, the headline scrolling at the bottom of the screen read. "Giant robot?" He scoffed. "This can't be real. It completely stretches all sense of belief in reality that we'd have some sort of tech apocalypse at the same time we're having a mythological one."

As if to prove him wrong, the image on the screen cut from a neatly dressed reporter behind a desk to a shaky cell phone video of what was unmistakably a giant bronze humanoid standing in the middle of an unnamed city. The robot—if that was what it was—was weaving in and out of buildings and looking around the area in confusion. The creature was enormous, standing taller than the seven-story building next to him.

"Where is this?" Zoe asked as the bronze man stepped on a car and crushed it.

Jason hoped the car had been empty.

"You're never going to believe this," Selene replied. "It's in İzmir."

"That seems like a hell of a coincidence," Zoe said.

"Unless it isn't a coincidence at all," Colin said.

"What do you mean?" Kalli asked.

"I guess it's possible that the news is right and that some giant prototype robot escaped from some lab somewhere. But I wouldn't buy that. I'd bet you my considerable bank balance that the bronze guy is Talos," Colin said.

"And who or what is Talos, for those of us who don't have PhDs in boring old stuff?" Selene asked.

Jason wanted to laugh at her sarcastic question but held himself back.

Sam picked up the story. "Talos was a giant bronze statue that was supposedly built by Hephaestus and then sent by Zeus to the island of Crete to protect Europa—one of Zeus's many lovers—and the children they had together. Talos was said to stride around the island three times a day and heave boulders at any approaching ships."

They all jumped when a loud crash came from the television. The live footage showed a car that looked like it had crashed into a building. As they watched, Talos bent down and grabbed a different car from the side of the road before hurling it at another building. The gawking pedestrians had to dive out of the way to not get crushed.

Jason found himself horror-struck and a little baffled. "But this isn't Crete. It's not even Greece," Jason said. He felt ridiculous pointing it out, but someone needed to say it.

"Not today, it's not. But back when Talos was alive—the first time, I guess—the western coast of what is now Türkiye was part of the Greek empire. In fact, it changed hands many times and was part of Greece off and on for hundreds of years," Sam said.

If Jason were ever at risk of forgetting that Sam was a professor, it was explanations like this one that never failed to remind him. "That still doesn't explain why this Talos dude isn't where he's supposed to be. Why would he be in İzmir when he's supposed to be in Crete?"

"I think it's one of two reasons. Possibly both of them," Colin said. "The first reason is that Europa—the woman he was charged with guarding—is long since dead. His mission is over, and therefore he's no longer tied to the island where she lived. The second reason is you two. You're literally following in the footsteps of Jason and the Argonauts. Not only did you start in Volos—which was the part of Greece where Jason lived and where they sailed from—you then fought the bulls and dragon and retrieved the fleece. From then on, you've been encountering the same creatures that the Argonauts did thousands of years ago. First the sirens, then Scylla and Charybdis, and now Talos. Some sort of magic is re-creating the exact series of events from before."

Another boom came from the television, and Jason turned to see Talos smashing another car. Unfortunately, this one appeared to be a police car. The police officers were already out of the vehicle, thankfully, but they'd drawn their guns and were firing at the giant metal creature. "They're going to get themselves killed. They have no idea what they're up against or how to defeat him," Zoe said.

"Do we?" Jason asked. It was one thing to judge the police for going in with guns against an animated metal statue, but the thing was a hundred feet tall. What options did they even have?

"Yes. Talos only has one vein. It's full of ichor—the blood of the gods—and it runs from his neck to one of his ankles. That vein is closed with only a single nail. If you can remove that nail, the ichor will bleed out of him and kill him," said Sam.

On screen, Talos lifted one giant foot and stomped on a food truck, crushing it flat to the pavement. Panicked police officers and citizens dove behind cars and buildings to avoid flying shrapnel. People were going to die. Jason was surprised it hadn't happened yet.

"We need to get over there," Zoe said. "Guys, I'll have to call you back." Without another word, Zoe hung up the phone and started pulling on the same clothes she'd worn the day before. They still hadn't had a chance to replace the luggage they lost in Corinth.

"As we can see, the Police Special Operations Department is not having any noticeable success against the robot that continues to cause massive amounts of damage to downtown İzmir. The creature is only a few streets away from the port of İzmir, which is the largest port in Türkiye. Damage to the port could have catastrophic consequences for the country's economy and supply chain," the female reporter said.

Her male colleague interrupted: "Breaking news. We've been given an update that the government of Türkiye has scrambled their military forces. A contingent of tanks belonging to the land forces was doing live-fire exercises in the vicinity and will be rerouted to the city to help address the ongoing threat. Military personnel should be on-site within the next thirty minutes."

"Tanks? This is going to get ugly fast," Jason said as he pulled on his own clothes. "There are civilians all over the place. What in the hell are they thinking?"

As if he could overhear Jason's question, the television reporter spoke again: "The police are mobilizing to start evacuating buildings near the creature. We're told that the police and military will be setting up a perimeter around the current location, barricading streets, and preventing all nonofficial personnel from entering the zone."

"How are we going to get through that?" Jason asked.

Zoe chewed her lip. "Any chance you have a spare press pass hanging around?"

Why hadn't he thought of that? Press passes weren't exactly an all-access pass to everything, but they certainly helped. "Actually, yes. In my bag." He rummaged through the small backpack he'd been carrying and dug out the lanyard with his credentials on it.

"Great. We'll make do," Zoe said. She spun on her heel and headed out of the hotel room but paused when she reached the door, then turned to face him. "Whatever happens out there, I need you to promise me that you'll stay safe and out of the way. I can't focus on saving the city if I have to worry about you blundering headfirst into danger."

He met her eye, hoping she saw the annoyance in his. "First, super flattering. I appreciate your faith in me. It's not at all like I stayed cool under pressure and solved that dragon riddle while risking being flambéed by the bulls." She tried to speak, but he cut her off. "Second, I'm coming with you. End of discussion. Whether you admit it or not, you need my help. I won't be left behind like an afterthought. We're partners."

She sighed but nodded. "Fine. Just . . . don't get dead."

He would take it.

They made it to the lobby, where the woman who had checked them in the day before was back on duty. Zoe marched to the hotel doors, but as she reached them, the woman behind the desk called out, "You don't want to go out there. Haven't you seen the news?"

Zoe gave the woman a withering look. "Of course I know what's going on. That's exactly why I'm going. I'm the only one that can stop it."

The woman gave her a confused look but didn't bother to respond. Jason shrugged and followed Zoe out into the chaos.

Based on the news coverage, Talos was several blocks north of their current location, between their hotel and the port. The horrendous roar Jason heard as soon as he set foot outside confirmed that. So did the giant bronze man suddenly stomping his way down the boulevard in front of him. Several police officers chased him on foot, and police cars trailed in his wake. Zoe started running after them, and Jason did his best to keep up.

Unfortunately, Talos veered into the narrow streets that made up the Kemeralti Bazaar. The bazaar had been continuously expanding since the sixteen hundreds and was a maze of tightly packed, sometimes-winding roads that had a mix of shops and restaurants, one of the most popular and well-known parts of the city.

That cultural heritage was under siege. Talos was crashing through the streets and smashing anything in his way. He crushed vehicles and knocked over vendor carts full of colorful cloths, fruits and vegetables, and fresh fish.

One of the police officers pulled their weapon and took a handful of shots at the monster currently shoving his enormous foot through the front of a clothing store. Terrified screams of pedestrians and shop owners alike split the air as the bullets ricocheted off Talos's metallic skin and embedded into the building's walls.

The officer, realizing his mistake, immediately holstered his weapon and started ushering people away from the monster. The problem was the volume of people in the marketplace. The streets rapidly clogged with people trying to flee in panic. The officer shouted a few commands in rapid-fire Turkish, which Jason didn't understand. The people either didn't hear the police officer or ignored him entirely, since absolutely nothing changed, and civilians continued to race around in terrified circles, trying to escape.

"We need to get Talos out of here," Jason called to Zoe. "This area is too tightly packed. People are going to get trampled!"

She nodded to show that she'd heard him, then quickly glanced around.

Talos took the opportunity to smash his considerable fist through an antique store, sending glass and metal flying everywhere. Jason ducked behind one of the few intact cars to hide from the flying debris. He grabbed his phone from his back pocket and turned on the video app to start recording. He cautiously peeked around the trunk of the car and saw Zoe run up to the two brave police officers still trying to fend off Talos.

She obviously spoke Turkish, because the men were nodding along with her as she pointed in various directions, and they made a plan for how to corral Talos out of the bazaar. They each nodded, then split up. Luckily Talos had stepped in front of a side street that would lead out of the marketplace and toward the relatively open area beyond. They just had to get him to move in that direction.

The first officer, using a shoe store as a cover, took up a spot on the right. The second officer went to the left, concealing himself behind a tiny grocery store. Zoe stood tall right in the middle of the street, nothing standing between her and the hundred-foot creature who finally realized that she existed.

Talos started to swing his enormous fist in her direction, but she raised her hands, flames pouring out of them. The monster flinched, dodging away from the fire. With a smirk, Zoe slowly advanced, shooting fire in short bursts, aiming for Talos's feet and hands. Jason followed a short distance behind, trying to keep the action in sight but not wanting to get in the way.

The monster started to retreat down the short side street as Zoe and the officers paced him, keeping the pressure on and forcing him back. With a roar, Talos emerged from the bazaar and back out onto the main street. Zoe kept up with her fiery assault until she'd pushed Talos into Konak Park. Waiting on the other side of the park—between the paved promenade and the Aegean Sea—were two tanks, gun turrets pointed in their direction.

The army had arrived.

Zoe dropped her arms, letting her flames recede. Her shoulders slumped, and she started to weave from exhaustion. Just as Jason was about to run to her and catch her before she fell, Talos realized that the threat had stopped. With a mighty bellow, Talos swung his oversize arm and sent Zoe flying through the air and into the side of a brick building.

Jason's heart jumped to his throat. "Zoe!" he screamed and ran toward her limp body.

Chapter Seventeen

*W*AS THIS WHAT DEATH *felt like?*

Zoe couldn't move. Every square inch of her screamed in agony. It hurt to breathe, and she was afraid to shift even slightly, unsure what might be broken.

"Zoe!"

She heard someone scream her name, but her foggy brain couldn't figure out who would be calling for her. It was a man, so it couldn't be Kalli or Selene.

She managed to wrench open her eyes a fraction and look around. She was lying in a pile of bricks that had probably come from the damaged wall next to her. Turning her head slightly, she saw a park and a giant bronze monster destroying an intricately designed clock tower in the middle of the promenade.

Everything came flooding back: Talos. The fleece. Jason. She needed to get to him. If Talos was still alive, then the whole city was still in danger. *Jason* was still in danger. She tried to sit up but failed.

"Whoa, don't move."

Jason's voice was like music to her ears. He was alive and well. At least for now. It was her job to keep him that way. She was an Amazon, he was a human, and this situation was far more dangerous than she'd realized back at the hotel. She needed to get him out of this environment and back to safety. But first she needed to figure out how to stand.

Zoe once again started to sit up. Jason's hands came to her shoulders to stop her, but she glared at him, and he removed them. "You need to leave," she said weakly.

He stared at her like she'd grown another head. "What on earth are you talking about? Why would I leave? I told you we were partners."

She stayed seated while she waited for her head to stop swirling. "It's not safe for you. You could get hurt." At least her voice was stronger this time.

"*I* could get hurt?" Jason asked angrily. "Zoe, that dick threw you into a wall. You should be in a hospital right now. In fact, how are you not dead?"

She was already shaking her head and wishing it didn't make her feel like she was staring at cartoon birds flying around her head. A hospital wasn't an option. Not with Talos still on the loose. "I'm an Amazon. We're less breakable than your average human. Plus, I'm the only one who can stop him."

Jason rolled his eyes at her. "Let the army handle it. Remember the tanks with the really big guns?" He gestured vaguely over his shoulder to where the military was, indeed, pointing their mounted tank guns in Talos's direction.

"It's not going to work," Zoe said as she slowly pushed to her feet. She felt slightly less like she was dead and more like she'd been run over by a truck. Or, you know, thrown into a brick wall.

"Humans have evolved since Talos last walked the earth. Regular bullets might not be able to take him down, but hopefully a 120-millimeter tank-fired bullet will do the trick." Jason still had his hands out in front of him as if he was expecting her to go down at any moment. To be honest, she wasn't sure she wouldn't.

A loud crack split the air and made them both duck and look for the source. One of the tanks had fired its main gun at Talos. Unfortunately, Talos saw it coming. He smacked the shell out of the air and sent it right back in the direction it came from. The ammunition hit the tank, which exploded with a resounding boom and sent shrapnel flying in all directions. The second tank was smack in the middle of the impact zone and buckled under the force of the explosion.

"You were saying?" Zoe asked. Their crouched position next to the pile of bricks gave them inadequate cover to fully hide.

"Zoe, are you really up for this?" Jason asked, looking her straight in the eye. "I know we haven't known each other long, but you mean more to me than I thought possible in such a short amount of time. I don't want you getting yourself killed."

Jason's words were like a balm to her tattered soul. As weird as it was, she felt the same. She had no idea when Jason had started to creep into her heart and settle there, but he had. Which was why she had to do what she now knew was her only option. If Jason wouldn't leave on his own, then she was going to have to make him leave. She couldn't risk him. She wasn't sure her heart could survive if something happened to him.

She sent him a somewhat sad smile. "The same goes for you. I couldn't take it if you died, so you can't be here, Jason. *I need you to go back to the hotel.*" She pushed her power into the words, compelling him to comply.

She watched his face become a blank mask as his own will was wiped away and her power took root in him. It wouldn't last forever, thankfully. But it would last long enough for her to deal with Talos and make sure he couldn't harm Jason. Or anyone else, for that matter.

Jason looked at her in mild confusion and then said, "You know, you're right. This place isn't safe for me. I'm going to head back to our room." Without another word, he turned and headed away from the giant monster and back toward their hotel.

With one less thing to worry about, Zoe directed her attention back to the threat she needed to neutralize. The remaining army personnel had been engaging Talos with whatever weapons they had at their fingertips. One person had a rocket launcher on his shoulder. Before Zoe could blink, a rocket went flying.

Talos caught it and crushed it in his hand.

The explosion startled him enough that he dropped the remains of the rocket with a roar, grabbed the tank that hadn't exploded, and Hulk-smashed it into the ground. The soldiers scattered like rats.

Zoe charged into the fray. She knew Talos reacted to her fire, so she dug into her very low magical reserves and shot flames at his head, attempting to draw his attention from the soldiers as the remaining ones tried to regroup.

It worked. Talos turned and growled in her direction.

Great. She had his attention. What was step two?

The nail. She had to get to the nail. It was the only way to kill him.

Zoe ran directly at Talos, hoping to duck between his legs and get to his heel. No such luck. Talos kicked one of his enormous legs, forcing her to tuck and roll sideways. As a distraction she shot a quick burst of flame in his direction and tried again.

The results were the same. No matter what she tried, Talos anticipated her moves. Plus, given how long his legs were, it was trivial for him to simply sidestep or even step directly over her, preventing her from reaching her goal.

His last move at least let her get a good visual of the nail. While it may have been small in relation to Talos himself, it was still enormous. The head of the nail was probably the size of Zoe's torso. She hoped that by the time she finally got her hands on it, she had enough strength left to yank it out of place.

Zoe crouched behind a large bush to catch her breath and regroup. The fire thing wasn't working. He already knew about that power, and he seemed to be less and less afraid of it, since the fire didn't seem to be doing any actual damage to him. She needed something new.

Talos batted a seagull away from his face, making the bird squawk loudly and giving Zoe an idea. She closed her eyes and concentrated. Seagulls were much easier to influence than the dragon had been. She soon had several dozen birds at her beck and call.

She rose from behind the bush like an avenging angel and compelled the birds to attack Talos's face. They wouldn't be able to do any damage to his hard metal exterior, but maybe they could be the distraction she needed to get up close and personal with the monster.

Talos was instantly distracted and started swatting the birds away from his face. Zoe gave the seagulls enough of a push to keep them circling and dodging out of the way of the monster's eager hands. She sucked in a deep breath and ran for it. His feet were right in front of her. If she could make it to his heels, she would have a shot at stopping this.

Her ruse had worked. Zoe wrapped her arms completely around the head of the nail and yanked with all her remaining strength.

The nail didn't budge.

She tugged again. And again. Nothing happened.

Except Talos finally figured out what she was doing. He kicked his leg like a dog trying to shake off its wet paws. Unfortunately, Zoe was still holding on to the nail. She lost her grip on the slippery metal in midair, and for the second time in the last thirty minutes she went flying. Thankfully this time she didn't smash into a building. She tucked and rolled as she hit the ground, coming to a stop just before smacking into a park bench.

For a moment Zoe wanted to stay right where she was. She was out of ideas. The police had tried to stop Talos and failed. So had the military. Modern weapons didn't seem to have any effect on him whatsoever.

She'd been so certain that if she could get to the nail, she'd be able to remove it and put an end to his rampage. Even that had failed. She'd been unable to remove it, even with all the brute force and strength she was imbued with as an Amazon warrior.

Maybe it wasn't about brute strength.

She slowly sat up as one last desperate idea popped into her head. Talos was a magical creature. Maybe only magic could stop him.

She had one last magical gift in her arsenal. It was her weakest ability, but maybe, just maybe, it was the one that would end this once and for all. Her telekinesis didn't work over long distances, so she was going to have to get close to Talos for this to even have a hope of working. She was also going to have to let go of the control she had of the seagulls and focus all her power on this one objective.

Zoe reached deeper within her wells of magic than she'd ever done before. She pictured Kalli and Selene and the rest of her Amazon sisters. She pulled up an image of Jason's face.

She could do this. She *would* do this. For them and for him.

With a resolute breath, she once again walked straight at the monster that might very well kill her. When she was no more than fifty feet away, she stopped. Talos realized she was back and reached for her. Zoe aimed her palm at the nail in his foot and yanked with every mental and magical thread she had.

"Time to bleed, asshole!"

With a screech of wrenching metal, the nail pulled free.

Golden fluid—the ichor of the gods that was keeping Talos alive—poured freely onto the ground. Within seconds, the area had sprouted a heartbreakingly beautiful garden overflowing with flowers unlike Zoe had ever seen.

Unaware of the miracle happening on the ground beneath him, Talos weaved slightly on his feet before tipping over and tumbling into the sea with a splash that sent waves in every direction and capsized several small boats.

She'd done it. Talos was dead. She barely had time to enjoy that fact before she blacked out.

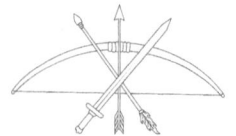

Chapter Eighteen

J ASON WAS PISSED.

He'd gotten all the way back to the hotel and up to the room before he realized something was wrong. Why would he have gone back to the hotel when the fight was still going on? It didn't make any sense. Something inside him was telling him that the hotel was the right place to be, but his brain couldn't make sense of why. He never would have abandoned Zoe in the middle of a battle like that.

The only thing that made any sort of sense was that she'd done something to him. She'd been cagey about her powers anytime he'd asked, and she'd given a suspiciously vague answer when asked why she thought the dragon had suddenly dropped them in the sea. He'd bet more money than he could afford to lose that she'd put some sort of whammy on both him and the dragon.

Zoe had used her magic on him and had sent him away like he was a small child being banished to his room. She'd taken away his free will and forced him to do what she wanted. When he caught up with her again, they were going to have a long talk about what was and wasn't acceptable behavior with someone you were . . . involved with.

He didn't know what to call the thing that he and Zoe had going on between them. It wasn't like they could say they were in a relationship. Not really. They'd known each other for five days. Yes, they'd slept together, but what did that really mean?

And it wasn't like they could truly be together, could they? She was thousands of years old. He was thirty-four. There was a world of difference between them. She'd seen things and experienced things he would never comprehend. Imagining the dozens of lifetimes she'd lived, his own life experiences seemed to pale in comparison. His life's goal was to get a job at an international news station. Her current goal was to save the world. They weren't even in the same league.

Glancing at his phone, Jason realized that both Noah and his boss had tried to get ahold of him. He fired off a quick email to let them know he was all right and update them on the situation, and then he tucked the phone back in his pocket.

He grabbed his small backpack, hefted the fleece onto his shoulders, then glanced around the hotel room for anything else they might have left behind. There was nothing.

He stormed through the hotel lobby and didn't even bother to check out at the front desk. He needed to get back to Zoe as quickly as possible. Who knew what had happened since he'd been gone?

The street was eerily quiet after the constant crash and boom that Talos had made as he ripped his way through the city. A sour feeling settled in Jason's stomach as he pictured all the horrible things that could have happened to Zoe while he wasn't there to help. Not that he could be a lot of help in the physical sense, but maybe he could have helped in a different way.

Heart in his chest, Jason jogged as quickly as he could back to Konak Park, hoping that the action hadn't moved farther away. The swirling police lights and caution tape told him he was in the right spot. The shiny bronze foot sticking out of the water next to the pier told him what had happened to Talos.

But where was Zoe?

He pulled out his phone and grabbed footage of the scene, all the while keeping an eye out for Zoe's head of shiny blond hair. He walked up to the caution tape line and flashed his press badge at the officer, hoping it would get him some information.

"I'm looking for a woman who was here a few minutes ago, fighting that." Jason pointed at the statue sticking out of the sea. "Her name is Zoe. Any chance you can point me to her?"

"I don't know anyone named Zoe," the man said in slightly accented English.

Fine. He'd just have to find her himself.

"But you may want to head in that direction," the officer continued. "There was an ambulance over there checking out some of the people who were severely injured during the incident. I may have seen a blond woman over there."

Zoe was severely injured? Jason took off running in the direction the man had pointed.

"Get off me! I told you I was fine." Zoe's irritated voice was a welcome sound.

Jason came skidding to a stop as Zoe emerged from the back of the ambulance. She had a handful of bandages and gauze wraps on her cheeks and arms, but other than that appeared intact.

Jason pulled her into his arms and squeezed until she let out a groan. "Maybe not so tight, though," she said. He immediately loosened his grip and took a step back. She didn't let him retreat, though, and tugged him against her. "You're alive."

"Me?" he asked incredulously. "Of course I'm alive. You didn't even give me the choice to stay and help. You forced me to leave, didn't you?" Zoe at least had the decency to look ashamed, so he knew he was right. "We will be discussing that at some point, but put a pin in that for a moment and tell me what happened here. Are you hurt?"

He pulled Zoe over to a park bench as he listened to her recount the battle. He had to admit, he was somewhat shocked by everything she was describing. The truth was all around him, though. The wreckage of the tanks, the hundred-year-old clock tower that was smashed to smithereens, the giant statue that was now likely a permanent part of the Aegean Sea, and Zoe herself.

When she was finally done with her story, Jason pulled out her phone and handed it to her. "You need to call Kalli and Selene and check in. They need to know what happened."

She recounted her story once more for her queen and Kalli's crew. Kalli listened mostly in silence, but when Zoe came to the end, Kalli finally spoke. "Are you okay?"

"I will be," Zoe answered after a heartbeat. "I can't afford to stop right now, so adrenaline has been my friend."

Jason knew what she was talking about, but adrenaline got you only so far. Eventually Zoe was going to crash and crash hard. Again.

"Selene says the plane is waiting for you in the İzmir airport. Get there. Do not pass go. Do not collect two hundred dollars. And whatever you do, do not fight another monster. Get your ass back to Themyscira pronto," Kalli barked at Zoe, who winced.

"Understood, my queen."

"How are we supposed to get to the airport?" Jason asked.

"I'm sure we can find a taxi," Zoe said as she stood gingerly.

They made slow progress through the damage and rubble left behind after the fight. A man in military garb approached them before they'd made it out of the park. He had a fresh-looking cut across his cheek, and his green camouflage uniform was covered in dust and debris. The Turkish soldier snapped to attention next to them, so Jason and Zoe stopped walking.

Jason glanced around. There weren't a lot of military uniforms among the chaos of the recovery efforts. He was probably one of the few survivors of Talos's attack.

"Ma'am," the young officer said. "I wanted to thank you personally for what you did. As bad as things are, they would have been much worse if you hadn't been there."

Zoe nodded at him in acknowledgment. "I'm glad I was able to help. I'm only sorry I wasn't able to stop him sooner."

The man—who appeared to be in his late twenties—looked stunned. "Our forces were having no success against that robot. Creature. Whatever it was. You were the only one with any success. I'm glad you were here to help. I will be telling my superiors about everything you did and how we would have failed if not for you."

Zoe blushed. "You don't have to do that. I'm not in this for the credit."

The man bobbed his head once. "Nevertheless, you'll get it. From everything I can tell, your people need the good press. Ms. Harper, Mr. Bloom." The man nodded to each of them before spinning around and heading back to the wreckage of the tanks.

Zoe looked at Jason, a deep vee forming between her brows. "We didn't give him our names."

"I guess he's been following along with the news," Jason said.

Zoe sighed. "One more thing I'll have to report to Kalli, I guess. Come on. Let's get out of here."

They finally managed to get back to the main road and hailed a cab to take them to the airport. They slouched together in exhaustion in the back seat for the short ride. Jason wanted to bring up the magic conversation, but it didn't feel like the right time. Instead, he let Zoe have a bit of peace and quiet as she zoned out while staring through the windows at the passing buildings.

When they arrived at the airport, they made their way to the area where they kept the private planes. Sure enough, Selene's Gulfstream was waiting for them, door open and steps down. Jason dragged himself—and the fleece—inside the plane.

Marcus, the same attendant from their previous flight, greeted them. He took the fleece from Jason's outstretched arms and safely stowed it in a wall compartment. Relieved of his burden, Jason flung himself into one of the extremely comfortable cabin chairs. Zoe sat down across from him, almost hesitantly. He wanted to make her feel better, but he was still too irritated at her for her magical overreach, so instead he kept silent.

They were quiet during the entire takeoff procedure. Only once they had reached cruising altitude did Zoe finally speak. "You're mad at me."

"Damn right I am," Jason responded. He crossed his arms over his chest and waited for her to continue.

She slumped in her seat. "I probably shouldn't have compelled you to leave."

His eyebrows winged up. "Probably? That should have been *definitely*. Just because you have the power to do something doesn't mean you should."

"I was trying to keep you safe," she said. "I wouldn't have been able to stand it if you'd been injured and I could have done something about it." She shifted in her chair as much as the seat belt allowed.

She looked like a kicked puppy, all sad eyes and uncertainty. As much as Jason didn't want to rake her over the coals, it was important that she understood boundaries. "Believe it or not, I understand that. I have no desire to see you hurt either. However, whatever we have between us, however new it may be, it won't survive if we don't trust each other. You can't take away my autonomy whenever you damn well feel like it. Free will is what makes us human. Free will may even be the very thing that keeps us alive."

She nodded. "You're right. I know that more than you can imagine. This isn't the first time I've made this mistake." She paused, but when all he did was stare at her, she finally continued, "Fifty years ago, I was involved with a man named Max. He was a New York City police officer, and he found himself on a pretty big case involving the Mob. We'd been together long enough that I had told him about myself, so he knew what I was and at least some of what I was capable of doing.

"One night he was preparing to go on a warehouse raid. There was some sort of big shipment coming in, but the cops couldn't figure out what it was supposed to be. Drugs, guns, girls, it could have been anything. My radar had been pinging off the scales, so I convinced him to let me come along. I figured my Amazon abilities could be useful."

Jason had a feeling he wasn't going to like where this was going. "What happened?"

She crossed her legs, her foot bouncing. "We showed up to the supposed meeting site, but no one was there. Not that we could see anyway. We breached the warehouse and started clearing it one room at a time. Finally, we got to the last remaining room. My instincts were going haywire that we were about to stumble on them and that they would kill Max. We could hear some sort of noise from the room beyond but had no idea what it was. I took matters into my own hands and compelled Max to leave the warehouse. I figured I could probably take out the Mob goons on my own and then let him claim the credit for the collar." Zoe trailed off like she couldn't bear to finish the story.

"What happened to Max?" Jason asked gently.

She sniffed like she was holding back tears. "He died. He was shot point-blank when he walked out of the warehouse and straight into the gathering Mafia thugs. The noise I'd heard was nothing more than two guys playing cards and smoking cigars while they waited for everyone else to show up."

He unbuckled his seat belt and moved to sit next to her. He gripped her hand tightly, and she squeezed right back. "What did you do?"

"I tried to save Max, but I was too late. I wanted revenge, and I could have taken out a bunch of those goons, but even Amazons have limits. There's no way I could have taken out all twenty of them by myself. Instead, I got out of there. Max's body was dumped into the East River and only recovered after it washed up on shore."

Jason put his arm around Zoe's shoulders and squeezed. "If using your magic contributed to Max getting killed, it seems like it could be dangerous. Why did you keep using it?"

She sat upright, pulling away from his embrace and staring him in the eye. "That's the thing. I did stop using it. Before Interpol showed up outside of Themyscira, I hadn't used my magic in fifty years. Did you think I intentionally set the bushes on fire?" She gave him a baffled look.

Thinking back on the footage Noah had captured, it seemed obvious by the way Zoe had been shaking her hands and stomping out the bushes that she hadn't been setting things on fire on purpose. "No, I guess not. Then what happened?" he asked.

She slouched back against the soft gray leather of the airplane seat. "I'm not entirely sure. I think it was probably a combination of being back in Themyscira again and the stress of the situation. I was basically acting as a double agent who wanted nothing more than for everyone to become friends. It was a bit exhausting, to be honest. My guard started to slip."

He couldn't imagine what it must be like to be in her shoes and have lived her life. She had so much power at her fingertips that she could conjure with a mere thought, and for fifty years she'd held it in check, never letting it slip out. Her self-control was amazing.

"That explains why you started using magic again and the fire wielding. It doesn't explain why you chose to use compulsion again, knowing what happened to Max."

"I guess everything seemed like it was going so well. Nothing had blown up in my face, so I figured I had it under control. I am sorry, though. It was wrong of me." Her gaze dropped.

"Well, this time there was no harm and no foul. I'm still among the living, and Talos will wallow forever at the bottom of the Aegean." He tucked her back under his arm and gave her a sideways hug. "You have to promise me that you'll never use compulsion on me again."

She nodded vigorously. "I swear."

"I believe you," he said as he leaned in and kissed her lips gently. It didn't stay gentle for long, though. Zoe shoved the armrest up and leaned into him, kissing him soundly, her tongue sneaking out to dance with his. He groaned as his cock started to go stiff beneath his jeans. "Is it true that this plane has a bed?" he gasped out between kisses.

"Follow me," Zoe said as she rose to her feet and tugged him toward the back of the plane.

Jason knew they didn't have long, but he intended to make the most of what time they did have. As soon as the door to the bedroom clicked shut, he tumbled them onto the surprisingly soft mattress. He captured her mouth with his, reconnecting in a way beyond words. It felt like it had been weeks since they'd been together rather than just over a day.

A firm shove on his shoulder had him rolling onto his back. "You're mine," Zoe said as she sat up next to him, staring warmly down into his eyes. "Now ditch the clothes." She waggled her eyebrows, making him chuckle and do as she asked.

As soon as they were both naked, Zoe pounced. She crawled on top of him, her warmth and curves an exquisite torture as she rubbed herself all over him. Her mouth latched on to his neck and sucked hard enough that he suspected he was going to have a hickey, but it felt so good. She moved down his torso, kissing her way along the light trail of hair that led to his crotch.

Before he could even take a deep breath, she fastened onto his cock, her tongue laving over the tip several times before she fully engulfed him in the wet heat of her mouth. She bobbed up and down several times, adding a hand at his base, where her mouth couldn't quite reach.

Jason let out a guttural moan of pleasure. "You're killing me," he whispered.

She released him with an audible pop. "We can't have that," she said with a wink. She moved up his body until she was hovering over his hips. She grabbed his hard length and lined him up at her entrance before sinking down with a groan of pleasure.

For a few moments she stayed frozen in place, and Jason was able to enjoy the sensation of her body gripping his like a glove. Then she started to move, rising and falling on him like she was riding a prized stallion.

The bliss spread through him and made it difficult for him to think about anything other than the amazing woman above him and how unbelievable it was that he was allowed to be with her this way.

He jolted himself into motion, reaching for her breasts, which were bobbing temptingly in front of him. He cupped them, shoving them together and running his thumbs over her nipples, drawing them into tight peaks.

Zoe's head fell back, and he could tell that she was getting close, just like he was. He dropped one hand between her thighs and pressed on the tight bundle of nerves of her clit. She shattered, coming with a filthy groan, her movements slowing and stuttering.

Jason grabbed her hips and pumped a few more times before he followed her into the abyss.

Chapter Nineteen

Z OE KNEW THEY COULDN'T stay curled up in bed forever, since the flight from İzmir to Samsun wasn't long. She didn't want to move, though, so she snuggled up to the man she was coming to care for. She wasn't quite ready to use the L-word, but she couldn't imagine a man more perfect for her. He had put up with all her neuroses and had even forgiven her for using compulsion on him. She had really stepped in it by doing that, but thankfully he'd accepted her apology.

The world still existed outside the shell of the private jet, but she wasn't ready to confront it. She wanted to stay in their bubble for at least a little while longer.

For the first time in a long time—maybe even forever—Zoe's mind wandered to the future. She'd focused her entire life on what she needed to do that day or in the next few days. She'd never stopped to think about what her life could look like if she did something completely different.

The entire time she'd been exiled from Themyscira, Zoe's main focus had been on tracking Eris and trying to prevent her from doing bad things. She'd never been able to bring herself to kill her—that was a step too far that she hadn't been willing to take against someone who was still her sister—but she'd sabotaged Eris's operations and saved innocent people dozens, if not hundreds, of times over the centuries. Zoe had been doing it so long that it had felt like her eternal burden. That her whole immortal life was going to revolve around finding and stopping Eris.

But Eris was gone now. Kalli had killed her three weeks prior during the raid on Themyscira, after Eris shot Sam. Zoe no longer had that self-imposed burden on her shoulders.

What was left?

She was no longer an Interpol agent. She no longer had to chase down Eris. Once this current standoff situation was dealt with—assuming some trigger-happy foreign military didn't blow Themyscira off the map—what would she do?

Zoe glanced up at Jason's face, which was relaxed as he napped. Was it possible that she could have some sort of normal life—at least some twisted definition of normal that involved her being immortal while being with Jason, who wasn't?

Kalli and Selene had managed to make it work with their boyfriends. Kalli and Sam were even engaged and would hopefully start planning their wedding as soon as everything died down a bit. There was a difference between them and Zoe and Jason, though. Sam had been granted immortality by their mother. Harmonia had hand-delivered a bottle of nectar to him after he'd jumped in front of a bullet to save Kalli's life. That wasn't exactly a repeatable event. Colin had also managed to make himself immortal, though through almost no fault of his own. Selene had been stabbed and drowning in the Fountain of Youth, and Colin had unknowingly waded in to save her, thereby changing his own fate.

Zoe's mind flashed back to the basement of the building in Rome that housed the Fountain of Youth. Knowing the dangers that the fountain had presented to the generations of men who had controlled it in the past, the Amazons had agreed among themselves that they couldn't allow anyone access to it again. Through Zoe's Interpol connections and Selene's security business, they'd managed to permanently seal off the room that housed the fountain. They also had guards stationed on the door around the clock as an added precaution.

The fountain wasn't an option anymore.

And who knew if Jason even wanted to be immortal? It wasn't exactly all it was cracked up to be. Zoe had lived through hundreds of lifetimes. She'd seen ancient wonders being built and modern marvels being erected all over the globe. Honestly, she was just . . . tired.

"What are you thinking about so hard?" Jason asked softly.

She smiled into his shoulder, where her head was resting. "Trying to figure out what comes next." She traced her finger on his bare chest, making invisible doodles.

"What do you mean?" His hand started caressing her upper arm from shoulder to elbow and back.

"Let's say we get through this current crisis and everything works out in some mutually agreeable way. Then what?" Zoe turned her head to look him in the eyes. "What does the future look like for Jason Bloom?"

He smiled and kissed her lightly before leaning back against the pillow to apparently give her question some real thought. "My focus for the last several years has been to make my way up in the news industry. *The Truth Report* isn't bad, don't get me wrong, but I've always wanted to be a nationally known hard-hitting journalist like Anderson Cooper or Dan Rather—minus the scandals, of course. Every move I've made, even traveling to Themyscira, was with that singular goal in mind."

She could absolutely see that for him. Jason was hard working, dedicated, and intent on getting the truth out to the world. "I think you would do an amazing job." She gave him a quick peck on the lips. "And now we have to hustle back into our clothes, because we're about to land."

The SUV they'd driven to the airport was still waiting for them when they deplaned. They made the short drive back to Themyscira and pulled up as the sun was setting. Zoe was astounded how much the crowd of people and tents outside the city had grown. Their vehicle was immediately swarmed by the press, the authorities, and representatives from at least five foreign nations. Zoe saw flags from the United States, Türkiye, France, Germany, and the United Kingdom. That was more than there had been the last time she'd talked to Kalli.

A handful of cameras swiveled to film their approach to the city. Dozens of men in uniform stood at the sides of the dirt road that led from the main road down into the valley where Themyscira was situated. Thankfully they didn't block their SUV from entering, but the situation was unsettling.

Zoe slowly descended the hill and parked the large vehicle in the small parking lot near the Royal Hall. As soon as she cut the engine, they were surrounded a second time, this time by her sisters and their boyfriends. She and Jason climbed out of the car as the small crowd started peppering them with questions.

"Are you all right?" Kalli asked.

"Did Talos really destroy half of İzmir?" Colin asked next.

"How did you get the nail out of his foot?" Sam chimed in.

"You didn't damage my plane, did you? Or have sex in it?" Selene asked as she stared at the hickey on Jason's neck.

"Which answer would disturb you more?" Zoe asked sweetly, making Selene laugh. "All questions will be answered inside."

Jason shouldered the rolled-up fleece—which was still rocking its amazingly clever black trash bag disguise—and the small party moved inside the building and out of sight of any telephoto lenses. As soon as the door closed behind them, all eyes turned to Jason, who stared back blankly.

"Jason, I think they're waiting to see the fleece," Zoe stage-whispered to him.

He jerked, then blushed. "Oh, right." He walked over to the end of the long center table and ripped the plastic off his precious cargo.

With a flourish worthy of a magician, he unrolled the fleece to the hungry gazes of his rapt audience.

Sam and Colin immediately gravitated to the fleece, running their hands gently over the coarse, almost wiry texture. Colin pulled out a jeweler's loupe and started examining the golden strands up close. The shimmer was duller under the dim interior lighting than it had been in direct sunlight, but it was still obvious that it wasn't an ordinary sheep's skin.

"So now that we have the fleece, what exactly do we do with it? We don't want to wave it in front of our unwanted visitors like a red cape in front of a bull before we know what it's capable of," Kalli said to the room at large.

All eyes turned to Sam and Colin. They exchanged a look. "I have no idea," Sam finally said.

Colin nodded in agreement. "The fleece is a fascinating artifact, and definitely more than simple wool, but the myths don't explain *how* the fleece provided protection to the city of Colchis, only that it did."

"So do we just hang it from the rafters and hope for the best?" Selene asked. Zoe wasn't sure whether she was joking.

"If the fleece is a magical artifact, Zoe should be able to tell that, right?" Jason asked. "She sensed Medea's illusion on the top of that mountain, so it seems logical that she would be able to sense something as powerful as the golden fleece."

Zoe shifted uncomfortably as everyone turned in her direction.

It was Kalli who finally asked, "Do you feel or sense anything from the fleece?"

Zoe wanted to say yes, but the real answer was no. She didn't feel magic on the real fleece any more than she had on the replica. But Selene's suggestion of hanging a sheepskin from the roof didn't seem like nearly enough for the fleece to offer the protection it was rumored to provide. "Honestly? No," Zoe responded.

"Well, crap. Now what?" Selene asked.

A heavy silence descended while they tried to come up with ideas.

Sam cleared his throat. "Should we hang it anyway? I mean, best-case scenario it works as is. Worst case, we're no different than we are now."

"And how ridiculous would we look if we hung a shiny sheepskin in the center of town and it turns out that it doesn't do anything?" Selene asked loudly. "Maybe I should go back to plan C or F or Z or whatever we're on these days. My people can acquire whatever weapons we need. I can have them here in three days." She crossed her arms and stared down Kalli as if waiting for her to agree.

Zoe's skin wanted to crawl at the very idea of the Amazons being in an arms race with the rest of the planet. There was no way they would win that sort of competition. There simply weren't enough Amazons to go around, no matter what weapons they had at their disposal. Plus, once tensions like that started, it would be a long time before they cooled off again. If they ever did.

"So was our whole epic adventure a waste of time?" Jason asked, his agitation getting the better of him. "We stared down not one but three creatures that breathe fire. We almost died from crashing into a stupid island. We could have drowned in a whirlpool or gotten eaten by snake-head lady. And that's not to mention the giant bronze

dude. I refuse to believe that we went through all that for nothing."
His voice had gotten steadily louder the longer he talked.

"No," said a timid voice, entering the heated debate. Zoe turned
to look at the newcomer, only mildly surprised that Ariadne had
joined them. She was the one who had come up with the idea of
going after the fleece in the first place. "Nothing was a waste. I agree
with Sam. We should proceed as we intended to. Hang the fleece
proudly in the center of town."

Kalli nodded. "It makes sense to me. As Sam said, there's no real
downside." Kalli turned to address Zoe directly. "Take some time
to recover from your confrontation with Talos, then see what you
and your magic can do. Hopefully we don't need to conjure some
fire-breathing bulls or track down that damn dragon, but if that's
what it takes, we'll do it. We're Amazons. We protect what's ours."

Pride swelled in Zoe as she watched her queen. Kalli, like Zoe and
Selene, had been away from Themyscira for thousands of years. She
had only recently reclaimed her throne and her rightful place as their
leader, and she was born for the role. Zoe was honored to serve under
Kalli's rule.

"Yes, my queen," Zoe said as she bowed.

She left the fleece on the table and turned to leave the Royal Hall,
Jason hot on her heels. "Where are we going next?" he asked.

"I don't know about you, but I'm starving and exhausted. So
food, then nap. I'd ask your place or mine, but I think the answer
is relatively obvious." Zoe circled the outside of the Royal Hall
and stopped in front of a storeroom. She grabbed meal rations and

bottled water for both of them, then headed across the town square toward her house.

The houses in Themyscira had been built thousands of years prior and were constructed of stone, then chinked with mud and clay. They were also tiny by modern standards, though the tiny-house movement might give them a run for their money.

She pushed open the wooden door and stepped back for Jason to precede her into the dwelling. He stopped dead in the middle of the one-room house and looked around. There wasn't much to see. She owned a tiny table and one chair, which she'd shoved as far into the back corner as possible. The focal point of the room was the queen-size bed she'd somehow managed to maneuver through the tiny door and which took up most of the floor space. When she'd first arrived back in Themyscira after thousands of years away, her first upgrade had been a newer, softer bed. Well, her first upgrade had been requesting porta-potties, but her second upgrade had been the bed.

Since there wasn't a lot of room to pull out the chair—and she had only one anyway—Zoe sat on the edge of the bed and patted the spot next to her, indicating that Jason should join her. She handed him his packages of beef jerky, nuts, and dried fruit before tearing into her own.

"Is this your normal dinner?" Jason asked as he awkwardly tore into a piece of dried meat.

"Of course not. We eat hot, cooked food just like the rest of the world. I just didn't feel like taking the time tonight. We may have upgraded some things"—she patted the mattress fondly—"but you're not yet going to find a full kitchen with indoor plumbing and electricity here in Themyscira. We have a few propane camp stoves and a generator we've brought in for the time being. We'll get there."

He smiled before popping a cashew in his mouth. "I have no doubt."

Zoe finished her unsatisfying meal and set the wrappers on the table to dispose of later. As she was getting ready to crawl under the covers and pass out, her phone dinged with a news alert from *The Truth Report*. Already nervous she wasn't going to like what she was about to see, Zoe clicked on the link, and a reporter's face filled her screen.

"I'm Trent Wimbly coming to you live from Themyscira, Türkiye." Jason perked up and shifted around on the bed to watch the news report over her shoulder. "*The Truth Report* has acquired shocking footage from earlier today. As you may already be aware, a giant bronze man was seen wreaking havoc in downtown İzmir, Türkiye. More than twenty people were killed, including military members, police officers, and civilians. Authorities are still trying to figure out where the monster came from, but *The Truth Report*'s exclusive footage might shed some light onto the situation."

The reporter disappeared as cell phone footage started to play. Jason's face was the first thing Zoe saw. "I'm Jason Bloom with *The Truth Report*, coming to you live from İzmir, Türkiye, where a mythical being is currently terrorizing the city."

The camera panned around, and Zoe was front and center, huge columns of fire shooting out of her hands. Talos was in the background of the shot, and beyond him, you could barely make out the Turkish tanks and the shining water of the Aegean. From the angle the footage had been taken, it wasn't clear whether she was aiming for the monster or the tanks. The video changed to a different angle, and Zoe and Jason both jumped when the tank closest to the camera exploded in a fireball, sending shrapnel in all directions and damaging the tank next to it.

The footage cut off, and the reporter was suddenly back on screen, the town of Themyscira barely visible over his shoulder. "The footage you just saw demonstrated the extreme power these so-called Amazons have at their fingertips. Are they self-appointed protectors as they claim to be or a dangerous menace that needs to be stopped before they hurt anyone else? I'm Trent Wimbly from *The Truth Report*, and we bring you nothing but the truth." The clip ended abruptly.

Zoe had never felt more betrayed in her life than she did right at this moment. Long seconds went by in total silence before she could finally bring herself to break it. "How could you?" she choked out. "After our conversation earlier about being able to trust the person that you were with, you went and did something like this."

"Zoe, it's not what you think," Jason said, his eyes wide with panic.

She brutally cut him off. "You also told me on the plane that you were willing to do almost anything to get ahead in the news business, so I guess I shouldn't be shocked that you did exactly that." This was the third time that he'd put her front and center on the international news stage, but this time was so much worse. "At least the first time I just looked like a fumbling buffoon who couldn't help setting a few accidental fires. *This* footage was deliberately edited to make it look like I blew up those tanks." She picked up her phone and hurled it across the room. It hit the stone wall and shattered into hundreds of pieces.

"Zoe, I can explain," Jason said as he grabbed her hand.

She tugged away from him. "I'm sure you can. I hope you enjoy your Pulitzer and that it keeps you warm at night."

"Wait, no. That's not what happened here," Jason said as he turned to face her more fully. "Just let me explain."

Zoe stood and calmly walked to the door. "No, I think I've done enough of that, don't you? Get out. Now. Before this mythical being starts terrorizing something else."

Jason ran his fingers roughly through his hair and let out an exasperated huff, but he did as directed. "I never intended for something like that to be broadcast. I'm going to figure out exactly what happened, and when I do, I hope you'll listen to me."

Zoe shut the door in his face. Her instincts had told her she shouldn't have trusted him. She should have followed her gut. Instead, she'd let Kalli and the idea of good press convince her to give Jason a chance. Look where that had gotten them.

Zoe fell face-first onto her bed, yanked the covers over her head, and screamed into her pillow.

She tossed and turned most of the night, unable to get Jason's treachery out of her head. She must have passed out eventually, because she woke with the sun streaming through her window. She could have used a few more hours of sleep, but oh well. It had been a trying few days. Her magic was almost completely depleted after the fight with Talos, and food and rest were the only way to get her magical stores back to full capacity. Not to mention the absolute betrayal from Jason the night before and the toll that had taken.

Thankfully she felt at least slightly stronger than she had the night before, and she wanted to have a go at the fleece. Maybe she hadn't felt anything from the fleece because her magical stores had been too low for the fleece's magic to register.

Hopefully that was all it was.

Zoe slipped out of bed. She grabbed a clean outfit from the small trunk she had along the far wall, pulled it on, and slipped out into the dawn.

Themyscira was always the most peaceful first thing in the morning, before everyone in the town was up and about. The Amazons never truly slept—there was always a team on watch, regardless of war or peace—but the lookouts and soldiers were hidden from sight, and she could pretend she was the only one in the city, at least for a few moments.

She decided to take a detour and headed to the beach, which just so happened to be in the exact opposite direction of the Royal Hall and the fleece. No matter, she'd get there soon enough. She crossed to the water's edge and pulled off her shoes so she could walk through the gently lapping waves.

"Harmonia? Mom?" Zoe hadn't known exactly why she'd come to the beach, but communing with the gods felt right. "I know you can't talk to me directly—I'm not Kalli—but I figured I would give you a heads-up about what's going on in case you haven't been paying attention. Things down here are . . . not great. We're all fine, for now, but if we don't figure something out soon, this could very easily be the end of the Amazons. We're up against a foe that we never could have foreseen, and we may not come out victorious. We'll do what we can, but unless I can figure out how to make the golden fleece provide its protections to Themyscira, our luck might run out."

Zoe leaned up against a boulder and closed her eyes, breathing in the cool morning air. It wasn't the easiest when your mother was an immortal wood nymph and your father was the god of war. You couldn't exactly pick up the phone and hit speed dial to get ahold of them. She could use any guidance they could offer, but since Kalli was the only one with the power to directly interact with the gods, Zoe wasn't likely to get what she was seeking.

With a final sigh, she opened her eyes. Something green caught her eye, and she turned her head to find an ash leaf on her shoulder—the exact same type of tree her mother called home.

Reverently, Zoe plucked the leaf from her shirt and tucked it carefully between her palms. "Thanks, Mom." She knew now that Harmonia was watching. Zoe had to do everything in her power to save her sisters and her home and trust that her mother would do anything within her power to assist.

Filled with determination, Zoe headed back up the main road through town, aiming for the Royal Hall. She stopped dead as soon as she reached the town square. There, smack in the middle of the field they used to graze goats, was a giant post standing straight up, reaching for the stars. The post appeared to be the trunk of a tree with all its branches trimmed off, then shoved unceremoniously into the ground. At the top of the tree trunk, barely moving in the breeze, was the golden fleece.

All right, let's do this.

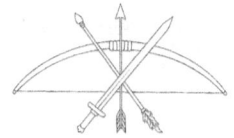

Chapter Twenty

J ASON WOKE UP ON a cramped cot that had been shoved into the corner of the Royal Hall. After Zoe kicked him out the night before, he'd had no idea where to go. He'd briefly thought about climbing up the hill to crash with Noah, but he'd been too worried that he would run into that rat bastard Trent. He wanted nothing more than to throttle the man. Instead, he'd returned to the hall and begged for a place to sleep from Kalli, who had conjured an extra cot out of some random storage room somewhere.

When Jason had reached out to his boss at the studio and to Noah the day before, he'd given them the full account of everything that had happened, including Zoe's role in fighting and defeating the monsters. Yes, he had included the footage of Zoe fighting Talos—even the bit where she'd been thrown into a wall—but he hadn't sent any footage of the tanks blowing up. He hadn't even been there when it happened, so they must have gotten that from someone else. Someone at *The Truth Report* had deliberately edited the footage to look like Zoe blew up those tanks. Jason needed to figure out exactly what had happened, and he needed to get Zoe to listen to him.

Rolling out of bed—or cot, really—he tugged on his same filthy outfit from the day before and decided to make it a priority to get more clothes as soon as possible. *Did Amazon deliver to the Amazons?* The thought made him chuckle. He could probably borrow something from Colin for the time being. They appeared to be about the same size.

After finding Colin and dealing with the clothing situation, Jason felt at least 75 percent better. He could use a hot shower to go with the clean clothes, but the lack of indoor plumbing was going to make that difficult. He could figure out how to take a bath later. Right now he needed to find Zoe.

He tried her house first, but she wasn't there. Jason walked slowly through the town, having much more appreciation for what he was looking at now that he'd spent so much time with Zoe. The houses were small but functional and had stood the test of time. The town was laid out very simply, with the road going through the center and buildings off to either side. The Amazon lifestyle was fairly rustic, and their architecture and buildings reflected that. As far as he could tell, only a handful of buildings weren't homes, and those were things like a jail, an armory, a horse stable, and the storage building where they'd gotten food the night before. And, of course, the Royal Hall, where they gathered for large events or petitioned the queen.

He circled back to the town square. Sometime overnight the Amazons had erected a giant pole in the middle of the square and hung the fleece from it like they were staking their claim. And there, at the base of the tree trunk turned flagpole, sat Zoe.

"Hey, you," he said as he came up behind her. "What are you doing?" He sank to the ground next to her, joining her staring contest with the golden fleece.

She let out an angry huff. "Not that it's any of your business, but I'm trying to make it work." She leaned back against her hands, feeling the coarse grass beneath her palms. "I had this hope that if I got enough rest and ate enough food, suddenly my magic would connect with the fleece somehow. That I would know what to do. Guess what? It didn't work."

Jason set his hand next to hers on the short, stubby grass and intertwined his fingers with hers. She immediately retreated a few inches. He let her go. "Maybe it's not a matter of magical force. Maybe there's something else we're missing."

She glanced at him out of the corner of her eye, then immediately looked away. "I hope the answer isn't animating fire-breathing bull statues. I can compel animals to do things, but I do not have the power to bring statues to life."

"How long have you been out here trying?" he asked.

She wiped a bead of sweat off her forehead and grabbed her phone to check the time. "Four hours maybe?"

He shook his head. She was going to overtax herself. She'd been using a lot of magic in the last several days, and that was after a self-admitted magical detox that had lasted for fifty years. Zoe need-ed to cut herself some slack. "You need a break. Let's go grab an early lunch and see what the big brains have come up with."

"I don't need you to tell me when to eat. I've been feeding myself for thousands of years. Pretty sure I can keep doing it without you." She glared at him.

Jason lifted his hands to indicate he was backing off. "I have no doubt of that. But doesn't something warm in your belly sound good right about now?"

Zoe's stomach rumbled, giving away any lie that was about to fall from her lips. "Fine," she said as she stood and brushed the dirt off the seat of her jeans.

"This isn't all on you, you know. You have a whole civilization at your back, trying to figure this out. We'll get there." He tried to console her, but she narrowed her eyes at him.

She glanced up the hill at the ever-expanding row of tents full of people who were probably spying on everything they were doing. "I just hope we figure it out in time."

They went inside the Royal Hall, where a war room of sorts had been set up at one end of the central table. Colin and Sam were both heads down, poring over books. Colin also had a shiny new laptop perched nearby, and he was regularly flipping back and forth between the book in front of him and whatever he was reading on the screen.

Selene was across the room at a second table, seemingly teaching a few of the Amazons how to use a propane stove to cook food faster and easier than you could over a firepit. Jason steered them in that direction first, waiting behind one other Amazon before they could get their hands on what appeared to be a delicious-smelling soup with chicken and vegetables. They grabbed drinks and headed over to sit next to Sam and Colin.

"Have you found anything?" Jason asked.

Sam turned to look at him and blinked in confusion, like he had no idea Jason had sat down beside him. "What?" Sam asked, clearly baffled.

Zoe had to hide a smirk. "You two look like you've been hard at work. Have you found anything we can use yet?" she asked, repeating Jason's question.

Sam shook his head as if to clear it, then said, "Oh, right. Maybe."

It was like pulling teeth. "And what might that be?" Jason asked between spoonfuls of the soup.

"Well, I stumbled on a myth online that might help," Colin said, "but the good professor here is trying to substantiate it in a written record somewhere more official." He put air quotes around the word *official*.

Sam bristled. "It's not so much a myth as a prophecy, and I put very low stock in the mythical predictions of an unknown source you stumbled on by googling."

Between Sam and Colin was noticeable tension that Jason wasn't privy to, but at this point it seemed like they should try anything that might help.

Zoe appeared to feel the same way. "Care to share with the rest of the class, handsome?" She winked at Colin and earned a glare from Selene, who had overheard what Zoe said from her position across the room. Zoe sent her a brilliant smile, then turned back to focus on Colin.

"Yeah, let me pull it up." He opened a tab in his browser, then tapped away at his keyboard. *"The Fates await when the stars align, magic unfolds at the frozen shrine. Trials and dangers awake and breathe, waters churn and monsters seethe. Gold comes forth with fire and shine, to await another of the chosen line. A boundary spreads to protect and deter, others' intent to guess and infer. For any that intend to harm or destroy, the boundary will react and deploy."*

"Maybe it makes an actual barrier, the way that Hermes's veil used to?" Zoe asked. "It might prevent people from getting in or out of Themyscira."

"Maybe," Sam said reluctantly. "But I don't understand the bit about intent. Hermes's barrier was mostly a visual and mental thing. It hid Themyscira from sight, and once you left the protection of the veil, you forgot the city existed. That's not the same as intent at all."

They chewed on that for a bit.

Jason contemplated the brief rhyme, trying to figure out what it all meant. "The frozen shrine is probably referring to Medea's illusion. Specifically, the fact that the fleece and its protectors were frozen in time until Zoe came along and unlocked it."

Zoe picked up the thread, abandoning her soup in the process. "The churning waters are probably a reference to Charybdis, and the monsters are almost too many to count at this point."

Colin nodded. "I agree, and the gold coming forth is probably a reference to the fleece. It's the last part that has me puzzled. What would the chosen line be?"

"You don't think it means an actual line, do you?" Jason said, tracing a line on the table with his finger.

"It's more likely to be a hereditary line," Sam said.

"I'm going to guess it's probably Jason and Medea's line," Zoe said. "Most of the prophecy has something to do with what happened to us while we worked to find the fleece and release it from Medea's spell. She's the only one that could have known what would happen. It's the only thing that makes sense."

Colin and Sam were nodding. "That's my belief as well," Sam agreed.

Lead settled into Jason's stomach. "So what you're saying is that we need to find someone in the here and now that is a descendant of Jason and Medea. Anyone else see a problem with that? How in the world would we trace a family tree going back three thousand years?"

"Damn it," Zoe said as she slapped her hand on the table and made everyone jump. Her hand slowly slid off the table and her shoulders slumped as she stared morosely into her now-cold soup. "I was hoping this would give us a new lead. Something else to try. I guess we're back to square one. I'll keep trying whatever I can think of."

Zoe pushed up from the table and left her food behind for someone else to clean up. Jason hesitated. He felt bad making someone else clean up after them, but Zoe wasn't in a good headspace. He needed to chase her down. "Sorry, all. I need to go deal with that," he said and gestured to Zoe.

Sam and Colin both gave him nods like they knew exactly what he was talking about. "Amazons, am I right?" Colin said quietly enough that Selene shouldn't have been able to overhear.

"You'll pay for that one!" Selene yelled from across the room, clearly having heard him anyway.

"Looking forward to it," Colin replied cheerily as he went back to his research.

Jason chuckled as he followed in Zoe's footsteps. Colin was more than welcome to his spicy redhead. Jason would take his flirty blonde any day of the week. Speaking of which, his fair-haired temptress was back at it, camped out at the base of the makeshift flagpole. She was staring at the fleece as if she could imbue it with power using nothing more than her gaze.

He crossed over the tough green grass until he was standing next to her. "Come on, you need a break."

Zoe gave him an irritated look. "Didn't I just take a break? Not to mention, I'm likely the only person in this entire town who can figure out how to activate this damn thing and protect Themyscira from *that*." She pointed up the hill at the tents on the ridge.

Jason shrugged but refused to let her off the hook. "That may be, but you can't do it if you're burned out. You need to regroup and gather your energy . . . or health. Mana. Whatever it is that you burn when you throw fireballs," he said.

Zoe looked at him out of the corner of her eyes then immediately focused on the fleece again.

Fine. If she wasn't going to leave, then he would have to camp out next to her. Whatever she thought of him after the news broadcast the night before, he wasn't going to leave her. She might be needed to save the world, but whether or not she wanted to admit to it, she needed him to keep herself sane.

Her eyes narrowed as she squinted at the fleece, high on its lofty perch. Sweat popped onto her brow as she strived to make something, anything, happen.

Jason couldn't stand to see her struggling like this. Without a thought of the consequences, he came up behind her and gently put his hands on her shoulders. He had no magic of his own, so if the only thing he could do was physically support her while she strained, that was what he would do.

The moment his hands made contact with her bare shoulders, Jason could tell something was different. This was no mere friendly or sexual contact. No, something more was going on. He felt a tug behind his navel as his fingers clamped down on her shoulders like they would never let go again.

With a bang and a surge of intense energy, a wave of power traveled from him, through Zoe, and up the pole into the fleece. A dome of golden light sprouted from the top of the flagpole and encircled the town.

Jason started to smile before he was blown backward across the field. His head cracked into a boulder, and everything immediately went black.

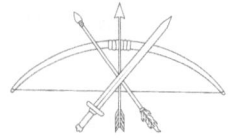

Chapter Twenty-One

WHAT HAD SHE DONE? Zoe stared at Jason in horror as he lay on the ground, his head perched awkwardly on a rock, blood pouring from one of his temples.

She had done that. Her magic had done that.

Jason might have pissed her off and may have gone behind her back to conspire to make her—and the Amazon people—look bad, but she never wanted to hurt him. It was even worse that it had been a total accident. Something her magic had done without her even realizing it was going to happen.

She was an Amazon and a former law enforcement officer. She wasn't immune to hurting people, but if she did, it was for a reason. Not this. Never this. Her inability to control her powers had led to the man she cared about being injured. That was unacceptable.

She was frozen in shock. She didn't know what to do. They didn't have medical facilities in Themyscira, and there was a wall of military and reporters camped outside their boundaries. She didn't have time to deal with them.

Zoe crouched next to Jason, her hands impotently running over his body and face, trying to revive him. What would she do if she'd killed him? If he never woke up? This was all her fault.

"It's okay. I've got this," a no-nonsense voice said next to Zoe's ear.

Selene squeezed Zoe's shoulder once, then bent down to check Jason's pulse. She must have been satisfied with what she felt, because she scooped him up and strode confidently in the direction of the SUVs. Zoe followed at a slight distance, not sure whether she should stay behind or follow along. After all, it was her fault Jason was injured. She should probably be as far away from him as humanly possible.

Selene glanced over her shoulder when Zoe lagged behind. "What are you waiting for? Get up here!" Selene rolled her eyes and gestured to the rear door of one of the SUVs.

Zoe lunged forward and opened it, watching Selene as she carefully laid Jason in the back seat and did her best to get the seat belt around him. Selene left the back door wide open, hurried around the large vehicle, and climbed behind the driver's seat but didn't go anywhere.

Selene lowered the passenger-side window. "Are you coming or what?" she asked. When Zoe continued to hesitate, Selene finally yelled, "Get in the damn car, Zoe!"

Zoe crawled into the back seat next to Jason, still not speaking. She rooted around in the rear of the SUV until she found a towel and pressed it against the blood seeping out of Jason's head wound.

Selene threw the car into reverse and peeled out of the parking spot and up the hill. She didn't bother to stop for the overly curious military folks. Instead, she powered right through them, forcing them to jump out of the way or risk being run over.

"So how did that feel?" Selene finally asked Zoe as they were on the main road.

"How did what feel?" Zoe asked quietly, refusing to make eye contact with Selene in the rearview mirror.

Selene gave Zoe a look that meant she should know exactly what Selene was talking about. "Almost murdering your boyfriend. How did that feel? Was the grudge worth it?"

Zoe shrank in on herself, avoiding Selene's pointed glare. "He's not my boyfriend."

Selene closed her eyes for an alarming amount of time, considering she was driving. "Sure. Let's go with that. You're sleeping together. You've spent every waking moment together for days. He stares at you like you have the sun shining out of your ass, but sure. He's not your boyfriend."

Zoe wanted to deny everything Selene was saying, but she couldn't. She and Jason were sleeping together. They did have a strangely close bond that didn't make any sense, except that it did. But did he really stare at her like that? Debatable. Zoe gazed down at his pale face, desperately wishing he would open his beautiful blue eyes and look at her.

"Obviously we've grown close over the course of our travels, but he betrayed me. He had his news organization publish multiple video clips that made me look not only incompetent but dangerous. How is that okay?" Zoe wanted to rage, even as she cuddled his head on her lap. She hadn't wanted to hurt Jason, but she was still angry at him.

Selene glanced at her as she merged onto the highway. "Obviously it wouldn't be, if that is what actually happened. But, Zoe, are you *sure* that's what happened? Because the guy I've seen doesn't seem like the type of man that would betray the woman he loved that way."

Zoe's head whipped up, and she pinned Selene's gaze in the mirror. "He doesn't love me."

Selene full on hooted as she took the exit off the highway that led to the hospital. "You keep telling yourself that."

It wasn't possible, was it? There was no way that Jason could be in love with her when they'd known each other for such a short time, and for half of it she'd been mean to him. Okay, yes, she'd also flirted with him, but that was just what she did. It was like breathing.

And what did she feel for Jason? She definitely cared for him. It was impossible to go through what they'd been through together over the last few days and not have developed an attachment. He was sweet, supportive, and gorgeous to boot. Not to mention they had great chemistry in bed. But did that translate to love? She wasn't sure she was quite there yet.

She glanced down at him, tracing her fingers gently along the side of his face. Whatever her feelings were, she didn't want to see him injured.

They screeched into the emergency room ambulance bay, and Zoe threw open the SUV door. Someone from inside must have seen them arrive, because a team of people hustled outside with a gurney. Zoe could have hefted Jason out of the back seat and onto the mobile bed by herself, but instead she took a step back and let the professionals do their thing.

Zoe glanced from Jason on the gurney—which the team was rushing into the hospital—to Selene.

"Go. Be with your man. We'll be fine without you, at least for a little while," Selene said.

Zoe nodded and rushed through the automated doors and into the air-conditioned environment inside. Jason had already been wheeled back into the emergency room, so Zoe went to the check-in desk and told them everything she knew about him, which honestly wasn't all that much, considering how close they had become. The woman behind the desk directed her toward the waiting room, and Zoe trudged her way there, her feet feeling like lead the whole way.

The only thing she could do was wait.

Zoe sat and watched the people go by, some mildly injured, some severely injured and being rushed into surgery. She saw loved ones and friends, people who were distraught over whatever was going on, and some folks that seemed to take it all in stride, as if being in the emergency department was another random day for them.

With the man that she cared for somewhere behind those closed doors, it left Zoe with a lot of time to think.

She had caused this. Her powers were the reason that Jason was in the hospital. She had no idea how injured he was or if his injury was minor or fatal. She knew from experience that head wounds were tricky. They always bled like hell, but you couldn't tell what the real damage was until they'd done scans. It certainly wasn't a good sign that he'd still been unconscious when they'd arrived.

What on earth had made her think that using her powers again would be without consequence? She hadn't had much of a choice when they kicked in and she started lighting stuff on fire, but she could have worked much harder to shut it all down again.

Even so, it felt so good. She'd denied herself access to her powers for fifty years. She'd cut off something that was as much a part of her as her arm or her leg. When she'd originally forced herself to stop using magic—after Max died—it had been hard and painful. Every day she'd had to fight against her natural instinct to use the gifts that she'd been given. But as time passed, it had slowly gotten easier. That magical limb had shrunk and atrophied, and it had felt, well, not normal, but at least no longer as painful to ignore.

For fifty years she'd lived her life, closing herself off from real love because it was too painful and instead sustaining herself on more surface-level relationships and flirting. She hadn't felt the need to tap into her magic for anything, even during her more recent adventures following Eris around the globe and cleaning up after her messes. So why, right when she'd met a man who could potentially mean so much to her, did her powers have to suddenly rear their ugly head?

Not that her powers were always bad. Her powers had saved their asses several times during their quest to retrieve the fleece. Not to mention whatever the giant golden glow was that had spread from the fleece the moment Jason had touched her in the town square. As unbelievable as it seemed, she'd managed to get the fleece to work. Themyscira was now protected by magic even she couldn't fully understand, and she was sort of an expert on the subject.

Why it had happened was another discussion altogether. If Colin's rhyming couplets were anything to put her faith in, there was only one explanation for it. Jason—her Jason—was a descendant of Jason and Medea, the last owners of the fleece. All this time they'd been joking about his namesake, and it was truer than either of them had realized.

What did that mean? Did it have to mean anything? Maybe it was sheer coincidence—though with everything that had happened recently, she had reason to doubt coincidence even existed. Maybe it was the Fates, and those three old ladies were staring down at them, ready to cut the strings to one of her or Jason's lives.

And maybe, just maybe, it meant that Jason was supposed to be here. That she was destined to find him, and they were fated to work together. Or perhaps, even more outlandishly, they were fated to be together. She wanted to scoff at the idea, but it settled softly in her stomach, warm and comforting. And surely, if they were inevitable, then something as silly as a misleading news report or a magical overload wouldn't be the thing that tore them apart, would it?

"Ms. Harper?" a voice in front of her asked somewhat impatiently, as if it wasn't the first time he'd called her name.

She glanced up into the dark eyes of a middle-aged man wearing scrubs and a lab coat. His eyes narrowed as he waited for her to respond. "Yes?" she finally blurted out.

The man nodded before glancing down at the piece of paper he was holding in front of him. "Mr. Bloom is going to be fine. He took a hard blow to the head and has a mild concussion, but other than some swelling and a nasty headache, he should be perfectly fine."

Relief whooshed out of her. She hadn't killed him. His injuries sounded relatively minor in the grand scheme of what could have been. "Is he awake? Can I see him?"

The man nodded. "Yes, he's awake. He's been asking for you." He gestured for her to follow him.

It seemed that all hospitals, regardless of the country, were more or less the same. The beige walls, the light-colored tile that squeaked beneath her shoes, the beeping of machines coming out of each room they passed. Finally, the doctor stopped outside a room in the middle of an endless corridor and gestured for her to head inside.

Zoe's stomach suddenly felt like butterflies had taken off in a hurricane. Her mouth went dry, and she licked her lips like it would help, full well knowing it wouldn't. Yes, the doctor had said that Jason had been asking for her, but that didn't necessarily mean he would be happy to see her. Maybe he wanted to curse her out for landing him in the hospital. It wouldn't be like she didn't deserve it.

The doctor cleared his throat, startling her. She glanced into his impatient gaze. He gestured to the room once more, and she stiffened her shoulders. She could do this. She could take whatever Jason was going to throw at her, whether it was physical or metaphorical.

The sound of her footsteps must have alerted Jason to her presence, because he was blinking his eyes open by the time she made it to the foot of his bed.

"Hey, you," he said quietly.

"Hi, Jason," she replied, not meeting his eyes. She glanced around his utilitarian room, noticing that the drapes were drawn against the bright afternoon light. That made sense given his head injury. The light probably hurt his eyes.

Several tense moments went by, broken up only by the low beeping of his heart monitor. "I see we're still not talking."

She wasn't quite sure what to make of the quiet words. "No? Yes? I'm not sure . . ." What did he want from her? Should she get down on her knees and grovel? "Do you want to talk to me?" she finally asked, venturing a glimpse at his pained expression.

His jaw dropped open slightly before he slammed it shut. "Did you even ask me that?" He made a low noise that sounded like a mix between a grunt and a growl. "Don't you think we have a few things to discuss?"

Zoe hung her head in shame. Of course he wanted to discuss it. She shouldn't be shocked. She swallowed hard and then said, "Yes, we do." She took a deep breath and let it out. She braced herself and said "I'm sorry" at the exact same time as he did.

"What do you have to be sorry about?" she asked. "It was my magic that landed you in the hospital. I'm the one that screwed up. None of this is your fault," she said vehemently.

His mouth dropped open for the second time. "Are you kidding me? I'm the one that sent the footage of you to my network. The footage that they strategically doctored to make it look like you were the one to blow up those tanks instead of Talos. If anyone is to blame for starting this whole thing, it's me." He gestured between them as if to encompass everything that had happened in the last twenty-four hours.

She sank down onto the corner of his bed, the fight draining out of her. "It's not your fault."

He shook his head as if to clear it, then groaned in pain. "How could you possibly know that?"

She tilted her head to the side and ran her fingers over the rough texture of the blanket she was sitting on. "Well, I don't *know* know. But I figured it out. Or at least Selene did and then smacked me over the head with it."

A relieved smile ghosted over his lips. "So you really don't blame me for what they broadcast? It wasn't particularly flattering. To you or the Amazons."

She tugged on a loose string she'd found in the blanket. "No, I don't blame you. You've been nothing but supportive and have honestly seemed like you wanted to do everything you could to help us."

Jason's smile spread. "Damn right." He leaned back against his bed, relaxing into the thin mattress. "I can't have the woman I love be ostracized by the entire planet. I need to figure out why the studio did what they did, since it was clearly deliberate. Maybe if I corner Trent, he'll know something . . ." He trailed off, clearly lost in thought.

Zoe's brain short-circuited. "Um, excuse me, did you say that you loved me?" She practically squeaked out the question.

Jason's smile turned smug. "Obviously."

Zoe launched herself off the bed and began pacing the tiny hospital room. "No, not so obvious." She yanked out her ponytail holder and hastily fixed her hair into an even higher tail. "How can you even say that?"

Jason's smile dimmed and his eyes narrowed. "What are you talking about?"

She threw her hands up as she continued to pace. "How can you possibly love me? I'm the one who landed you in the hospital. My power exploded and gave you a concussion, Jason!" She wanted to shout at him to see reason, but she was aware that they were in a hospital with other patients, so her words were more of a whisper hiss.

His tension visibly eased as he relaxed against the mattress once more. "Did you intend to injure me?" he asked.

She shook her head vehemently. "No! Of course not."

"All right," he continued in that maddeningly calm tone. "So what do you think happened then?"

She finally stopped pacing and stared at him from the foot of his bed. "Colin's prophecy. As ridiculous as it may have seemed, it must be true." She stared at him as if he should be able to read her mind. "I had been trying for hours to use my magic to make that damn fleece do something, anything. Nada. Zip. Zilch. You walk up, touch my shoulder, and BAM! Glowy gold lights, some sort of wild dome thing I haven't figured out yet, and you're being blasted to oblivion."

"Is that what happened?" he said as if simply asking what time it was.

"Yes," she continued to angrily whisper. "My power landed you in the emergency room, Jason." It was obvious. Zoe had no idea why he wasn't picking up on it.

"Huh." He rubbed his fingers over his jaw. "I guess that makes me a descendant of Jason and Medea. That's pretty cool and something I'll have to contemplate later. However, if I really am their descendant, that means that it was the prophecy—or more likely Medea's power that fueled the prophecy—that landed me in the emergency room. Not you."

Zoe froze as Jason's words penetrated her panicked thought process. Was he right? She hadn't made the prophecy, so she wasn't the one who had demanded someone of the correct bloodline be part of the ritual. The fact that his presence had been required wasn't her choice. So maybe it wasn't her fault after all? Yes, the explosion of power had been what had injured him. But had she really been the source of that eruption? Or had she merely been its vessel?

Jason smiled softly and held his hand out. Without thinking, Zoe crossed the tile floor to grasp it. "Are you going to leave me hanging out here all alone?" he teased.

It took her a moment to figure out what he was talking about, but once she did, she blurted out her answer. "No. Of course not. I love you too." She leaned over him and gently touched her lips to his.

Jason tried to deepen the kiss, but she pushed him back with a soft chuckle. "Maybe take it easy for a little bit while your noggin is still recovering. Who knows what we're going to have to face next." She traced her hand gently down his cheek and gave him one more peck on the lips.

"Yes, ma'am. Whatever you say."

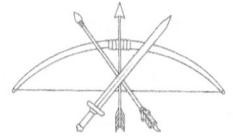

Chapter Twenty-Two

J ASON WOKE UP TO a persistent buzzing. He shook his head, trying to clear it, and immediately regretted his decision. He groaned as the giant knot on his forehead throbbed and instantly made his headache worse.

He blinked several times, bringing the room around him into focus. Right, he was still in the hospital. They'd wanted to keep him overnight for observation, but with any luck they would send him on his way first thing.

The view was the same from the day before—the boring beige walls not giving him anything interesting to look at—with one exception. There, curled up and fast asleep in a very uncomfortable-looking armchair, was Zoe.

His heart softened when he looked at her. The hospital staff had tried to ask her to leave the night before, and she'd firmly and politely told them where they could shove it. The nurse who had asked the question must have seen the news, because she gave Zoe's hands a wary look before backing slowly from the room.

The persistent buzzing started again, and this time Jason was awake enough to process that it was his cell phone, which had the ringtone turned off but was doing its best to vibrate off the bedside table. He grabbed it and glanced at the screen. It was his boss. Roger Westfield had been the CEO of network that hosted *The Truth Report* for ten years. Normally Jason had a decent relationship with the man, but with everything that had happened over the last few days, he had no idea if that was still true. With a reluctant sigh, Jason swiped to answer the call.

"Hello, Roger," Jason said quietly, doing his best to not wake Zoe and simultaneously not make his headache worse.

"What's this I hear about you being in the hospital?" Roger barked loud enough that Jason pulled the phone away from his ear to save what was left of his eardrum.

"It's not a big deal. Just a small bump to the head. I should be out this morning." Maybe if he downplayed the injury Roger would let it go.

"My sources are telling me there was some sort of explosion and you went flying through the air."

Jason could practically see Roger's beard and mustache twitching with agitation. "Would your sources happen to be Trent and Noah?" It made the most sense, considering they were still camped outside Themyscira.

"Does it matter? Answer the damn question."

Roger had always been hard to read. Jason wasn't sure whether he was asking out of genuine concern for his health or because one of his assets was injured and out of play. Honestly, it could go either way. "Tell you what. I'll answer your question if you answer mine."

Roger spluttered. "That's not how this works, Bloom."

Jason adjusted his position slightly on the hospital bed in a futile attempt to get more comfortable. "Isn't it? We're a news organization, Roger. We make our living based around an exchange of facts."

A long put-upon sigh came down the airwaves. "Fine, what do you want to know?"

Jason caught a slight movement out of the corner of his eye. He glanced up and saw that Zoe was awake and staring at him from across the room. He pulled the phone away from his ear and pressed the speakerphone button. "Why did the footage of Zoe Harper in İzmir get cut to make it look like she'd been the one to blow up the tanks instead of the giant bronze guy?"

Zoe sucked in her breath sharply but otherwise didn't move or say anything.

Roger paused before responding. "Look, here's what you need to know about that. Sometimes we have to do things we don't want to do. A decision was made, and we followed through."

Zoe's eyes narrowed, but she didn't say anything. She also had no idea who he was talking to.

"Roger, you're the CEO of the network. It seems like you could have overruled any decision that *someone* made."

"Not this time, Bloom. This decision was hand-delivered to me by men wearing suits and carrying badges and guns, all right? America might be the land of the free, but that freedom lasts only as long as the government doesn't want a different outcome."

Jason's jaw dropped open. "Are you telling me that the US government forced you to alter the footage so that it looked like Zoe was the bad guy?"

"Did you hear me say those words?" Roger cleared his throat loudly, and Jason got the hint.

"No, sir. I did not." Jason glanced at Zoe and saw his own shock reflected on her face. "Thank you for the information. And to answer your question, yes, there was a minor power surge yesterday, and I was caught in the middle of it, but the doctors have assured me that it's not serious and I'll be on my way shortly."

"Glad to hear it." There was a pause on the other end of the line. "Oh, and Bloom? Whatever you're doing over there, keep doing it." With that parting comment, the call ended.

Zoe slowly got up out of her chair and perched on the end of his bed. "So that was your boss, huh?" she asked tentatively.

"Yep. That was Roger." He wished she would come closer to him so he could at least hold her hand. He wiggled his fingers in her direction, and with a slight smile she moved up on the bed until she was sitting near his hips. He grabbed her hand and brought the back of it to his lips for a gentle kiss.

"He seems like a good guy," she ventured as she rubbed her thumb over the back of his hand.

Jason nodded. "It was touch and go based on how he answered that question, but yeah. It seems like he really is one of the good ones, despite evidence to the contrary." He paused, searching deep into her eyes. "What do you think it means?"

Her lips flattened. "What do I think it means that the US government set me up? Nothing good, that's for damn sure. It could mean they're setting themselves up for some sort of action and need the court of public opinion to agree that we're the enemy. It probably also means we need to get our asses back to Themyscira before anything else happens. I'll go talk to the nurse and see about getting you out of here." She stood up and walked to the door but then turned to look at him. "I'm glad you're all right, baby. I don't know what my life would be like if I didn't have my valiant dragon rider by my side." She sent him a soft smile then left.

With Zoe greasing the wheels, the hospital had him discharged in less than fifteen minutes. Hospital procedure said they had to take him out in a wheelchair, but as soon as they were outside, he stood and stretched. Selene was waiting for them behind the wheel of a large black SUV. Zoe opened the rear passenger door and ushered him inside. He was pleasantly surprised when she followed him rather than taking the front. She buckled up, then grabbed his hand and squeezed it.

"I see you two worked things out," Selene said with raised eyebrows.

"Just drive, Selene," Zoe said.

With a quiet chuckle, Selene turned back around and did exactly that.

"So catch us up. What's happened since yesterday?" Zoe asked.

Jason was eager to hear what had been going on. Zoe had mentioned the golden dome thing the night before, but that was all he knew. That wasn't much to go on.

"So after your power went kablooey," Selene started.

"Medea's power," Jason corrected. He wasn't going to let anyone blame Zoe for what had happened. Zoe squeezed his hand again with a smile.

Selene glanced at him in the rearview mirror and gave him a slight nod. "After Medea's power sent out that shock wave, the fleece started radiating a golden aura of some sort. It projected a glowing dome over the entire valley—including Themyscira—but it stops short of all the outposts, tents, and vehicles gracing our doorstep."

"What do you think it does?" Jason asked, uncertain whether he was asking Selene or Zoe. It didn't matter, really, since they both shrugged.

"It's some sort of protection, that much is clear from the myths," Zoe said. "But it obviously isn't a hard barrier. It lets people through it."

Selene smirked. "It lets *some* people through it."

That was intriguing. "The three of us have been through it, you more than once. Who didn't it let through?" Jason asked.

"I may or may not have been taunting one of the Interpol dudes. Things got a little heated, and he tried to come at me, but instead he bounced off the barrier and fell on his ass. Don't worry," Selene said, cutting off Zoe before she could ask. "He's fine, just a bit of a bruised ego. I may have laughed at him." Selene shrugged not quite apologetically.

"Selene," Zoe said exasperatedly. "We're trying to deescalate something that could turn into an international incident and has the possibility of getting people killed. Please try to remember that." She pinched the bridge of her nose.

"He started it," Selene said defensively.

"What are you, five? You're four thousand years old. Act like it," Zoe snapped.

"So we know the barrier is selective about who it lets through," Jason said, trying to redirect the conversation. "What was the prophecy again?"

"The Fates await when the stars align, magic unfolds at the frozen shrine. Trials and dangers awake and breathe, waters churn and monsters seethe. Gold comes forth with fire and shine, to await another of the chosen line. A boundary spreads to protect and deter, others' intent to guess and infer. For any that intend to harm or destroy, the boundary will react and deploy," Selene said. When both Jason and Zoe looked at her in surprise, she shrugged again. "What? I'm in love with a nerd. He's been a bit obsessed about it."

"Well, that seems clear. The barrier can sense people's intentions. Anyone who intends to harm anyone or destroy anything won't be allowed through. That's brilliant. It seems like that will be good enough to protect the city," Jason said.

Zoe waggled her hand back and forth. "That depends. Can the barrier detect the intentions of a bullet? Or worse yet, a missile?"

"Let's hope the gathering military forces don't test that," Selene said as she pulled up to the ever-growing tent city between them and the golden boundary to the valley.

Jason swallowed thickly. The military presence—and the media involvement—had only grown since they'd arrived two days before. Men with machine guns and sidearms seemed omnipresent. Everywhere he looked there was a sea of camouflage in various shades of green, beige, and brown. Including the US Marines standing in front of the car, blocking the only road in and out of the town.

"This can't be good," he muttered quietly.

Tension vibrated off Zoe so palpably that Jason could feel it on the other side of the car. "Selene, whatever you do, do not make this worse than it needs to be," Zoe said quietly as one of the marines came to the driver-side window.

Selene rolled the window down and addressed the uniformed man standing beside the car. He had pale Caucasian skin that looked to be on the verge of sunburn, and a buzzed haircut so short it was practically impossible to tell what color his hair might be. "What can I do for you?" she asked.

"Ma'am, this is an active military zone. I'm afraid we can't allow civilians in or out of this area. I'm going to need to ask you to turn around and head back the way you came."

Selene smiled, but Jason could see the predatory glint in her eyes as she sized up the poor man and took in every detail of his uniform. Her eyes lingered over his name tag and his insignia. "Then I guess it's a good thing I'm not a civilian, isn't it, Sergeant Evans? It just so happens that we live here."

Surprise flickered over the man's face before he schooled his expression. He ducked slightly to look inside the vehicle through the open window, his gaze skating over Jason and Zoe in the back seat.

"Can I get your name, ma'am?" the sergeant said as he stood tall once more.

"Sure. I'm Selene, that's Zoe, and this is Jason. But please stop calling me *ma'am*. It's making me feel every one of the four thousand years of my life." She smiled sweetly again, clearly doing her best to unsettle the poor man.

The marine blinked, then turned and called out to one of the men standing at parade rest in front of their vehicle. "Gunny!"

A large Black man whose muscles filled his uniform until it was practically bursting walked over and stood next to the sergeant. "Sergeant Evans." The new man addressed the sergeant with a head nod.

"These are the folks we were told to be on the lookout for, Gunny," Evans said, practically snapping to attention.

"Thanks, Sergeant Evans," the newcomer said before stepping around him and peeking in the open window of the SUV. Once he looked his fill, he stepped back and placed his hand on his sidearm. "I'm Gunnery Sergeant John Haskins. I'm going to need Mr. Bloom to step out of the vehicle and come with me. My superiors would like to ask him some questions." He gestured to one of the tents with armed guards standing at attention at every entrance.

Jason's stomach dropped. The US military wanted to question him? Possibly detain him? This definitely didn't feel right. He was a US citizen. The military should not be able to arrest him, if that was their intention.

He sent a panicked look in Zoe's direction, but she gave a subtle shake of her head, so he kept his mouth shut. Better to let the two nearly invincible warrior women handle this.

"Oh, that sounds like a smashing idea. We'll get right on that," Selene said with an eye roll.

"Mr. Bloom is wanted for questioning regarding aiding and abetting a terrorist threat against the United States," Gunnery Sergeant Haskins said. "I'm not going to ask again." He pulled his sidearm from its holster and aimed it at Selene.

"You think we're a terrorist threat?" Selene practically screeched.

Zoe cut her off abruptly with a brisk headshake. "Don't risk it, Selene. Not even you can come back from a headshot."

Sergeant Haskins glared through the open window into the back seat and aimed his gun in Zoe's direction. He cleared his throat loudly and obviously.

"All right!" Jason couldn't stay quiet anymore. He had no desire to surrender himself to the US military, especially for something he didn't do, but he wasn't about to sit around and let this asshole shoot Zoe. "I'm getting out now."

"Do it slowly," Haskins said. He backed away from the car slightly but kept his gun trained on the door as Jason slowly opened it.

"Damn it, Jason," Selene muttered under her breath.

Zoe let out a distressed noise behind him as he slid out of the vehicle. "I'll be fine," he said with more confidence than he felt. He gave her a small smile. She didn't return it. "They just want to ask me a few questions."

Even he didn't believe that.

Jason raised his hands to show he was unarmed. The gunnery sergeant didn't lower his weapon. "Sergeant Evans. Please escort Mr. Bloom inside. The major general is waiting for him."

Evans gestured with his M16 rifle for Jason to precede him up the small incline toward the tent. "So this major general," Jason asked loudly enough that Zoe and Selene would still be able to hear him. "Is he the guy who ordered my network to broadcast doctored footage of Zoe to make her look like a villain?"

Evans's eyes narrowed, and he tightened his grip on his service weapon.

"What's the matter, guys? Can't handle that a bunch of women are more powerful than you are?"

Without warning, Sergeant Evans slammed the butt end of his rifle into Jason's stomach, knocking the wind out of him. Jason keeled over on the ground, desperately trying to inhale, but it was like his lungs had stopped working. No oxygen was getting in or out. Black spots danced in front of his eyes, and he started to panic.

The doors to the SUV were flung open. "Oh, hell no!" Zoe yelled as she sprinted in Jason's direction, reaching his side in seconds. She immediately yanked the rifle from Evans's hands and clocked him upside the head with it, knocking him out cold.

"Breathe, baby. Just breathe." Zoe crouched next to him, her voice low and soothing. "In through your nose. Out through your mouth."

Jason tried to do what she asked, sucking in as much air as he could manage until his lungs started working normally again. His vision finally cleared enough to see that while Zoe was keeping him company, Selene was taking on the remaining marines single-handedly. She was holding her own, but reinforcements were heading in her direction, and she wouldn't be able to take them all on.

"We can't stay here. We need to go." Zoe pulled him to a standing position, wrapped her arm around his waist, and practically dragged him to the SUV. She unceremoniously tossed him in the back seat. "Selene, time to go!" Zoe yelled as she dove behind the wheel of the vehicle and slammed the door shut.

A deep rumbling started from somewhere behind the marines. The fight paused as everyone turned to watch as a giant boulder rolled down the jagged cliffs and straight for the uniformed men and women. Selene had the presence of mind to fling herself into the SUV as the marines dove out of the way of the massive projectile.

"The seismic activity around here is pretty strong, folks. Keep a close eye out for falling rocks," Selene tossed out the window as Zoe floored it, heading straight for the golden barrier that was their salvation. Several men and women from other countries' military forces jumped out of the way of the speeding vehicle, but Zoe barely blinked. Within seconds they were through the blockade and within the relative safety of the dome of protection.

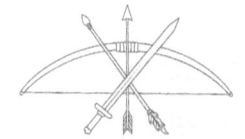

Chapter
Twenty-Three

HAD SHE REALLY DONE that? Zoe couldn't believe that she'd purposefully aimed a giant boulder at US military forces. Granted, the marines had attacked first, but she hoped she hadn't killed anyone.

On the other hand, what would the military have done if Jason had made it inside their tent? Would they have arrested him? Hurt him? She would like to believe he would have been safe. He was not only an American but a journalist at that. The amount of backlash the government would have gotten for imprisoning a journalist was hard to fathom. Of course, they had also mentioned trumped-up charges of aiding terrorists—otherwise known as the Amazons—so who knew how bad it would have gotten if Jason had been in their custody?

"Was that you?" Jason asked quietly as they drove down the hill and into town.

Zoe nodded. "Yeah, it was." She pulled the SUV up next to the Royal Hall and threw it in park.

"Nicely done," Selene said, then hopped out of the vehicle without a second glance.

Zoe started to follow her and reached over to open her door, but Jason's hand on her shoulder stopped her.

"Hey, don't do this," he said as he reached between the front seats, grabbed her chin, and turned her to face him.

"And what exactly is this?" Zoe asked.

Jason leaned in and pressed a featherlight kiss to her lips before pulling back and staring deep into her eyes. "You feel guilty when there's no need for you to. They started that fight. We were within our rights to defend ourselves."

The corner of Zoe's mouth twitched and she almost smiled. "Hate to break it to you, darling, but the rights of an American, a Brit, and a French citizen all on Turkish soil are murky at best."

Jason's lips thinned, but he didn't give up. "Nevertheless, you did what you had to do, and everyone is fine."

"Speaking of fine, how's your stomach?" The visual of that idiot marine slamming his gun into Jason's midsection replayed in her mind. She wanted to shudder. Hearing him gasping for breath had been terrifying, even if she'd known deep down he would be fine.

"Tender, but I'll live."

She took a deep, cleansing breath. She needed to shake off the confrontation and move on. What's done was done.

"Let's go talk to Kalli and figure out what the next steps are. If they're going to stop us every time we enter or leave Themyscira, they've effectively created a blockade for supplies. This place has always been self-sufficient by necessity, but damned if I want to go back to living that way. I've gotten used to modern amenities, and I don't feel like giving them up now."

By the time they made it inside, it was clear that Selene was already informing the others about what had gone down. They were coming in at the end of Selene's rant. "They're tightening the noose, Kalli. I refuse to be trapped here for all eternity. There are people I care about out there, and I have a business back in London that isn't going to run itself. Not to mention the fact that they have effectively cut off our food and weapons supplies. Who knows what they'll do to the next person who tries to leave."

Crowds of Amazons were pouring into the Royal Hall. Breakfast was long since over, so they weren't there for food. Feet shuffled and low murmurs passed throughout the gathering warriors.

"Have you seen their weapons?" Melina asked her neighbor, a tinge of fear in her voice.

"They tried to block Selene and Zoe from returning, and they attacked Jason," Psyche added quietly.

Frona crossed her arms and glared. "I think we should take our chances against them. We're the Amazons. We can win any battle."

"Hush," Ariadne said. "This is an enemy we're not prepared to face. The queen has told us that much."

Kalli climbed the few steps that led to the dais on the far end of the room—where the throne rested—but didn't sit. Instead, she lifted her arms, signaling for silence. Her rapt audience turned to face her, and an uneasy stillness fell over the crowd.

Wanting to show support for her queen, Zoe squeezed her way from the back of the room to the front, pulling Jason in her wake.

Kalli addressed her people, "Sisters, I understand your unease and your discomfort. This has been a trying time for all of us. The strangers on our doorstep came with talks of peace and friendship, and yet days later have turned against us and deny us our freedom. Up until now, I have been firmly against approaching them with force or anger. I did not want our ire to be the thing that tips the scale from peace to war. However, with this latest escalation against our people"—Kalli's gaze swept the room and landed first on Selene, then on Zoe, and finally on Jason—"we can no longer sit idly by and let the trap close around us. It is our time to show these men and women who they're truly dealing with."

A cheer went up, almost deafening in its intensity. The conviction she saw on Kalli's face wiped away any remaining doubt Zoe might have had. Kalli had also lived in the world among humans. She was engaged to a human. Her queen knew exactly what they were up against and the potential consequences of their actions just as well as Zoe did.

But Amazons didn't back down from a fight. They didn't allow themselves to be intimidated. They stood up for what they believed in and fought for what was right. The idea of Amazon warriors alive and well in the world today might be a scary concept for presidents and dictators alike, but that didn't mean the Amazons had to kowtow to the fear of others.

"Sisters—and lovers," Kalli said with a longing smile toward Sam, "I cannot tell you what awaits us. This may be the end of us, the culmination of our lives. It is possible that the Amazons are about to march into their final battle. But even if that is the case, we will do it with our heads held high and our honor intact. We will not strike first, but we will fight to the last breath."

Another shout went up, this one loud enough to shake dust from the rafters.

"Suit up and fall in!" Kalli yelled.

"To arms!" the Amazons replied as one.

Organized chaos reigned as the warriors filed out of the room en masse to don their armor and grab their weapons. A few short moments later, the only ones left in the room were Kalli, Sam, Selene, Colin, Zoe, and Jason.

"Sam, Colin, Jason," Kalli said, addressing each man in turn with a sad smile and tears in her eyes. "I am not your queen and cannot order you to do anything—including ordering you to stay here. I also cannot, in good conscience, ask you to accompany us to what very well may be the death of us all."

Sam invaded Kalli's personal space before leaning down to give her a soft kiss. "I may not be an Amazon, but you are my queen in every way. Where you go, I go."

"And Red would be lost without me," Colin chimed in. "She wouldn't even know which way to point a gun, am I right?" He nudged Selene, who flicked his arm with her finger before leaning her face into his neck and taking a steadying breath.

Zoe gazed into Jason's gorgeous blue eyes, silently begging him to stay behind. "Jason, I know we haven't known each other long, but that doesn't matter to me. I've been alive for thousands of years, and I've never met anyone quite like you. I love you."

Jason tapped his index finger against her lips. "Stop right there, Zoe love. I know I'm the only mortal person inside this glowy golden dome, but that doesn't mean I'm going to be left behind. Give me Kevlar and a sidearm and I'm with you. To the end." He grabbed her behind the neck and dragged her mouth to his. The kiss went on and on, a mating of tongues. It was only after someone rather rudely cleared their throat that Zoe remembered they were still surrounded by people. She took a step back and gently wiped her lips, still feeling the warmth of his mouth on hers.

Kalli cleared her throat again, holding back tears. "Now that that's settled, everyone suit up. The fate of our world hangs in the balance."

"But no pressure," Selene muttered, making Zoe chuckle.

Their small band split up to head their separate ways. Zoe grabbed Jason's hand and marched him out the front door of the Royal Hall and straight toward the armory. "Have you ever fired a gun before?" she asked as they walked.

"Yes, though I'm not going to lie, it's been a minute," Jason replied.

Zoe nodded once. "You stay glued to my side, and if shit hits the fan, you bail, you got me?"

"I'll stay glued to your side because there's no place I'd rather be, but I'm not going to run. If you die, I die. And to make sure that we do everything we can to prevent that . . ." Jason pulled out his phone. He hit a number on speed dial. When the other person answered, he simply said, "Be ready. It's going down," then hung up the phone.

Zoe had no idea whom he'd called but didn't waste time trying to figure it out. With an exasperated huff, she opened the door to the armory and grabbed the first bulletproof vest she saw. She flung it over Jason's stubborn head and then yanked the Velcro tightly into place. He gasped at the pressure against his injured torso, and she winced in apology. Next, she grabbed a gun belt and wrapped it around his hips. She plucked a Beretta semiautomatic pistol off the shelf, checked the magazine to make sure it was fully loaded, then slid the weapon into the holster. "Only in the case of emergency," she said, trying to stare him down.

He smiled and gave her a quick peck on the lips. "Yes, ma'am."

She repeated all the same motions for herself, and when they were both as protected as she could make them, she turned and led him back to the town square. There, right beneath where the fleece was gently swaying in the breeze, hundreds of Amazons were lined up to march into battle. She bypassed the rank and file of her sisters and walked straight to the front of the formation to stand side by side with Kalli, Selene, and their men.

"Amazons, move out!" Kalli shouted with a raised fist.

As one, they marched forward, one troop following the other down the long center road through town. The rhythmic pound of footfalls resonated through Zoe as she looked around her hometown for what was quite possibly the last time. She glanced at her tiny house before resolutely staring straight ahead again. Now was not the time for sentiment.

Their activity had not gone unnoticed. By the time their battle formation had reached the incline to take them out of the valley, the golden barrier separating them from the outside world was lined with the faces of men and women, some in uniform and some not. None of them attempted to cross over, but all watched with undivided attention. Noah was front and center, his camera capturing everything.

With no more than a silent hand gesture from Kalli, their force came to an abrupt halt.

Kalli sent Zoe a quick nod, and Zoe took a step forward, drawing all eyes to her. She scanned the crowd until she found one face in particular. Staring directly into her former boss's eyes, she began, "When Interpol first arrived in Themyscira, I still had hope. Hope that peace was possible, even between civilizations as different from one another as the Amazons are from the rest of the modern world. That hope was quickly shattered when instead of openness and understanding, we were met with fear and hostility."

Matis at least had the grace to look ashamed.

"Your forces have been camped on our boundaries for days. I understand that our sudden appearance in the world caused a shock, but nevertheless, we're here, where we've been for thousands of years. We have granted you leniency and attempted peace talks with some of your leaders, because we do not want to be at war with you, with the world. That being said, that indulgence lasted only as long as it took you to threaten our people. Today was that day, and our patience is at an end. I would like to speak to the men and women in charge. Don't worry, I'll wait," Zoe said with a snarky smile. "But not long." She fell into parade rest and cast her icy-blue gaze over the gathering crowds.

The trained soldiers on the other side of the barrier glanced in confusion between the phalanx of Amazons and their own commanding officers. Zoe even caught sight of her old pal Gabriel hovering in the background, trying to smother a grin as he watched the standoff.

Several tense minutes went by, but the Amazons didn't flinch. Not one person moved a muscle as they stared down their potential adversaries. Finally, one man in camouflage fatigues broke ranks on the other side of the dome. Gunnery Sergeant Haskins sent a long stare in Zoe's direction before pivoting and crossing to a nearby tent. When he returned, he was accompanied by a handful of other men and women. The crowd parted for them as representatives from the US military, Interpol, the UK, France, Germany, and Türkiye spread out in an evenly spaced line facing them.

Zoe glanced at Kalli, who took it from there.

"I am Kalliope James, queen of the Amazons and citizen of this world. In fact, I suspect that you've already done your homework and found out that I'm also an American citizen. If you go back further than the last hundred years or so, I'm also British, French, German, Greek, and—through eminent domain or simply the fact that we were here first—Turkish." She paused and let the silence stretch between them.

The American general broke first. "Well?"

Zoe noticed Kalli crack a tiny smile before schooling it. "I told you who I am. Who might you be?" Kalli asked, cool as a cucumber.

The general's jaw twitched, but he answered, "Major General Vaughan Calvino of the United States Marine Corps."

Kalli acknowledged his introduction with a slight tilt of her head. "And Mr. Laurent, how lovely to see you again." She dipped her head at the Interpol agent.

Zoe was amazed Kalli was able to say that with a straight face. Personally, Zoe still wanted to punch her former boss in the nose.

Each leader introduced him- or herself until they reached the leadership of the Turkish military. "General Ahmet Ergan, Turkish Land Forces."

Kalli relaxed her stance slightly and smiled. "Thank you all for introducing yourselves. Things are much more friendly when we know each other, am I right?"

General Calvino rolled his eyes. "I don't know what you think you're doing here. You are quite obviously outgunned, outmanned, and outclassed. What threat could you possibly pose to the likes of us?"

Kalli broke ranks and slowly approached the dome, the royal circlet glinting in her soft brown locks. "General, I understand that you truly believe that. You look at the two hundred of us and see a laughable force compared to the might of the US military complex. However, there are several key things you seem to have forgotten. First and foremost, we can always leave"—she stuck her arm through the golden barrier to prove her words—"but you can never enter.

"Secondly—and this one almost seems like it would have been impossible to forget, but here we are—the Amazons have powers unlike anything you've ever seen before. Amazons, ready yourselves!" Kalli yelled.

Zoe conjured two fireballs and started juggling them. Selene snarled and grabbed a gun in each hand, her knives glinting cruelly in the sun. Behind them, the crackle of lightning traveled between Ariadne's hands, and frost permeated the air from Frona's fingertips. One by one each of the Amazons did whatever they needed to do to conjure their power and show it off to their opponents. And in front of them all, standing guard like the warrior queen she was, Kalli raised her hand to the sky, and blue light spread from the ring on her finger. The queen's ring. The ring that let her wield the power of the gods.

Almost in unison, as if they'd planned it that way, the wall of generals, agents, and civilian leadership took a step back. General Calvino drew his sidearm, though it remained pointed at the ground.

"So, General," Kalli asked casually, her ring emanating power that everyone could no doubt feel, "do you really want to try your luck against us?" Kalli's arm flashed through the barrier once more, grabbing Calvino's arm before he could blink and bringing it up so that his gun was pointed directly between Kalli's eyes. "Are you ready to take that risk? Are you ready to gamble your life that the bullet from your gun will hit me and not ricochet directly back at you, killing you instead? Or perhaps assume none of our powers are fast enough to stop a speeding bullet before it can do its job?"

Kalli let go of General Calvino's arm, but he left it exactly where she'd placed it. His arm was rock steady, not quivering the tiniest bit. His jaw clenched and his eyes narrowed. It was obvious he wanted to take the risk and put a bullet through Kalli's head for the way she'd challenged him. It was equally clear that he wasn't sure whether she was right or not.

Seconds stretched into minutes. No one moved. Zoe's fire crackled merrily in front of her as if asking to be tossed at the nearest enemy.

Then she remembered Jason. The man who was standing next to her with no magical gifts of his own. He had a gun clutched loosely in his hand, and that was about it. If this confrontation came down to a firefight—literally or figuratively—Jason would be at a severe disadvantage. She was suddenly far less certain how she wanted this altercation to play out.

A ringing phone split the tense silence. Gunnery Sergeant Haskins answered it with a clipped "What?" He listened to whoever was on the other end of the line before crossing to General Calvino. "Sir, you need to hear this."

Calvino didn't bat an eye. He used his free hand to yank the phone out of Haskins's hands and put it to his own ear. "What is it?" Silence pressed in as everyone waited for the next move, the next command. "Damn it," the general said as he took the phone away from his ear.

Zoe noticed that he hadn't hung up. Whatever news he'd gotten wasn't good, but also wasn't something he could easily dismiss. He brought the hand holding the phone to his forehead as if whatever he was about to say pained him greatly. He took a deep breath and then dropped his hand and clicked the button to put the phone on speaker.

"Can you say that one more time, Captain?" he asked, irritation and anger lacing his tone.

"Yes, sir. Sources have confirmed something that we can only call a minotaur rampaging through Crete. The creature has the head and torso of a bull, but the lower half and legs of a man." The audio cut out for a few seconds before the man on the other end of the line returned, with a slightly more panicked tone of voice. "And there appear to be several bird-snake hybrid things attacking Athens. This is beyond anything my men know how to deal with."

General Calvino focused his stare at Kalli. "You. You caused this."

She shrugged nonchalantly. "It's possible." She paused. "It's also probable that we're the only ones that can help you stop it. Minotaurs? Basilisks? That definitely sounds like something you're ill equipped to handle. Tell me, General. How exactly would you go about trying to subdue a basilisk—or, as your captain calls it, a 'bird-snake combo'?"

The arm holding his gun started to vibrate. "I'd walk up and shoot the damn thing," he snarled.

Kalli nodded once like that was exactly what she'd expected him to say. "And you would be dead twice over if you tried. Not only can a basilisk kill someone just by looking at them, but they can also shoot toxic venom at prey several meters away."

The general lifted his gaze to the sky like he was praying for patience.

Kalli didn't let him stew for long. "General, my troops have spent their lives dealing with foes exactly like the ones you're currently facing. We might be persuaded to help you. For the right price." She buffed her nails on her Kevlar vest as if the standoff meant nothing to her.

Once again, silence rang through the gathered troops until one voice carried above them all. "We side with the Amazons." General Ergan of the Turkish Land Forces took a steady step forward. "These women have proved their worth to us. Zoe Harper saved the city of İzmir from a rampaging monster. We threw the might of our police and our military at that bronze beast, and nothing even slowed it down. Without Ms. Harper, İzmir would be nothing but ruins. What you did for our country will never be forgotten," he said as he bowed his head in Zoe's direction.

"And don't forget that a few weeks ago, Selene single-handedly prevented the citizens of Rome from being entranced by some psycho dictator," Gabriel yelled from the back.

Matis turned around and glared at his agent. "That psycho dictator was one of them. An Amazon!"

"Yes, Nyx was one of ours," Kalli acknowledged. "But I can assure you her beliefs are not shared by the rest of us. She has been dealt with and will no longer be bothering anyone."

"General," a loud voice said from the direction of the phone that General Calvino was still holding. "Sir, what would you like us to do?"

Calvino's finger twitched on the trigger before he slowly lowered the gun back to his side. "What is your price?"

Kalli tipped her head to the general. "Our price is simple. Peace between our people and yours." Kalli gazed from one leader to the next, staring each one in the eye before landing on General Ergan. "And, with your permission, we would like to continue to occupy Themyscira. I'm afraid we've grown quite fond of our home over the last several thousand years." She smiled broadly, which he returned. "Oh, and I'd like that peace treaty in writing, of course," Kalli said, directing her words at General Calvino.

Zoe held her breath and could feel the women and men around her doing the same. This was it. This was what would determine their future. Whether they would live, die, or spend the rest of their lives fighting.

"Your terms are acceptable," Calvino said, spitting the words out like they left a bad taste in his mouth.

"Wonderful. Amazons, as you were," Kalli said in a normal voice, but everyone in the surrounding area heard her loud and clear. Zoe doused her fire and Selene sheathed her weapons. The crackle of electricity died behind them, and the frost gave way to the warmth of the day. Around them, each of the Amazons dispelled their powers and returned to parade rest. "Now, who should we talk to about helping you dispatch those monsters?"

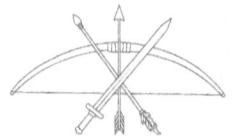

Chapter Twenty-Four

J ASON COULDN'T BELIEVE IT was over. The various militaries
had agreed to Kalli's terms, and each had signed the peace treaty
she'd demanded. Of course it had helped that the whole encounter
had been broadcast live not only on *The Truth Report*, but on every
station that had a team on-site.

The Amazon troops had returned to the city and were now
preparing for a feast and celebration that he was told would last well
into tomorrow. The relief was palpable. Selene had already called
whoever it was that was on the other end of her magical procure-
ment line, and cases of wine and beer had arrived along with the
food.

Jason wasn't quite sure what to do with himself. He'd spent his
entire adult life trying to be the best reporter he could possibly be.
He'd wanted to climb the ranks and jump from one network to
the next until he was on top of the world—figuratively speaking,
of course. However, this experience with Zoe and the Amazons had

changed him. It wasn't that he no longer wanted to be a reporter. He still firmly believed that getting the truth out there for the world to see was his higher purpose, and watching the encounter between Queen Kalliope and General Calvino had only solidified that.

But now he had other things to think about. He sat in the corner of the Royal Hall and watched Zoe as she moved easily among her sisters as they prepared for the party. She fit in here among her family. He knew she loved him, and he loved her more than he ever imagined he would ever love someone, but where did that leave them? His job and life were in Washington, DC. Her life was here. She'd spent blood, sweat, and tears to secure the future for her sisters. He couldn't ask her to come back to the US with him. It would be cruel. It also didn't help that she would live forever, and he would only live to be seventy-five or so, if he was lucky. And since he was already thirty-four, he only had around forty or so years left to enjoy his life with Zoe.

As if she sensed his eyes on her, Zoe glanced in his direction and sent him one of her joyful smiles. One of the ones he hadn't seen in a few days as they'd fought and clawed their way across Europe and the Middle East. Something in his expression must have clued her in to his conflicting thoughts, because she handed the rag she'd been using to wipe the table to someone else and came to sit next to him.

"Hey, babycakes. What's up?" she asked as she casually bumped his shoulder with her own.

He couldn't do it. Not now. The last thing he wanted to do was ruin this joyous celebration with his insecure and troubled thoughts. Zoe and her sisters deserved to be happy. He wasn't going to take that away from them. "Nothing. Just rehashing the last few days in my mind." It wasn't a total lie.

"I get that. We've been through a lot, you and I," she said, tapping his knee with her index finger.

"We certainly have." As surprising—and often terrifying—as it had been, it was an amazing experience. He'd had his eyes opened to a world of possibilities, and it was all thanks to the woman sitting next to him. "You know what I want to experience next?"

She turned to him with a glowing look. "What's that?"

"I want to know how immortals celebrate a battle victory, even if it was a bloodless one." He leaned in and kissed her luscious pink lips. His concerns could wait. Tonight was for celebrating. They could figure out logistics tomorrow.

A slight ruckus by the door to the hall caught his attention, and he glanced over to see what was going on. Much to his surprise, Noah, Trent, Gabriel, and a few others from the occupying forces were standing at the door, looking like lost puppies, uncertain where to go.

"Uh . . ." Jason started to stand and go kick the interlopers out.

Zoe put her hand on his arm to stop him. "It's all right. We invited a few friends." She waved the group over.

"How did they get through the barrier?" Jason whispered as the group approached them.

"Easy. They don't intend to harm us." With a shrug, she stood and went to greet her Interpol friends.

Noah and Trent came to sit next to him. "So, this is where you've been hanging out," Noah said with a laugh. His eyes roamed over the Amazons, some of them dressed rather skimpily, their toned and fit bodies on display with no shame. "I can't say I blame you."

Jason smacked his arm. "Don't be a pig."

Noah put his hands up in surrender. "I'm not trying to be insulting. This place is really something, isn't it?"

"It sure is," Jason said as he looked around the stone building that had been occupied for longer than he could comprehend. The weapons on the walls spoke to a history of battle, but the tapestries showed the simpler, more beautiful side of life.

"Do you think you could introduce us to any of your new friends?" Trent asked.

Jason let out an unintentional laugh. "No. But feel free to introduce yourselves. Just remember, they can eviscerate you without hesitation if they choose to." Confident his warning would keep his coworkers in line, at least for now, Jason leaned back and allowed himself to enjoy the party.

As Zoe had promised Jason, the celebration went through the night and into the following morning. Amazons spilled from the Royal Hall and into the town square, laughing and toasting to their victory. A cheer had gone up as they watched several of the occupying forces pack up and head out. The number of observers diminished by the hour.

Zoe was happy that everything had worked out. Kalli had been the queen they'd all needed her to be, and the Amazons were safe. At least for a while anyway.

But there was something else still nagging at Zoe. She and Jason had talked at the hospital, and she knew he didn't hold her responsible for putting him in the emergency room, but she couldn't shake the realization that for the second time in her seemingly infinitely long life, she'd injured a man she loved.

She glanced from the golden fleece, which was still dangling from the makeshift flagpole and giving off its protective ward, to her hands. She had done that, with Jason's help, of course. But her powers were what had allowed her people to come into the negotiation the day before from a position of strength instead of weakness.

She had spent her entire life fighting the good fight. Most of that time she'd been following one step behind Eris, cleaning up her messes and interrupting her plans whenever possible. She'd worked with law enforcement through the decades both formally, like with Interpol, and informally, like when she'd helped Max out on his cases. That had both been for personal reasons—their police databases allowed her to more easily track Eris—and because she believed in the side of good and wanted to catch bad guys and put them in jail. It had been her lifelong mission.

But Eris was dead. Zoe no longer worked for Interpol. For the first time in her whole life, she was entirely without a purpose. Maybe she didn't need to keep doing what she had been doing.

Maybe she could stop.

The idea settled idly on her shoulders as she looked around at her sisters, who tripped and laughed their way to their houses to finally get some sleep. Kalli had promised the world powers that the Amazons would help them fight whatever magical creatures had been unlocked when Zoe broke Medea's spell—something else that was her magic's doing. If she hadn't unleashed Medea's magic into the world again, the monsters might have stayed in whatever hole in Hades or Tartarus that they'd crawled out of.

She watched as dozens of her sisters passed by, some off to their assigned patrols, others looking for another mug of beer. Either way, there were hundreds of Amazons who could carry the mantle and help save the world from whatever threatened it.

Maybe it didn't have to be *her*.

For the first time in a long time, Zoe had other priorities. And her main priority was walking toward her at exactly that moment. Jason's blue eyes gleamed as he sent her a soft smile. He reached her side and pulled her into a hug, his soft mouth planting a gentle and healing kiss on her lips.

"Hey, there you are," he said as he pulled back. He didn't let her go, though, keeping her snug against his warmth.

This man was everything to her. She didn't want to be anywhere he wasn't. She didn't want to picture facing the long centuries of her immortal life without him. There was no magical water source or scheming mother that was going to swoop down and ensure that Jason could live forever. He was a mortal man, and he would live a mortal's life. He would age and grow old, and suddenly she wanted nothing more than to do exactly that right by his side.

"Good morning, handsome. Did you enjoy your first Amazon party?" She ran her fingers down his chest. Even through the fabric of his T-shirt she felt the firmness of his muscles and the warmth of his skin.

He chuckled. "The first? Does that mean I should be expecting a lot more of these? I'm not sure my liver can handle it."

A terrible thought crossed her mind. What if Jason didn't want to stay with her long-term? Yes, they'd exchanged I-love-yous, but she also knew he had plans for himself and his life. What if she wasn't a part of those plans?

She shook her head resolutely, refusing to let the negative thought take root. She wanted to be with him, and she was going to be damned sure she did everything in her considerable powers to make sure he felt the same.

"So, I was thinking," Zoe started.

"We should probably discuss some things," Jason said at the same time.

Her heart sank. "Do we need to be sitting down for this conversation?" She tried to make it a joke, but it didn't come out that way.

"No? I don't think so?" He sounded as unsure of himself as she was.

"Well, I was having a few thoughts of my own, so why don't we take a walk," Zoe said. She shoved her hand in the crook of his elbow and tugged him into a walk, heading for the beach.

Silence stretched between them as if neither of them wanted to go first.

"I want you to move to DC with me," Jason blurted.

"I'm planning to give up my powers," Zoe said simultaneously.

Jason's jaw dropped. "Wait, what? Why would you give up your powers? They're a part of you."

"You want me to move to DC with you?" she asked hopefully.

"Of course I do, but that's not the most important thing we have to discuss right now," Jason said, running his fingers through his hair.

Zoe couldn't disagree more. "Actually, I think it's the most important thing in my world right now." She wrapped her hand around the back of his neck and brought their faces within inches of each other's. "Jason, do you want to be with me? To spend the rest of your life with me?"

Confusion clouded his eyes before it cleared. "Of course I do. I'm surprised you even have to ask."

Soothing warmth spread through Zoe's body. "So your plan involved what, exactly? Us spending a few decades together and then me having to live centuries without you?"

"I mean, that's not ideal, but what are the options? You're immortal and I'm not. There aren't really any alternatives." Jason's hand came up to cup her jaw. "I don't want to lose you, Zoe. I'll take you for however long I can get you."

Zoe leaned in, her lips finding his in a searing kiss. "And I have no intention of living forever and having you be a constant ache in my heart. That's one of the primary reasons I want to give up my powers, though not the only one."

"What do you mean?" he asked carefully.

"My powers are too powerful to exist in the world. I've only abused them a few times, but when you pack as much of a punch as I do, a few times is still too many. Plus, I'm ready to retire. My heart and my mind can't keep putting strangers in front of myself and the people I love. I truly wish that there were no more bad guys in the world and that everyone was safe. But I also know that I've done my time. I've put in the work, and I've helped stop hundreds or thousands of bad situations. Murder, theft, rape, arson. You name it, I've stopped it or helped people recover from it. I'm tired, Jason. Now is my time to focus on me. On us. On what we can be together."

A soft smile crossed his lips. "Is it even possible?"

"Perhaps with some divine intervention," Kalli said behind them, then wiped a tear from the corner of her eyes. "Are you sure about this, my sister?"

Zoe took a step away from Jason but never let go of his hands. "I've never been more sure of anything," she said to her queen.

Kalli bowed her head and cleared her throat. "Then it shall be as you say." Sam came up behind Kalli and put his arm around her shoulders for a quick squeeze.

Behind Sam and Kalli, Selene and Colin emerged from the Royal Hall and came to stand beside the others.

"Zoe, you've been my sister so long I don't know how to say goodbye," Kalli said through her tears.

Zoe tried to lighten the mood. "Well, it's a good thing you won't have to for at least a few decades."

Kalli let out a choked sob and reached for Selene's hand to squeeze it tightly.

"Zoe Harper. Amazon warrior, sister, and friend, I commend you for your service to the Amazon people and the world. As a reward for your dedication and service, I will do what you ask, no matter how much I wish you would choose another path." Kalli gave her a glare but softened it with a smile. "Harmonia and Ares, mother and father. And to any other gods that care to listen in, Zoe has proved herself to be the best of the best. An exemplary Amazon warrior. One that has done everything that was asked of her not only willingly but bravely through the long years of her life. Now, as a boon to her and a reward for her servitude, I ask that you remove her powers. Grant her wish to be made mortal so she may spend the rest of her days with her true love."

Kalli's ring once again glowed blue with the sparkling power of the gods whose powers she channeled. Zoe felt the warmth of the blue light circling her, spinning like a painless hurricane, lifting her from her feet and surrounding her with what truly felt like the love of her parents. For the second time in her life, she felt like she'd spoken directly to her mother and that Harmonia approved of her decision.

The blue light dissipated, dropping Zoe gently back on her feet. Her legs buckled, but before she could fall to the ground, Jason's strong arms snaked around her waist and held her up, tucking her close to his chest like he never intended to let her go.

"Did it work?" Jason finally asked.

"Why don't we let Zoe tell us," Kalli said with a fond smile.

Feeling slightly steadier, Zoe stood on her own two feet, pushing away from Jason far enough to free her hands. She spun in his embrace so that her back was to his chest, then focused on the inner flame that was the source of her powers.

Nothing. That core inside her that she used to conjure fire, move things with her mind, or command animals and humans was just . . . gone.

She flicked her hands like she was purposefully trying to set the brush on fire, but nothing happened. Her hands stayed cool, and the bushes were saved from a fiery death.

Tears leaked out of her eyes as Jason tightened his grasp around her. She was free. No more accidentally setting things on fire. No more forcing people to do whatever she thought was right, only to have it blow up in her face.

Kalli and Selene approached her, and Jason released her but didn't go far. She felt the warm embrace of her sisters' arms, and she buried her face in Kalli's neck as Selene came from behind and snuggled close.

"Thank you," Zoe whispered.

"I love you, sister," Kalli said.

"More than life itself," Selene said.

Zoe reveled in the love and comfort her sisters provided for a few extra minutes before pulling back. "I'm moving to DC with Jason."

Kalli straightened, dabbing the corners of her eyes with her shirt. Even Selene appeared to be crying, though she would never own up to it. "It's a lovely town. What are you going to do there?" Kalli asked.

Zoe glanced at Jason with an excited smile. "I have no idea, but I know it's going to be amazing."

"Well, I know a women's shelter that could use some additional hands, if you're interested," Kalli said.

"That sounds just about perfect," Zoe said.

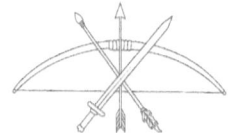

Epilogue

ARIADNE HAD SPENT HER entire life surrounded by her sister Amazons. For the first part of their lives, they had traveled the countryside fighting battles and defeating monsters. It was what they lived for. What they were good at.

Then the barrier came. The first one, to be clear. Queen Kalliope had asked Hermes to create a veil that would separate the Amazon homeland from the rest of the world. She had done it with the best of intentions. Ariadne truly believed that. Their people had been dying at an alarming rate, and the veil was the means that Kalli used to protect them from the outside world and make the world forget they existed.

Then Queen Kalliope had been exiled. Nyx had taken over as queen, though not one that had been selected by her peers, as was custom. She'd taken control by force and ruled with an iron fist for more than two thousand years.

Hope had entered Ariadne's heart once more only after she'd seen the triumphant return of Kalli and her chosen few. They had stopped Eris from destroying their people. A few days later—after taking down the veil—they'd stopped Nyx from enslaving the entire world.

Ariadne was still trying to comprehend the vast nature of the modern world, but she was confident she would get there. Queen Kalliope, Selene, and Zoe had been doing their best to introduce the Amazons to the marvels that were now possible. When Selene had been in trouble in Rome, Ariadne had been honored to be one of the select few her queen had chosen to accompany her on the flying machine that took them to Rome in a matter of hours rather than weeks.

It was the last few days, however, that had shaken her to her core. The Amazons had always been the most adept fighting force in the world. Or so they thought. Their recent semi-violent introduction to the weapons and soldiers of the modern era had come as a shock to them all. Everything she knew was wrong or outdated. She needed to learn, and she needed to do it quickly.

The flat box lying next to her on the table—which she'd heard Selene refer to as a phone—started to buzz. Ariadne glanced at it out of curiosity but didn't touch it. It wasn't her place. The buzzing stopped momentarily, but then quickly started up again once more. The glass screen had someone's face on it and a name she recognized from hearing Selene talk. Ambrose was calling—Selene's son through some sort of logic that escaped Ariadne.

Trying to make the noise stop, she poked at the dots on the screen. Green had to be good, right? Maybe that would make the noise go away.

"There's a damn dragon!" a man's voice yelled through the tiny device.

"Um, hello?" Ariadne replied, not sure what part of the small box she should be addressing.

Ambrose's voice immediately became quieter. "You're not Selene. Why do you have her phone?"

Ariadne didn't feel the need to explain the situation happening outside with Zoe. "Selene is otherwise occupied."

Ambrose laughed. "Well, then she better the hell get unoccupied quickly. That damn fire-breathing beast is currently circling Big Ben."

Ariadne had no idea who Ben was, but he sounded important. "I'll let her know."

"You do that, sweetheart." There was a muffled click, and the phone went silent.

It had been less than a day since Queen Kalliope had negotiated a peace agreement with the occupying forces. In return, she'd promised that the Amazons would be there to protect the modern world against the magical one.

It sounded like their peace was over.

Ariadne couldn't wait.

Thank you from Elizabeth!

If you made it this far, THANK YOU for reading *Amazon in Hiding*. I hope you enjoyed reading this book and this series as much as I enjoyed writing it. Will there be more out of Themyscira? I guess you'll just have to wait and see.

Reviews and ratings are the life blood of independent authors. If you liked *Amazon in Hiding*, I hope you'll consider leaving a review.

If you want to be the first to hear announcements and updates about future books, please consider joining my newsletter. As an added bonus, you'll get exclusive content (like a glimpse of how Kalli became queen of the Amazons or other fun related scenes).

http://www.elizabethsalo.com/newsletter/

Acknowledgements

This book would not have been possible without a host of people who believed in me and made it happen. Among those I should thank are my beta readers, my copy editor James Gallagher of Castle Walls Editing, and my cover designer GraphicSoulArt. And, as always, my brainstorming partner/marketing director/social media coordinator/all-around go-to person Chris.

About the author

Elizabeth Salo is a Michigan native who loves magic, myths, and mayhem. She writes paranormal romance, romantic suspense, and urban fantasy books and is a sucker for a strong female lead. She firmly believes she should have been born with superpowers, but since she wasn't, she'll have to make do with writing about people who do.

She currently lives in Michigan with her family and more fur babies (and feathered babies, and scaly babies...) than is probably wise.

http://www.elizabethsalo.com/

Also by Elizabeth

Did you miss Kalli and Sam's story? Check out:

Amazon in Exile
Amazons of Themyscira Book One

Wondering what happened between Selene and Colin? Check out:

Amazon in Darkness
Amazons of Themyscira Book Two